I0609712

Michael G Kramer OMIEAust.

A Gracious Enemy & After the War
Volume Two

ISBN = 978-0-6455701-1-3

Table of Contents

Forward

This is a work of historical fiction. The names of people have been changed and most of the conversations are imagined. Other than that, this story illustrates well, the trials and tribulations of those whom we now call *"The Vietnamese Boat People"* Between the 26th of April 1976 and until now, more than 2,000 Vietnamese refugees came to Australia as *"Boat People"*.

However, since then, the Australian Immigration officials began to travel to various refugee camps throughout South East Asia to interview and select refugees as probable migrants to Australia. Since 1976, Australia has become home to a thriving Vietnamese community which has engineers, doctors, surgeons, and other professional people as many of their children. This story is about a cross section of Vietnamese people who were some of the *"Boat People"* arriving at Darwin during late 1978 and 1979. I have also included some history of the characters involved both while they were living in Vietnam, and later, in Australia.

In 1975, the Second Indochina War, also called the Vietnam War, ended with the withdrawal of the last American soldier from Vietnam. The American withdrawal from the American Embassy in Saigon was shameful and many were left to the mercy or otherwise of the victorious Vietnamese Army.

The events of the dark times for the people of Vietnam have already been well documented in my previous book, entitled "A Gracious Enemy & After the War Volume One". This book deals with events in

4

Indochina and Australia after the war. For those people who did not read "A Gracious Enemy & After the War Volume One", I have again included some of the events that occurred in the war years and before that time, but only briefly.

One thing that became very clear during my own war service is that those who are actively taking part in war-like activities very seldom hate their former enemies. The reverse in the case, with a great and grudging respect for each other developing between the veterans, even though they have been on opposing sides!

As I have stated before, I am an Australian Veteran of the Vietnam War. Like many other Aussie Veterans of that war, I see it as none of Australia's business. It was a shameful invasion of a sovereign country. Warfare was practiced against it but was not declared! Many of the actions of the Allied side were in fact war crimes.

These included the deliberate poisoning of large tracts of countryside, which included productive farmland and even entire villages. Since the war, it has come to the knowledge of people in the west, including myself, that thousands of Vietnamese people are still suffering from the effects of deliberate poisoning of farmland, villages, and the general countryside of Vietnam. The use of the chemical sprays and continued use of herbicides in saturation quantities can only be described as war crimes. It must be called genocide by biocide! To me, the resulting birth defects of so great a part of the population of Vietnam is perhaps the most disgusting aspect of the Second Indochina War! I always did my duties while fighting for the Australian

Army in Vietnam to the best of my abilities. Like many other Australians who served in Vietnam with the Australian infantry forces I soon came to realise that the whole Second Indochina War by the entire allied side, was both wrong and immoral. No-one other than the people of Indochina had any right to be there in the first place.

Although I am very much against the Second Indochina War or Vietnam War, if that is what you wish to call it, I am proud that I had the good luck to serve with the amazing men of the First Battalion Royal Australian Regiment (1RAR) in Vietnam during 1968 – 1969. I am still in contact with some of these amazing men. They included some members of the Australian indigenous population or Aboriginals if you prefer to call them that. In all cases these men were as good as any Caucasian and probably better than many!

The Vietnamese refugees were mainly people who had been supporters of the previous regimes in southern Vietnam before 1975, but also included some people who were in fact heroes of the Vietnamese resistance against the foreign aggression from France, the USA, and her allies. As the National Government of the Democratic Republic of Vietnam took over governing both north and south, some people had managed to take over the belongings of others by denouncing the persons concerned, resulting in that person being removed from society and unjustly punished.

I know some Australian Vietnam Veterans who say that they hate the Vietnamese people and have the unmitigated gall to call the Vietnamese people "Slopehead and Gooks!" I have found that those who actually mean this are normally those veterans who were not involved in the fighting because those of us who were, have a grudging and deep respect for our former enemies who made up the patriots of Vietnam and who are called Vietcong (American slang meaning Vietnamese Communist) and those who preceded them in fighting the French who were called Viet Minh by their own people. Since many of these people came to Australia, I have had the privilege of getting to know them and to work with them.

They are now a vibrant part of Australian society, with many of their children now being surgeons, doctors, chemists, police and even in the Australian military forces. So, let us now look at why and how many of these people came to Australia, the problems they encountered and how they have settled in and successfully become Australians!

1945 - End of Fascism in Germany & the Japanese Fascist Occupiers of Vietnam.

Prelude

As we have already seen in "A Gracious Enemy & After the War Volume One", the fall of France to the German NAZIS during WW2 changed nothing for the people of the French colonies and the French colonists simply continued to serve the Vichy French Government.

The change in Indochina was that the population there was now subject to both the Vichy French and the Japanese occupations and both of their laws. Indochina was the French name of their colonies of Cambodia, Laos, and Vietnam, with Vietnam being divided into three administrative regions to enable easy control of each region. These were Cochinchina, Annam and Tonkin.

So it was that after the fall of France in 1940, the French Indochinese Government served the Axis powers! In July of 1940, the French Governor General called Admiral Jean Decoux signed an agreement allowing Japanese soldiers to occupy the French bases across Indochina. By the end of 1940, Japanese armed forces occupied the north of Vietnam and the southern half of the country as well.

When I was serving as an Australian infantry soldier near Long Binh in 1968 and 1969, we noticed many groupings of small tanks in much of the background of the areas around Long Binh and its various villages. Years after my return to Australia, I was at the Gerogery Hotel when I was speaking to Kurt Wiegner. For some reason, we discussed Vietnam.

Kurt said, *"I was once a member of the Wehrmacht. After Germany had lost WW2 and became occupied by foreign forces, I needed a home to go to. Most of the people whom I knew had died during the war. Some of them had died from being front line-soldiers, while many others had died from having their homes bombed by the Allies!*

People should think of northern Europe as being a mass of ruins of bombed out buildings among which the people of various parts of France, Belgium, Holland, and Germany as well as Poland and the USSR were living among the ruins in the best way that they could. Into this mess of despair, men such as me were finally given clearance to move on by the occupying allied armies, depending upon which sector we lived in. At the time, I was released by the French into the French sector of western Germany and because I was homeless and confused, I opted to join the French Foreign Legion! I had thought that the discipline as practiced by the Wehrmacht was extreme, but that was nothing when compared to the discipline practiced by the French Foreign Legion!

After the French leader, Charles de Gaulle replaced Decoux, the French Governor of Indochina with General Eugene Mordant, it was found that Mordant liked talking too much and that distressed the Japanese who were still the occupiers of the French colonies. Now that they were becoming increasingly alarmed, the Japanese general Yuitsu Tsuchihashi held

9

an "O" group with other Japanese officers on the 5th of March 1945!"

The "O" Group of the 5th of March in Japanese Indochina

Lieutenant General Tsuchihashi addressed the meeting. He said, *"Gentlemen, it is now the 5th of March 1945 and during a South China Sea raid in January of 1945, American aircraft from their carriers sank twenty-four of our vessels as well as damaging another thirteen of them! We have a rather serious situation on our hands at the moment!*

The Vichy French Government that the French colonists of Indochina have pledged allegiance to, no longer exists, and I fear that Indochina and its French garrisons will become a direct threat to all Japanese soldiers. They could become part of an allied attack upon us! Therefore, I propose to strike first and thus nullify the threat! As well, when the American aircraft from the carriers attacked us, we managed to shoot down six of them. The crews of these aircraft were picked up by French authorities and they are currently housed in a Saigon Prison.

I have been in touch with the Vichy French commander called Decoux and I called upon him to surrender. However, he has declined to do so, and he is now about to be replaced by Mordant. I have approval from our Japanese high command to use my judgement about this and we shall move against the French forces before they become a problem to us. After all, they significantly outnumber us!"

Lieutenant General Saburo Kawamura now spoke. He said, *"I also fear an attack directly upon us which shall be considerably aided by the French colonists! I therefore completely support your plan to act first and stage a pre-emptive strike against the French by the launching* **"Operation Bright Moon"** *which is now the code name for the Japanese led coup d'état which shall disarm the Vichy French forces during or by the 9th of March 1945!*

The French have had a long history of cowardly behaviour and I strongly believe that they shall simply retreat when we attack them in order to safe-guard their rears! We should redeploy Japanese Forces right now so that we can stage the Coup d'état by the 9th of March!"

Coup d'état Against the French by the Japanese

During the first part of 1945, the French Colonial Forces in Indochina still greatly outnumbered the Japanese in South East Asia, and they comprised some 65,000 men. Of these, 48,000 were locally recruited *"Tirailleurs Indochinois"* serving under the command of French officers. The remaining French Forces were the French regulars of the colonial Army plus another three battalions of the French Foreign Legion. However, since the fall of France in June of 1940, there had been no replacements of personnel or supplies had been received from outside of Indochina. That resulted in only 30,000 French army forces who could be described as being combat ready.

On the 7th of March Lt. General Tsuchihashi spoke to several of his sub-ordinates. He said, *"Decoux, the bloody leader of the French forces in Indochina is wasting my time and he is just stalling in order to embarrass me! As well as embarrassing me, his stalling can result in either the British under Admiral Mountbatten or the Americans invading! I therefore order that an ultimatum be delivered to the French upstart called Decoux, telling him to surrender to us immediately!*

If he chooses not to comply, he shall find that Japanese Forces have moved into and now occupy every French centre! Fighting has taken place in Saigon, Hanoi, Haiphong, Nha Trang and along the northern frontier! As well, the 11th Régiment d'infantrie Colonial based at Martin de Pallieres Barracks was surrounded and their commanding officer, Lieutenant Colonel Moreau was arrested! There has been limited fighting in Hue! The Garde Indochinoise has been fighting us and I expect them to fall in about eight hours from now!

As well, I have been informed that at the Lang Son areas near the Chinese border, the French under the command of General Emile Lemonnier are holding out against all Japanese attempts to take over the French fortress complex at Lang Son! That must be rectified immediately, otherwise our Japanese forces will have enemies in their rears!"

Battle of Lang Son

At this point, came an interjection from a Japanese captain. He said, *"Sir, I am Captain Kayakawa, and I suggest that if you want to be successful in your coup d'état by the 9th of March 1945, then it may be better to just invite him and other*

12

officers of the French garrison at Lang Son to a banquet to be held at the headquarters of the 22nd Division of the Japanese Imperial Army. If he chooses not to attend, we can still bring him to task. I also suggest that we put all of this into play immediately because it is now the 7th of March, and you want the French to be overrun by the 9th of March! Therefore, it is time to act now!"

Due to French fears of invasion by Chinese forces, the French Colonial Army built a series of fortifications along the Sino-Vietnamese border. The main fortress was located at Lang Son, which is about eighteen kilometres from the border with China. The French named the main fortress as *'Fort Briere de l'Isle'*. It had a garrison of four thousand men, many of whom were Vietnamese from the Gulf of Tonkin areas. Commanding the garrison was General Emile Lemonnier, who was also the commander of the border region. He was known to be patriotic and stubborn.

He had served in the French army in 1914 when he was a lieutenant in the 25th Artillery Regiment and during that time, he received several commendations. After the armistice of 1918, he transferred to the French Colonial Forces. As a member of that force, he served with distinction in various regiments of the *'Artillerie Coloniale'*. Having impressed many others, he was made a Knight of the Legion of Honour in 1920. He continued to serve in French West Africa from 1925 to 1936. After returning to France, he left that country for the last time in 1937.

Lt General Tsuchihashi answered, *"Very well captain, go ahead and see if you can get that obstinate man to come to the banquet and if he does so, we can easily kill him! If he does not, we shall just have to take his forts by storm. One way or the other, we shall be victorious, and the French shall loose! In the meantime, I want all of the Vietnamese to be brought under our immediate control. No excuses shall be tolerated, just get it done!"*

So it was that Captain Kayakawa had an official invitation for the officers including the commander of the French force at Lang Son to attend a banquet at the 2nd division Headquarters. Upon being told of the invitation, it was immediately rejected by General Emile Rene Lemonier. He said, *"So, the near sighted little brown monkeys called Japanese want me to go to their headquarters for a banquet? Bloody bullshit to that! It has all of the hallmarks of it being a trap! I am not stopping other officers from attending but be warned! Those of you who do attend this this bullshit banquet will be putting yourselves into harm's way! I fear the worst from these untrustworthy heathens called Japanese! The little brown monkeys are attempting to deceive us! We can be certain that the so-called banquet is a trap from which there can be no escape!"*

Those French officers who had attended the banquet were arrested and taken prisoner. The Japanese captain Kayakawa demanded to know where the French general was. He was told, *"Sir, he never came. Apparently, he does not trust anyone who is not French, and even then, he is known to gather intelligence about that person before he sees him or her!"*

Captain Kayakawa said, *"So, it appears that we must take the French positions the hard way! Very well then! I want as much artillery as possible to be used against the French. Also, our Japanese battalions have the support of armoured units consisting of twenty-two light two-man crewed tanks! I want all of them to take part in our assault upon the French positions. We shall be victorious and have the French forts in Japanese possession by the 9th of March 1945. I will find the French General Lemonnier and he shall sign the document of surrender of all of his fortresses and men under arms!"*

The smaller forts surrounding the main French fort of Fort l'Isle were taken one by one until only the main fort was left. After sustained attack by Japanese artillery, infantry, and tanks, it also was about to fall, and that allowed Captain Kayakawa to find French General Lemonnier. Upon doing so, Kayakawa spoke to Lemonnier. He said, *"Well, you arrogant French arsehole, you have lost all of your smaller forts and soon, we shall have this last one as well! Do something for the good of your men and order them to surrender. Also, I need you to sign the documents of surrender immediately."*

General Lemonnier answered, *"Go to hell, you jumped up little brown monkey! I shall never sign any document of surrender! Fuck you because you are a near-sighted little brown slant eyed monkey shithead!"* Captain Kayakawa replied, *"You arrogant French arsehole! Both you and that other disgusting Frenchman called 'Camille Auphelle' shall be put to work in digging your own graves! While you are doing so, you shall be under the supervision of Sergeant Sato and his section.*

Be warned these men have just joined us after being transferred here from their previous posts as guards of Allied Prisoners of War who were building the Burma Railway. None of them will put up with any non-sense from the likes of you and you shall find that they just delight in watching white men like you, and other arrogant French suffer until you die!"

Having said that, Captain Kayakawa walked away while the two Frenchmen were left to the mercies of the brutal Japanese section. Sergeant Sato kept on at both men saying, *"Both of you lazy white men are working far too slowly! Get a move on with your work! You are only delaying the inevitable by being so slow and obstinate! Work faster and then you can die like men!"*

Both Auphelle and Lemonnier said to their Japanese tormentors, *"You want us to dig our own graves, therefore you can either dig them yourself or you can wait for as long as it takes, you fucking little brown monkey!"* Captain Kayakawa returned, and he was furious that there had been very little progress in the grave digging. He went to Lemonnier and said, *"I shall give you a final chance to redeem yourselves! Here is the official document of surrender of fort Briere I'Isle, sign it and you shall live!"* the French general replied, *"You little brown monkey, go and fuck yourself!"*

That aroused the fury of Captain Kayakawa who shouted, *"Sergeant Sato! You and your men shall now pinion the arms of both of these white men to their sides or better still, tie their hands together behind their backs! You shall then make both of them kneel. After that has been done upon my command of 'up', you are to lift the hands of both men up high and hold them at the new height! Because they have their hands tied, that will result in them leaning forward with their necks sticking out. I shall then behead both of them with my sword!"* After the war, Kayakawa was tried for war crimes and executed.

Japanese Find the Viet Minh Hard to Fight

The Japanese attempted to disarm a group of Vietnamese patriots, (the newly formed Viet Minh commanded by Ho Chi Minh and Vo Giap). The Japanese thought that the Vietnamese nationalists would readily defect to the Japanese forces. Instead, when six hundred Japanese soldiers marched into Quảng Ngãi, the Viet Minh ambushed the Japanese. The Viet Minh only lost three men killed in action (KIA) and another seventeen were wounded, but they killed one hundred and forty-three Japanese as well as wounding two hundred and fifty of them before they withdrew from their position. On the following day, a much bigger force of Japanese occupied the position after finding it empty.

At Haiphong, the Japanese assaulted the Bouet Barracks which also had the headquarters of Colonel Henry Lapierre's 1st Tokin Brigade. The Japanese used heavy mortar and machine gun fire. Attacking with ferocity, they took one French position after the other until the entire barracks fell, causing Lapierre to order a ceasefire. He refused to sign surrender papers for the remaining French garrisons in the area and chose instead to order the destruction of code books where-ever possible.

That meant that the Japanese had to use force to subdue the other garrisons. Meanwhile, the *Garde Indochinoise* had fought for nineteen hours against the Japanese before their barracks was overrun and for the next three days they resisted the Japanese in spite of hunger, disease, and betrayals. After that, three hundred of them of which one third were French, managed to elude the Japanese and escape to A Sàu Valley. There were also other actions against the Japanese in the north and in Laos. The Japanese attacks upon the French in the Northern Frontier was the scene of the heaviest fighting. Realising that they first had to take Lang Son, (strategic fort near the Chinese border with Vietnam.) the Japanese attack was delayed while they organised re-inforcements.

Independence?

Both before and after the Coup, the Japanese were trying to convince others that they had the interests of all Asian peoples at heart and they even said, *"We only invaded other Asian countries in order to remove the European and American white man from Asia. Stick with us Japanese, and together we shall make Asians great while we kick the whites out of the entire region! In order to do that, we will consult with you as to the best way forward in this glorious quest to remove the white man bully from all of Asia!"*

Due to instructions and orders that were sent by mail to the Japanese Chiefs of Staff commanding the conquered nations of French Indochina, an "O" among the Japanese General Staff was organised and put into place while the coup d'état was in the process of being carried out.

Present at the conference were Lt General Kayakawa, Lt General Tsuchihashi and captain Kawamura as well as many other Japanese officers. Also attending the conference were three men apparently not immediately connected with the Japanese. These were, Bao Dai of the Nguyen dynasty of the empire of Vietnam, King Norodom Sihanouk of Kampuchea, and King Sisavang Vong of Luang Prabang of Laos. Proceedings were opened by Lieutenant General Tsuchihashi. He said, *"Gentlemen, by the grace of Emperor Hirohito of Japan, we shall now set up your independent countries! We have set up already, the new Empire of Vietnam which shall be headed by Bao Dai, the last of the Nguyen dynasty.*

Bao Dai shall have the continuous assistance of the Yokoyama Seiko, who is the Japanese Minister for Economic Affairs of the Japanese mission in Indochina. He shall be the key advisor to Bao Dai. We also want Bao Dai to appoint a government of which we approve and that must be headed by Tran Trong Kim. The Empire of Vietnam shall be free to make its own laws, but they must first be approved by Tokyo! All collected taxes must be paid to Tokyo!

As well, the people of Vietnam can forget about freedom of expression and freedom of speech! All people who are found to be critical of Emperor Bao Dai of Vietnam or Emperor Hirohito of Japan shall be deemed to be disrespectful. Those who are disrespectful and also are found to speaking against the ruling classes of either Japan or Vietnam shall be guilty of treason."

"King Norodom Sihanouk, we are granting you and your kingdom of Kampuchea freedom, but you shall be guided by Japanese officials at all times! Do you understand?" King Sihanouk replied, *"I understand that you are granting my people a partial freedom which is always subject to Japan's approval!*

In short, you are saying that all three countries of Indochina shall look like they are free, but they will all have puppet governments that are subject to Japan! I think that is what you are saying!" Lt. General Tsuchihashi replied, *"Yes, Your Majesty, that is correct! You and the other rulers of Indochina can govern your people, but the final word in everything shall came from Japan and taxes must be paid to Japan on time!"*

King Norodom Sihanouk said, *"No matter how you portray it, what you are offering us is in fact just a continuation of Japanese occupation and interference in the countries making up French Indochina. By you saying that everything must firstly be approved by Tokyo, you are telling us that we, the people of Indochina do not matter and that you shall always control everything about us! Instead of lying to us all of the time, why is it that you unwanted Japanese people don't just leave us alone and go back to Japan where you have originally come from? It is because of your actions that many people of the West are openly calling Japanese 'Little Brown Monkeys!' If you did not treat all other people with distain, then perhaps other people would take kinder views of the Japanese!"*

As soon as he finished saying that there was a loud voice agreeing with what he had said. That was the King Sisavang Vong of Luang Prabang (Laos). He said, *"I totally agree with what has been said by King Norodom Sirhanouk of Kampuchea! (Cambodia) He has correctly told you that the freedom that you say that you have given us is not freedom at all, so instead of continuing with typical Japanese lies, just leave French Indochina and leave us all alone. If you were to do that, you would find that much of the world opinion would* start to favour Japan! So, just pack up and leave from our countries! We the people of Indochina are the only ones who have the right to be here!"

That in turn infuriated the Japanese overlords. Lt General Tsuchihashi now spoke. He said, *"Kindly get it through your thick skulls that it is only we, the Japanese who have the interests of other Asian peoples at heart! We are offering you and all Asians freedom if you join Japan to rid Asia of the menace of the Caucasian (white) race of oppressors! In order to achieve that, it requires you to do your part in ridding Asia of these European oppressors who take everything without asking and then just subjugate you!"* With that said, the meeting broke up and there was much distrust and bad feelings coming from it.

After Emperor Bao Dai, King Norodom Sirhanouk and King Sisavang Vong had left the "O" group, Lieutenant General Tsuchihashi spoke to the other Japanese officers who were still present. He said, *"Gentlemen, I do not trust that king of Kampuchea or the king of Laos at all! I gather by their attitudes, that they would much rather have the French back in control of South East Asia than Japan! It is because we cannot trust the kings of Kampuchea and Laos that I want contact made with the nationalist leader of Kampuchea. We must get him to come here and then we shall make him our puppet Prime Minister. King Norodom Sirhanouk shall have no say in the matter! He only rules in name and he shall remain loyal to Japan if he wants to or not!"*

The Japanese then contacted the nationalist leader of Cambodia called Son Ngoc Thanh, who was living in Japan, having been exiled from his home country. The Japanese military contacted him, with Lt General Tsuchihashi saying, *"I want you to return to Kampuchea! We, the Japanese shall help you to take power! Kampuchea has King Norodom Sirhanouk as its head, but you can quickly become Prime Minister with Japanese blessings!"* And so, he returned to Cambodia and became the Prime Minister.

However, in Laos, things were not going so smoothly for the Japanese! King Sisavang Vong favoured a return to French rule and refused to declare independence and found himself at odds with his prime minister. By the 15th of May 1945, the coup d'état was complete, and the independent countries were set up. General Tsuchihashi declared the operations to be complete and that released several brigades for use on other fronts.

Aftermath of the Coup d' état of 1945

The coup had resulted in heavy French losses. 15,000 French soldiers were prisoners of the Japanese. Two French soldiers were discussing the current situation and what they thought had brought it all about. Pierre Montague said, *"Hey Jacques, it has come to my attention that we lost fifteen thousand French soldiers as prisoners of the Japs! I began looking at the records of combat losses and I found that we only lost about four thousand and two hundred men killed in action (KIA).*

Many more were executed by such things as beheading by the Japanese heathens after their surrenders. About one thousand men were lost during the fighting or else they were beheaded by the Japs! Over three thousand of our soldiers reached Chinese

22

territory as part of the retreating French columns. Some of our native Indochinese soldiers managed to get away and re-join their original villages and towns in Indochina.

Meanwhile, in northern Vietnam, Ho Chi Minh has declared the independence of Vietnam and the formation of the Democratic Republic of Vietnam. His guerrilla army known as Viet Minh have started their campaign with the help of the American OSS (later to be re-organised and re-named as Central Intelligence Agency or CIA). The Americans supplied the Viet Minh directly with arms, money, and training. In return the Viet Mihn attacked many Japanese outposts and managed to overrun some of them. It was from this time forwards that the Viet Minh began their tunnels in order to remain an effective fighting force in spite of overwhelming numbers against them.[1]

The Viet Minh established their bases without meeting much resistance from the Japanese. They kept on establishing bases throughout Vietnam and including tunnel systems which proved to be invaluable for them. A famine had begun, and it helped to cause resentment towards the Japanese and French overlords. The hate of the Vietnamese people spread to include the Americans when bombing by the USA contributed to the misery caused by the famine!"

Viet Mihn Take-Over

Meanwhile, Japan surrendered when emperor Hirohito announced the surrender on the 16th of August 1945. Soon after, the Japanese garrisons handed control

---

[1] Those readers who want more detail about this time should read "A Gracious Enemy & After the War volume One".

over to Bao Dai and the United Party. That allowed the nationalist groups to take over public buildings in most of the major cities. Meanwhile, the Japanese occupiers did not oppose the Viet Minh because they were reluctant to give the French a foothold in Vietnam again.

The entire French colonial system had collapsed overnight. Meanwhile a major famine was beginning to take hold. The seizure and hoarding of rice and speculation considerably worsened an already bad situation. With the people ready to move in masses, the Viet Minh called upon them to intensify guerrilla activity and for the peasants to seize the stores of rice that were held by the Japanese. (Vien, 2009)

The August Revolution

In summer of 1945, the suffering and resentment of the Vietnamese people reached a climax resulting in revolutionary actions by both the political and military organisations of the armed struggle for freedom of the people and for freedom from hunger. Therefore, the rebellion spread throughout the country. The decisive force which led and co-ordinated these things on a nation-wide basis, was the Viet Minh Front.

On the 13th of August 1945, Japan surrendered. On the same day, the Communist Party of Indochina held a meeting at the level of a national congress. It was decided to adapt the following slogans:
-   End foreign aggression and seize back national independence.
-   Found the peoples' power.

On 16th of August 1945 the Viet Mihn held a National Congress in order to bring together the delegates from many political organisations, religious and ethnic groups. A number of speakers came up with the same sort of conclusions.

Typically, it was stated, *"We are at the cross-roads of gaining the freedom and independence of our country. In order to be successful in gaining freedom for our country, we must firstly see to it that we seize power from the hands of the Japanese and the puppet Vietnamese Government before the arrival of allied troops in Indochina and receive them in our capacity as masters of this country, the troops which come to disarm the Japanese. The main problem with all this to pre-empt the Allies, comprising Chiang Kai-shek, British, French, and American forces, all of whom want to occupy Indochina for their own interests!"*

This led the Congress to adopt an eight-point programme:

(1) Seize power and found the Democratic Republic of Vietnam on the basis of total independence. Arm the people. Strengthen the Liberation Army.

(2) Confiscate the property of the imperialists and traitors, and depending on circumstances, nationalise it or share it out among the poor.

(3) Abolish the taxes imposed by the French and Japanese and replace them with a just and non-punitive budget system.

(4) Guarantee the fundamental rights of the people: - human rights, - the right to private ownership, - Civil rights: universal

suffrage, democratic freedoms, equality among the ethnic groups, between men and women.

(5) Share communal land fairly, reduce land rent and loan interest rates, postpone repayment of debts, and provide relief to victims of natural disasters.

(6) Introduce labour legislation: an eight-hour workday, minimum salary, national insurance.

(7) Build an independent national economy, develop agriculture, and set up a national bank.

(8) Develop a national education system: fight illiteracy and introduce compulsory elementary education. Build a new culture, establish friendly relations with the Allies and countries struggling for independence.

The National committee for Liberation was elected and the functions of the provisional government were headed by Ho Chi Minh. He said, *"This hour is a decisive one for our nation's history. Let us all stand up and fight tenaciously for our own liberation. Many peoples of the world are rising up to gain their independence. We cannot lag behind. Forward! Under the Viet Minh banner* (red background with a large gold star in its centre), *let us march courageously forward!"* (Vien, 2009)

Vietnamese Opposition to Chiang Kai Shek

There were many external threats to the new nation, which were from countries outside of Vietnam. As part of the surrender agreements of the Japanese, all of Indochina was occupied above the 16th parallel by the armies of the Chinese Nationalist leader Chiang Kai-shek, while the south of Vietnam was occupied by the British Forces who were smoothing the way for the return of the French.

Chiang Kai-Shek's general called Li Han called for an "O" group to be held on the 29th of December 1945. Addressing the Chinese Nationalist officers present he spoke. He said, *"I have orders from Chiang Kai-shek to take over in the north of Vietnam! Our leader wants the remnants of the former nationalist parties in Vietnam to be imposed upon people of Northern Indochina. By that I mean all of Indochina, meaning the countries of Cambodia, Laos, and Vietnam!"* A Chinese major asked, *"And just how do you propose to do that sir? Northern Vietnam has a very popular set of leaders. In particular there are two of great importance. These men are known as President Ho Chi Minh and General Vo Nguyen Giap!"*

General Li Han replied, *"By using the army of our leader Chiang Kai-shek to enforce our wills, we should be able to install the previous nationalist leaders of Vietnam into power1 They will not be able to do anything at all, they shall just be our puppets and enforce whatever we tell them to!*

I have today sent an ultimatum to the new communist government of Vietnam demanding the immediate sacking of all communist government ministers and that the leadership of the government of the Democratic Republic of Vietnam is handed over to nationalist groups of Viet Cach and Viet Quoc. I also called for the immediate sacking of the President Ho Chi Minh!

The major said, *"Very amusing sir! Do you really think for just one moment that the people will do as you demand? If you actually believe what you have just said, then you are in for a rude awakening and that shall occur very soon, sir!"*

Frustrated that he could not force the government of Vietnam to sack President Ho Chi Mihn and his ministers, the general called for eighty seats in the National Assembly of Vietnam be granted to Viet Quoc and Viet Cach.

Ho Chi Mihn and General Vo Nguyen Giap were informed of that, and Ho Chi Mihn answered.

He said, *"We shall counter what Chiang Kai-shek and his army are doing! Chiang Kai-shek is a problem, but he is under threat from the revolution in his own country and he will find that even the continued support of the Americans cannot keep him in power! A far greater threat to the people of Vietnam and the other countries of Indochina, comes from the French colonists!"*

Allied Take-over

Meanwhile, in Paris, the then French president Charles de Gaulle, was speaking to those around him. He was heard to say, *"France shall regain total control of French Indochina! Let no-one have any doubts about that! It is entirely the fault of the arrogant Americans and their even more arrogant British allies and partners in crime that the heroic French defenders of Indochina lost against the Japanese! The morons commanding British, and the USA forces did nothing to aid the French people of French Indochina during the Japanese occupation.*

It is because of the inaction of the British and the Americans that all of French Indochina has been left in chaos by the Japanese occupation. I call upon the British and American governments to do something positive to return France's former colonies and territories back to France and to help France to install its will upon South East Asia in general!"

The result of that was to hold joint discussions between the British and Americans about the best course of action in French Indochina. Jointly, they decided that the British Forces under the command of Admiral Mountbatten would pave the way for the return of the French Forces to Indochina!

So it was that on the 11th of September 1945, British and Indian soldiers of the 20th Division under the command of Major General Douglas arrived in Saigon. This direct British interference in the affairs of the sovereign country of Vietnam was code named as **'Operation Masterdom'** by the British. It was a post WW2 conflict mainly involving the British-Indian infantry forces and it was putting the French back into control in French Indochina. It did not matter to the

British of how the feelings about the armed intervention by foreign forces were thought of by the Vietnamese, Laotian or Cambodian people!

What is beyond dispute is that the British actions in Indochina paved the way for the return of the French Expeditionary Army Group. As the French colonists returned to power in Indochina, they increasingly said to the local people, *"All of you people of Cambodia, Laos and Vietnam should now be thankful that France has recognised the monarchies and countries put into place by the Japanese. France shall continue to rule over all of Indochina, but each country within in shall have its own king or emperor.*

Each ruler shall have the power to conduct normal day to day running of their countries, but all laws passed, and all military alliances must be confirmed as legal by France! France shall always have the power to veto any law passed by any country! All resources shall be owned by France! French Law shall overrule all laws within all countries making up French Indochina! In Vietnam Emperor Bao Dai shall continue to rule. He shall have the power to appoint who-ever he like as his prime Minister and other ministers! Rebellion against the Vietnamese emperor and his officials shall be treated as rebellion against France and that is punishable by death!"

Those things were enforced, leaving the Vietnamese population more determined than ever to expel the foreign forces and those of the hated British and French in particular! While he was in command of the British forces in Saigon, General Gracey even re-armed Japanese Prisoners of War and then used them to enforce the return of the French Colonial Governments.

It was a similar story in Cambodia where King Norodom Sirhanouk undertook the role of being a puppet ruler for the French. While in Laos, King Sisavang Vong also had the power of being an absolute ruler, but always subject to French law and French interests. Over the years after World War Two, the American Central Intelligence Agency was to become increasingly involved in South East Asia.

Official American policy was to completely back-up the rule of corrupt officials in southern Vietnam after the Geneva conference on Indochina passed resolutions that wanted there to be a unification of Vietnam and stressed that free internationally supervised elections were to be held within a year from then. That did not suit the American aggressors. Instead, the Americans immediately set about the turning all of Vietnam below the 17th parallel into one huge American armed camp.

So it was that the administrations of the USA openly favoured telling Bao Dai what to do in order to rule in south Vietnam. The Americans then persuaded the French to put pressure upon Emperor Bao Dai to appoint Ngo Dinh Diem as his Prime Minister.

Bao Dai did as he was asked by the French and the Americans only to find that later, Diem was leading a plot to oust him and install Diem as the first President of South Vietnam which was then called the Republic of Vietnam. Meanwhile, the popular freedom fighting movement known as Viet Minh had by now established the Democratic Republic of Vietnam. The Americans regarded that as a threat to American interests and so, what was only the people of a sovereign nation taking back their own country, quickly developed into a major but undeclared war! It was a case of the super powerful USA, and its allies interfering where they had no right to be!

Operation Condor

This was the attempted weakening of Viet Minh artillery assaults against the surrounded French garrison at Dien Bien Phu. The French general Cogny, Captain Jean Sassi and General Navarre were discussing operations during an "O" group held to discuss ways of getting the Viet Minh out of their high ground positions overlooking the French garrison at Dien Bien Phu.

Captain Jean Sassi spoke. He said, *"My dear generals, I know that I can break through all of the enemy positions and with my men assisting, we shall create havoc for the Viet Minh! They shall lose their prized high ground positions as a result of what I can do to them!"* That aroused the interest of General Cogny who now spoke. He said, *"Do you really have a solution to the Viet Minh holding the high ground and having concrete casements built upon it for their artillery and mortars?"* Jean replied, *"Yes, you had better believe it! I shall lead the GCMA Malo-Servan commando unit which consists of Méo partisans through the jungle and cause havoc among the Viet Minh positions! First, we need to be air dropped about fifty kilometres away from Dien Bien Phu, after which we can walk through the jungle until we get to our objectives of the Viet Minh gun positions on the high ground surrounding Dien Bien Phu.*

Among my objectives shall be to force a breakthrough with the help of French Union soldiers based on Elaine Hill in order to surround the coolies supplying the Viet Minh combatants and to suddenly attack those weak "Little brown monkeys" using the element of surprise! When we achieve that, it will create much confusion among the enemy Vietnamese! In order for my commando to get close to the Vietnamese, my men and our Hmong partisan friends shall be wearing the black clothing of the Viet Minh and we are equipped with sub machine guns and rifles."

General Navarre said, *"Assuming that all will work out for the best, when can you have your force ready for action, Jean?"* Jean replied, *"We can be ready for action on the 30th of April, why do you ask?"* The general replied, *"If you can be ready by then, that is good! However, I don't think that you have let yourself enough time to get everything ready, after all, it is the 27th of April today!*

Jean's commando units consisted of several teams. The Sam Neua team was in the advanced position and closer to Dien Bien Phu. as it got closer to Sassi's team, they taped the way to the outpost in order to guide other French units. They were only a few kilometres from Elaine Hill, but they could not reach their objective and Elaine Hill fell to the Viet Minh on the 31st of April. This failed operation was followed by the cancelled 'Operation Vulture'.

Operation Vulture! Proposed Joint Assault by America and Britain to Help the French

The Background - the Viet Minh forces commanded by general Vo Nguyen Giap had surrounded the French at Dien Bien Phu. The Viet Minh could hardly believe that the French forces had been placed into a very compromising situation by having their forces placed on a flat area surrounded by high ground. That flies in the face of well-known tactics of *"Take and hold the high ground at all costs!"*

The French arrogantly thought that the Viet Minh had no artillery or mortars. However, the Viet Minh had captured Japanese Mountain Guns of 75 mm calibre. These guns were easily dismantled into component parts such as the breech, mountings, bipod or tripod, barrel, and wheels. These could then be easily transported to where they were required for use and re-assembled. As well, they had 81 mm and 82 mm mortars which were also used against the French with devastating effect! The Viet Minh attacked the French as of the 13th of March 1954.

The French tried to control things and even tried hitting back using their artillery and aircraft. These aircraft included thirty US supplied C-119 flying boxcars which had been converted into bombers which could drop napalm upon the Viet Minh artillery positions, and they were flown by American pilots! They were directly employed by 'Civil Air Transport', the name of this mercenary air unit. It was commanded by Major General Claire Lee Chennault, who had commanded the WW2 'Flying Tigers'.

Dien Bien Phu could only be supplied by air drop and the drop zone was shrinking fast because of Viet Minh gains of French territory and their artillery having a dramatic effect upon the French, many of whom were now either wounded or dead.

At an "O" group called to discuss the worsening supply and combat situations of the French, a colonel of the French forces called Jean Louis Nicot spoke his mind. He said, *"I am the officer in charge of aerial resupply, and I know that it is too dangerous for our pilots to be dropping resupplies from low altitudes. Therefore, I am ordering that all resupply drops from now onwards shall be changed from 2,000 feet to 8,000 feet altitude! That shall apply immediately! There shall not be any change to that command!"*

It was because of the increase in the altitude of the dropping height that accuracy declined, and many supplies fell into the hands of the Viet Minh. With these events causing near panic among the French based in Saigon, they pressed for the Americans to launch overwhelming airstrikes to save Bien Dien Phu.

Meanwhile, back in Paris, the French leader, Charles de Gaulle, was in conference with his military advisors. Addressing all of them he said, *"What is it about warfare that you clowns do not understand? Why is it that the cream of the French forces is bottled up in Bien Dien Phu which is in the far north-west of Vietnam and it is almost in Laos. Why is it that none of you clowns cannot beat the rag-tag army made up of the 'Little Brown Monkeys'?"*

That was answered by the French Chief of staff, called General Paul Ely. He said, *"President de Gaulle, the Viet Mihn whom many people including the British, French and Americans like to call 'Little Brown Monkeys', have both artillery and mortars which they use with devastating effect against all French forces at Bien Dien Phu. Part of the reason for that is the location of the Bien Dien Phu battlefield is surrounded by high peaks and the Viet Minh have been successful in getting their artillery to the top of those peaks which allows them to pour fire directly into the French base on the plain below them."*

De Gaulle could not believe what his ears were hearing. At first, he was stunned and after recovering his composure he said, *"God almighty! Am I surrounded by fucking idiots? Do you really mean to tell me that the entire French forces are on a plain overlooked by high ground upon which the VietMinh have placed their artillery which you told me they do not have?*

Are you people fucking mad or are you just stupid? All of you are senior officers of the French defence forces and none of you blinking idiots appear to know the fact that upon going to an area and setting up any type of base, you must firstly take and hold the high ground! God, save me from you fucking fools!"

General Paul Ely said, *"Cursing us will not improve the situation sir! The only way forward for France is for me to travel to Washington and plead the French case for American help directly to the American policy makers. I have arranged for me to be in Washington for just that on the 20th of March 1954!"* Charles de Gaulle replied, *"Well do not just fuck around this time! This time you must get things done!"* And so, General Paul Ely of France had a closed meeting in Washington with the US Secretary of State John Foster Dulles and the chairman of the joint Chiefs of staff, Admiral Arthur W Radford.

During the meeting, Admiral Radford said, *"General Ely, you worry too much! We have a plan which we shall give the code name of 'Operation Vulture'. Using this plan involves the use of sixty B29* bombers based in the Philippines and escorted by fighters from the Seventh Fleet. They shall bomb the fuck out of the Viet Mihn positions besieging the French at Dien Bien Phu!" Accordingly, General Ely came away from the conference with the impression that the Americans would intervene on the French side, and he reported to Paris that he had the co-operation of the USA.

Operation Vulture – the Plan

On the 24th of March 1953, the Secretary of State of the USA, John Foster Dulles said, "Indochina is the top priority in foreign policy, being in some ways more important than Korea because the consequences could not be localised but would spread throughout Asia and Europe!"

During a discussion between the chiefs of the General staff of the USA, involving what should be done about the freedom fighting activities of the people of Indochina, Vice President Richard Nixon was heard to say, "So, you are telling me that the slope-headed Gooks want and deserve freedom! Well, let me tell you how that will affect both the American and the British peoples! Firstly, by letting the people of Indochina become free and letting them decide what is or is not right for them and for the betterment of their people, we can expect that all of Asia will become a communist armed camp!

That must not be allowed to happen! Already, the British are fighting insurgents in the Malayan states of Malaya, Singapore, and in the outer Malaysian states of Sarawak and Sabah which are located on the island of Borneo. That area is now a problem in so *much as the rest of the island of Borneo belongs to Indonesia and the president of that country, Doctor Sukarno has official ties to the communist government of the USSR!*

We can therefore colour all of Indonesia either pink or red which shows that the Indonesians are extremely likely to either be or about to become communist or socialist! If the countries of French Indochina become free and decide to join with their Indonesian neighbours, the whole of Asia, other than Japan and South Korea will be aligned with communist governments or supporters of the communists!

Secondly, the Indochinese people must not be allowed to have independence from France because the French are keeping those slope-headed gooks in their place! They must never have freedom and they must always be controlled by western powers!

At the moment, the French are in difficult circumstances in the north-western part of Vietnam at a base area called Bien Dien Phu. The French commanding General has been foolish enough to site his base area on a large flat plain which is surrounded by hills and mountains!

The French are so arrogant that they believed the Viet Minh could never obtain neither mortars or artillery and even if they managed to do so, the Viet Minh could never get those weapons up the hills and mountains through thick jungle. However, not only have the Viet Minh obtained artillery and mortars, but they have also placed them upon the high ground surrounding the French base at Dien Bien Phu, which is now in great peril!

Accordingly, I propose that the USA joins with Britain and that together, we apply all of 'Operation Vulture', which will result in the Viet Minh being wiped out in their positions surrounding Bien Dien Phu and the French Forces shall thus be relieved! That will be the end of our current problem! I also favour the immediate sending in of American infantry and other ground troops to aid the French efforts in Indochina! So, gentlemen, let's get 'Operation Vulture' up and running before we all end up being sorry for not acting decisively when we had the chance do so!"

John Foster Dulles, the USA Secretary of State entered the conversation. He said, *"Vice President Nixon, I am most glad that you have this hawkish view as to what the USA must do in Asia to ensure French victory against the god damned gooks! I support completely your idea of sending American ground forces to Indochina to help the French maintain their sovereignty there!*

The only thing we lack is the will of the American people to enter another war, because World War Two is still fresh in the minds of many Americans who lost members of their families who died while fighting for the USA, and we are already fighting the North Koreans and Chinese in South Korea! I am hoping for the British to join us in implementing 'Operation Vulture', which will end the plans of the little slant eyed monkeys to become independent!"

Admiral Radford said, *"Gentlemen, I also support the immediate implementation of both the entire Navarre Plan and also that we implement 'Operation Vulture' in its entirety! It will be good to see those Viet Minh slope-heads wiped from the map and for the French to maintain control of the gooks!"*

Next, President Eisenhower spoke! He said, *"Whoa gentlemen! We must not act too hastily! For all of 'Operation Vulture' to be implemented, the USA must not act alone as world opinion will be decidedly against us! We do have the means to do this militarily, however, unless we are joined in 'Operation Vulture' by the British, we must abandon the whole idea!*

I have been having strategic discussions with the British leaders about all of this and I must admit that the British are luke-warm about the idea of us invading yet another Asian country without justification or provocation at best! Our British allies have told me that if the USA goes ahead and implements 'Operation Vulture' without consulting the British, that we shall be entirely on our own!

Their reason for having such a timid approach to the problem is that 'Operation Vulture' calls for using nuclear weapons against the Viet Minh positions or else using aerial bombing of those positions with napalm. The US Army Chiefs of staff are against the use of 'Operation Vulture' because of the likelihood that American soldiers will be drawn into a bottomless pit into which we shall be pouring the lives of thousands upon thousands of Americans! Therefore, as president of the USA, I rule that unless Britain joins us in 'Operation Vulture', it must be called off! Not only that but consider that fact that 'Operation Vulture' has several versions!"

There Were Several Versions

(1) Plans were draw up for the Americans to help out the French by suppling and crewing U.S. B-29 bombers, some of which were armed with nuclear weapons. Officially, the were no American ground troops or combat pilots actively assisting the French in Indochina. However, that does not account for the fact that American adventurers were active as pilots for the French through their connection with 'Civil Air Transport', the mercenary unit which was flying the thirty US supplied 'C-119 Flying Box Cars' which had been converted into bombers which were to drop napalm upon the Viet Mihn positions.

(2) This alternative version of 'Operation Vulture' required the sending of 60 B-29 bombers based in Gaum or the Philippines and supported by up to 150 fighter aircraft from the US Seventh fleet. This plan included the option to use up to three nuclear weapons on the Viet Mihn positions in support of the French colonial forces! That was supported by Admiral Radford, the chief of Staff of US Forces.

As well, American adventurers were serving as either outright mercenary soldiers or they were members of French units such as the French Foreign Legion. The USA was supplied the money for the French aggression against the people of Indochina, even though the USA was officially neutral. The USA directly supplied American arms and war materials to France[2]. In fact, America supplied 900 combat vehicles,

---

[2] Readers wanting more detail on this should go to "A Gracious Enemy & After the War Volume One".

15,000 other military vehicles, 2,500 artillery guns, 24,000 automatic weapons, 75,000 small arms, 9,000 radios. (Vien, 2009)

America also provided 160 F-6F Hellcat and F-8F Bearcat fighter aircraft, 41 B-26 light bombers and 28 C-47 transport planes. Pilots were also supplied but covertly, using the *'Civil Air Transport'* mercenary unit as a cover.

Even so, the Viet Mihn noose around Dien Bien Phu was tightening and the alarmed French sent General Ely to Washington in order to lobby the US administration to send US bombers to help lift the siege of Dien Bien Phu. Some of the US administration agreed with the French General Ely. Among them were Vice President Nixon, who wanted American ground troops to be sent in. As well, the Chairman of the joint chiefs of staff, Admiral Arthur Radford and the US Air force Chief of Staff, Nathen F Twining pushed for *'Operation Vulture'* to be fully implemented.

Advising against it was the US Army Staff General Mathew Ridgway. He was heard to say, *"We must not become bogged down in a land war against the Asian people, it would become a quagmire into which American units will sink without clear victories against the enemy! As to 'Operation Vulture', I think we should cancel it because it is likely to involve us in direct combat with either China or the Soviet Union and therefore, World War Three!*

We must not let that happen. When talking about taking on the Asian peoples now, America must get rid of the old delusive idea that America can do things in the cheap and easy way! I urge our president to consider that air power alone cannot defeat the Viet Mihn, they are fighting to take their own country back!

When the day comes for me to face my Maker, and account for my actions, the thing I would be most proud of is the fact that I fought against and perhaps prevented the carrying out of one of the most hare-brained tactical schemes that would have cost the lives of thousands of men!" Eventually common sense prevailed, and *'Operation Vulture'* was called off mainly due to British reluctance to proceed with such an aggressive idea!

Interference in the Affairs of Indochina Since 1950

There were many meetings between the American President and the general staff of the American Armed Forces which also included the entire USA cabinet. Of great concern, the continuing problem of the wars of liberation in South Eastern Asia!

It was during one these meetings that Richard Nixon spoke. He said, *"Mister President, you have been asking me and the other members of the cabinet of the United States of America to not spend so much money on the Indochinese War and to make sure that the USA has the correct outcome from the Indochinese liberation wars that fits in with our hard-line policies of supporting right-wing governments of whom we approve!*

It is now the year of 1950, and I want a military mission from the Armed Forces of the USA to immediately go to Indochina and actively advise the French Colonial Forces on all matters. That must also include increasing amounts of direct US military aid in the form of supplies of ammunition, weapons, vehicles, and radios which shall be directly supplied to where they are needed by the French in Indochina!

It is very clear that the USA must immediately obtain strong and legal footholds within Indochina that shall give us the right to permanently have US run and staffed bases within countries such as Vietnam. In that country, we have the French puppet ruler the so-called Emperor Boa Dai!

He is weak willed, and he is a push-over for anything that the USA wants done! However, I know that the Vietnamese freedom fighters called Viet Minh are also aware of that and they are likely to court his favour as well! We cannot let that happen!"

So it was that Richard Nixon was answered by President Truman. He said, *"All of what you have just said is all very well to say, but Richard, please tell me how you are proposing to accomplish it without getting us into a war with the Soviet Union or China?"*

Richard Nixon replied, *"It is now 1950, and I want to see the USA propose and implement a legal treaty of "Economic Co-operation" directly between Emperor Boa Dai of the southern region of Vietnam and the USA! The agreement must include the USA to having the right to equip, train and control a new armed force. In order to help us to effectively control things in southern Vietnam, I want to see Emperor Boa Dai appoint a staunch anti-communist like Ngo Dinh Diem as the replacement of Prime Minister who is currently the Japanese installed puppet called Tran Trong Kim. Just remember that he was installed by the Japs!*

As well, I recommend that we send a high-ranking mission made up of myself, General Daniels, John Foster Dulles, and support staff to sign, seal and deliver the "Economic Co-operation" agreement between Emperor Bao Dai and the USA which must contain clauses that allow the USA to do whatever we Americans think is correct, no matter how the Indochinese people feel about it! We must stop communism spreading! In time, we shall invade and conquer the north of Vietnam which is now called the Democratic Republic of Vietnam! Only then will we in the west be able to relax!"

Accordingly, the "Economic Co-operation Treaty" between Washington and Emperor Bao Dai was signed in1951. Four years later, in 1955, Ngo Dinh Diem ousted Emperor Bao Dai and became the first president of the Republic of Vietnam, a country which came into existence as a front for what was to become one huge American armed camp after fake referendums were held which were supported by newspapers in Australia, Britain, France, and most of English-speaking world

That resulted in much pressure being applied upon the French Administration which allowed the American agents to be installed into the Boa Dai puppet administration in return for vastly increasing amounts of military aid. By 1953, the USA granted the vastly increasing amounts of aid to the French administrators in return for the full implementation of the Navarre Plan which allowed American General O'Daniel to lead missions in Vietnam.

The Navarre Plan

US aid to the French in Indochina rose to 385 million dollars in 1953, covering 60 percent of the expenditure on the war. By 1954, this had risen to 80%. American arms totalled 25,000 tonnes per month in 1953 and 88,000 tonnes by July 1954. American missions led by high-ranking officials included the Secretary of State John Foster Dulles and Vice President Richard Nixon. Nixon participated directly in working out France's military strategy. Airlifts were organised in France, the Philippines and Japan to supply the French Expeditionary Corps and American pilots took part the operations against the Vietnamese people! (Vien, 2009)

Washington tried to prevent the holding of the Geneva conference on Indochina and failed in that attempt. The Americans then concentrated on undermining the accords and agreements reached at the conference and supported moves by the agents of the puppet Bao Dai administration for the unconditional surrender of the Vietnamese resistance and the grouping of imperialist and local reactionary forces in South East Asia into a coalition which would have allowed them to continue the war.

The scheme failed and the Geneva Conference closed on the 20th of July 1954 with the drawing up of agreements putting an end to the war. Meanwhile, the American administration in Washington had managed to persuade the French to accept Ngo Dinh Diem as Bao Dai's prime minister in June 1954. (Vien, 2009)

Repression and War

The Americans were not prepared to accept the peace agreements and immediately began to set-up a new strategy. The objective of which was clearly aimed at turning southern Vietnam into a new type of US colony which allowed the Americans to have a political and strategic base from which the USA could dominate South East Asia.

In September 1954, a South East Asian Military Organisation, (SEATO) was set up. That included (USA, Britain, France, Australia, Pakistan, New Zealand, Thailand, and the Philippines and was used as later excuses for unauthorised military aggression by the allies against Indochina.

On the 28th of April 1956, French soldiers finally left Vietnam, but the French side-stepped their responsibilities of implementing the Geneva agreements which provided for general elections to achieve a peaceful re-unification of North and South Vietnam. The French approved of and used the Japanese installed puppet emperor called Bao Dai and in 1954, the Americans got him to appoint Ngo Dinh Diem as Prime Minister of South Vietnam.

Having helped their puppet rulers of southern Vietnam set up an illegal armed force, the Americans decided to train it as well as equip it. The insignia of the ARVN, (Army Republic of Vietnam, meaning South Vietnam) were all originally based upon French designs. As the war dragged on, The Americans decided to change the rank structure of the ARVN as well as the insignia to resemble USA ranks more closely in 1967.

Hoa Lan Xuan at Phuoc Tan

Senior Corporal (rank insignia was three gold stripes surmounted by a silver stripe) Chi Dung Xuan was part of an ARVN (at this time, there was a transition between the Royal Army of Vietnam and the ARVN) sweep in the area surrounding Long Binh. His platoon was the 9th Platoon of the 2nd Battalion Royal Vietnam Army. His unit was to conduct a sweep of the villages surrounding Long Binh during the 19th of January of 1951. Chi Duc Xuan was in command of one of the smallest infantry sub-units in the Vietnamese Royal Army. That was what Americans call the eight-man squad commanded by a sergeant. In the Australian army the smallest sub-unit of the infantry battalions is the ten-man section which is commanded by a corporal.

The reason for the activity of searching the homes of the villages surrounding Long Binh was because Prime Minister Diem, (he became President Diem after he ousted the French puppet Emperor Boa Dai) of South Vietnam had ordered the constant searching of homes in villages, towns, and cities in an attempt to wipe out the patriots called Viet Minh, who had forced the French out of Vietnam. The Royal Army of Vietnam was a force conducting what had become common place in South Vietnam, the cordon of the entire towns or villages, followed by soldiers walking into the homes and physically searching them, much to the distress of the people of the town or village.

While the cordon and search of the village called Phuoc Tan near Long Binh was taking place, Senior Corporal Chi Dung Xuan was supervising the men of his section or squad if you wish to call it that. He and one of his private soldiers called Chien Chin Pham went into a house occupied by Bian Cai Ngo and her parents.

Seeing Bian Cai Ngo for the first time took away the breath of Chi Dung Xuan, for she was strikingly attractive. He said, *"What is your name my lovely lady?"* She answered, *"I am Bian Cai Ngo, and you are?"* Chi Dung Xuan answered, *"I am Chi Dung Xuan. I earn a living by being a soldier in the army. My rank is Senior Corporal, and I expect to be promoted to Senior Sergeant* (rank insignia was three silver stripes surmounted by a gold stripe) *soon. I can therefore offer you a secure income to live on. It is not much money, but it is always there. I want to make amazing love to you and to have you to myself by you becoming my wife. Will you marry me?"* Bian said, *"Yes, Chi, I will marry you."*

That was supported by her parents, with her father saying, *"Bian, if you love this man, why wait, marry him today, for tomorrow both of you could be dead! After all, Vietnam has been occupied by foreign forces for one hundred years now, and we are paying the penalty for letting that happen! First our own puppet rulers of Boa Dai and his Prime Minister called Ngo Dinh Diem were installed while the Japanese followed by the French imposed their wills upon us and now, the Americans have taken up where the French left off and they are constantly making us suffer!*

The latest problem being that the puppet ruler installed by the Japanese followed by the French with American backing called Emperor Bao Dai, has appointed Ngo Dinh Diem as Prime Minister. Diem in turn has announced that anyone who is even just suspected of having feelings that can be shown to be anti-French or anti-American, shall be deemed to be a socialist or communist.

*They will then be imprisoned in 'Tiger Cages'
on Con Son Island which is the site of French atrocities
against Vietnamese people by the French colonists!
Con Son Island is also the site of the old French prison
where many Vietnamese died! So, if you want each
other, marry now, and enjoy each other, for tomorrow,
neither one of you may be here!"*

Both Bian and Chi agreed that was the best plan
and they immediately made plans for the marriage.
After that, they made love, and they married on the
following day. Bian was fruitful and two months later
she had missed a period and was experiencing some
morning sickness. Eventually, she saw a midwife and
she confirmed that she was pregnant. So, she wrote a
letter to Chi, informing him that Bian was pregnant and
that the birth could take place on or about the 28th of
September 1951. After a normal pregnancy Bian went
into labour on the 26th of September 1951. A baby girl
was born and named as Hoa Lan Xuan on that day.

Meanwhile Chi was busy in his role of being a
senior corporal in the Royal Vietnamese Army (pre-
ARVN). He had asked to be promoted to senior
sergeant and that was quickly arranged when he paid
his lieutenant the sum of US$250.00. In 1951, that was
a lot of money. The ARVN forces and the previous
army of Bao Dai were always very corrupt. Also, the
members of the ARVN were recruited from the same
villages and towns as were the members of the Viet
Minh and later, their sons and daughters who were
patriots in the Viet Cong.

Whenever Chi could get leave, he would visit
his wife at her parents' home at Phuoc Tan. They did
not have much time together, but the times they had

were quality times and they constantly made love. After that, Chi had to return to his unit. Things kept on going in a similar way for seventeen years. Then, on the 26th of September 1968, the lovely Hoa was visiting friends in Phuoc Tan when she was noticed by an ARVN sergeant who was in the company of four American soldiers. The Americans had the ranks of one master sergeant, one corporal and two privates. The Americans were, Master Sergeant Ronald Buick, Corporal John Kelly, Privates Neville Williamson, and Brian Jones.

All of the five men were drunk, and they leered at Hoa, with ARVN sergeant Ho Anh Sang saying, *"Hey you beautiful girl, we want to fuck you, so you had better get your clothes off!"* Hoa ignored them and she kept walking past them. Suddenly, she was grabbed from behind and thrown to the ground. The American master sergeant who had done that was taking his pants off as he said, *"So you want to be a cock teasing Asian slut do you? Well, you will now get fucked by four American soldiers and one ARVN sergeant! We will fuck you and we will sodomise you! How will you like that you fucking Gook bitch?"*

While his four companions, held down Hoa, the master sergeant tore her clothing and completely stripped her. Then, the ARVN sergeant, the American sergeant, and the corporal and the two private soldiers all took turns in raping Hoa. She was being held down by the other rapists who then raped her when their turn came to do so! She had resisted and spat in the faces of each of her attackers. Having had his way with Hoa, the American master sergeant turned her over and then inserted his penis into her anus. While he did that he said, *"Well you little gook slut, how do you like being fucked up your arse? That is all that you gooks deserve!"*

Eventually, Hao's ordeal finally ended, and she barely managed to get back to her Phuoc Tan home. She was very emotionally upset, and she was still partly naked because her attackers had torn her clothes off before they all raped her. Being of a calm disposition in spite of her cloths being ripped open and dirty, she realised that she needed to cover her body as best as she could.

So, she covered herself as best she could with her torn and soiled cheongsam. She was crying as she entered her house, and her mother immediately knew that something awful had happened. After a long time, Hoa finally managed to calm down sufficiently to tell her mother what had happened.

In the weeks that followed, Hoa was horrified to think that she could been infected with a venereal disease. Concerned about it, she spoke to her mother about it, and she was told that it was likely she had a disease such as gonorrhoea and if that was left untreated, that the venereal disease had would wreak havoc with her ovaries, which could make her sterile.

After she had been informed of that, she said, *"It is bad enough that a woman gets attacked by a pack of cowards and gets fucked by all of them no matter how much she does not want that to happen. What these arseholes of men have done, besides raping me, is they may have infected me with a venereal disease and that may have taken away my birthright to have children!*

If any man ever tries that again, not just will I kill that arsehole, but I will castrate him before I kill him. I will do that, even if I have to wait up to five years before I can get him into situations where that becomes possible! In relation to the five men raping me, I want to see a qualified doctor so that I can firstly have the correct diagnosis and secondly so that I have the correct treatment if I do in fact have a venereal disease! If I ever see any of those men who attacked and raped me again, I shall see to it that I castrate the arseholes before I kill them That shall be done to all of them!"

Her mother called Bian, also was furious that Hoa had been raped and she thought that the five men who had committed that crime were adding insult to injury because they had raped Hoa on her seventeenth birthday. She said, *"Hoa, these men who have committed the crime of rape against you, do you know their identities?"*

Hoa replied, *"Mother, I only know and can confirm the identity of one of the men involved. He is ARVN sergeant Ho Anh Sang. He and his four American army friends not just raped me by fucking my vagina, all of them also raped me by fucking me up my bum! All I can tell anyone about their identities is that they are Americans, that one of them held the rank of master sergeant, one was a corporal and the other two of them were privates in the army of the USA! It should be possible to obtain their identities because of the fact that they are very likely to have come from the huge American bases at Bien Hoa or Long Binh!*

Bian said, *"Hoa, we must bring these low-grade men to justice! How about me going around the Long Binh and Bien Hoa areas and trying to find out the identity of the Americans? Once we have them, we should be able to begin prosecuting all of the men involved. I have written to your father who is currently near the 'Parrots Beak' area near the Cambodian border with his ARVN unit. When he reads that you have been raped and sodomised by the five men, I think that he will quickly come here, and he will take action against all men involved!*

Sure enough, a letter from senior sergeant Xuan arrived three days later. Bian spoke to Hoa and said, *"Hoa, your father's letter in answer to my letter to him, which informed him of the crimes committed against you, has arrived. He said that he is coming here for a month and that while he is here, he will take up the fight against the criminals who did those things to you! He has already started proceedings against ARVN sergeant Ho Anh Sang.*

The Military Police of ARVN known as QC has arrested him and the charges against Sgt Ho Anh Sang are in progress! While all of that may sound good to you, your father has warned that Sergeant Anh Sang is from a powerful family, and that he has powerful connections within the ARVN and the forces of the USA! Due to his debt, he was refused a commission to become an ARVN officer and he is bitter about that. He sees himself as a Vietnamese gentleman, but he has no scruples and he can never be considered as a gentleman, learned or otherwise! So, maintain your vigilance and never let down your guard, because that sergeant has powerful friends who will all be out to get you!"

The support of her mother steadied Hoa and she replied, *"Thank you mother, I think that we should do that and that both of us should go to the American bases. With luck, we may even be able to get sight of them. If so, we should be able to find out what their names are!"* That resulted in both women going to the American base at Bien Hoa. After arrival there, they entered the nearest orderly room of an American Unit they could find. As they walked not the orderly room, they saw corporal Rodgers who was sitting at the counter. Corporal Rodgers said, *"Look here ladies, this is the orderly room of a US military Unit, and no civilians are allowed in here!"* Both Hoa ad her mother could understand and speak English fluently and that resulted in Bian loudly saying, *"Corporal, I am Bian Xuan and I demand to see either your superior officer or the American Military Police!"* Corporal Rodgers said, *"Wait while I let Captain Williams know that you are here and explain what you want!"*

He then left the room leaving the two Vietnamese women talking to each other. Bian spoke to Hoa. She said, *"Hoa, although we may get lucky and the Americans may start investigating as a result, please don't get your hopes up too high about this! I caution you against becoming too hopeful of obtaining justice because it is far more likely that they will simply blame you for everything and then. After that, they will just not take any action at all! In short, I expect the low-life American aggressors to pretend to be doing something about the fact that your rapists are all still at large in the Bien Hoa and Long Binh areas, but they will only cover-up their crimes and nothing will be done!"*

At that point, Captain Williams entered the orderly room and spoke to the women. He said, *"Well, what is it that you two broads want?"* Bian spoke up. She said, *"Captain Williams? I and my daughter are Hoa here to report the assault and rape, including anal rape of my daughter Hoa. She was raped by an ARVN sergeant called Ho Anh Sang and his four American companions. They were one American master sergeant, one American corporal and two American privates, but we do not know their names!"*

The American Captain did not like what he was hearing, and he reacted by stalling. He said, *"It is all very well for you fucking gook broads to come into my orderly room and then make serious allegations against American soldiers! I do not believe you and I think that your daughter has brought this down on herself! I do not want to hear your allegations, so go away and do not come back!"*

Bian answered that with, *"Very well, Captain Williams, you have instructed us to leave and that is what we shall do! However, you have not heard the last of this, I was hoping to save you from a visit by the QC.* (ARVN Military Police) *However, your attitude is such that I am turning this prosecution over to my husband who shall be returning from the 'Parrots Beak' are soon!* Captain Williams replied with, *"Go away you stupid gook woman! Go away and live your lives without accusing Americans of anything! Just get used to the fact that Americans are here and that you gooks have to obey! Go home and forget about all of this!"*

So, Bian and her daughter Hoa left the American base and returned to their home at Phuoc Tan Village. As they were leaving, Bian spoke to Hoa. She said, *"Unfortunately, my daughter, this has turned out in the way that I was expecting! It is confirmation of the fact that the that the American oppressors do not care about Vietnamese people and that the see us as mere chattels and they think that they can do whatever they want to with us all at any time! Americans have made it very obvious that that they are the new rulers of our country and that they consider all Vietnamese people to be expendable!"*

Hoa had been silent because she was thinking of how to make a success of her life at future dates. She decided to speak to Bian about her hopes and desires. She said, *"Mother, I have been giving a lot of thought to what has happened to me and what my prospects for the future are! It is obvious to me that I have to forget about getting revenge upon the men who raped me for the time being.*

It seems to me that the best way forward for me is not have any relationships with males other than professional or religious ones. In order to advance, I think that I should enter the ARVN or the Police as a Reserve Officer. Either way, it will give me the status that I need to finally find at the very least, the ARVN sergeant Ho Anh Sang. Eventually, justice shall be mine!"

So, with, Hoa now attracted to the idea of serving the Government of the Republic of Vietnam (known as South Vietnam by the USA and her allies) as an officer in the ARVN. (Army of Republic of Vietnam) In order to achieve that, she was invited to hold interviews and undergo some tests at the ARVN recruiting office located in Ho Thi Ky Street of Saigon. After she had finally found the recruiting office, Hoa walked into it and spoke to the ARVN lieutenant who was manning the desk at the entrance to the office.

She said, *"My name is Hoa Lan Xuan and I wish to serve my country as best I can by becoming an ARVN officer! Can you help me to achieve that here and now?"* The lieutenant behind the desk, said, *"My name is Lieutenant Duy Nguyen Sang and I am the ARVN recruiting officer for this region of the Republic of Vietnam! I just absolutely love your looks, my beautiful lady! You say your name is Hoa Lang Xuan, and I cannot help but think that somehow, I have heard of that name before now, but I do not know if there is any connection to you. Time will tell! During the meantime, I have some simple written tests for you to complete before you can be admitted to Thu Duc Military Academy in the area of Thu Duc town."* Lieutenant Duy Nguyen Sang then gave Hoa the necessary tests, which she passed with high marks.

Finally, having completed the tests, the Lieutenant again spoke to Hoa. He said, *"Hoa, may I call you Hoa?"* She replied, *"Yes you can call me Hoa, in fact I do not care what other people call me, as long as it is not too late for my meals!"* Duy said, *"You have performed well in your written tests, now we are at what I consider to be the most critical point. We now go what is in your progress and advancement for me! To guarantee your entry to the academy, I need you to pay me US$580.00. If you do not pay it, you shall not enter the reserve officer academy at Thu Duc!"* That distressed Hoa, but she knew about the graft practised by officials in South Vietnam, and she had the money with her, ready to pay to whom-ever she had to pay.

Hoa reached into the bag she had with her and took out the money before giving it to Lieutenant Duy Nguyen Sang. She said, *"Well, Lieutenant, here is my money, now give me more information and let's get my entry to the academy going!"* Duy eagerly took the US$580.00 from her and he gave her a receipt for it. He said, *"Welcome to the officer class of the ARVN, Hoa!*

Since 1955, the school has been given the job of training cadre and specialists in addition to the infantry training which remains as the heart of its reserve officer output. Upon the completion of your training, you shall receive the rank of aspirant. (That is one level below 2nd lieutenant.) After you have completed your training which will take about twenty-seven weeks at the moment, you will graduate as an aspirant.

You shall serve up to four years as an aspirant reserve officer before you get transferred to other units or get to be able to hold a higher rank. Of course, all of that shall be made much quicker and easier for you if you pay the money that is being asked for. The more you grease the palms of the men or women in authority, that faster will be your rise in the hierarchy of the Army of the Republic of Vietnam! (South Vietnam).

Like most people in the southern part of Vietnam between 1945 and 1975, Hoa knew that in order to get ahead, she had no alternative but to pay the bribes to the people in authority in order for her to be successful. The corruption fuelled the greed of most officials in South Vietnam.

Hoa finally entered the academy at Thu Duc and began training as an infantry reserve officer. She completed all of the tasks set for her and did so both willingly and competently! So enthusiastic was she in her approach to her training, that many of the instructional staff at the Thu Duc academy were speaking to each other about her.

Typically, they would say to each other, *"I have never seen a more committed person attending the reserve officer training programme of the Republic of Vietnam! I think that whichever unit she ends up being posted to as an aspirant officer will be very fortunate because of her services!"*

Meanwhile, back in Long Binh, Lieutenant Duy Nguyen Sang was visiting his brother, sergeant Ho Ahn Sang. He said to Ho, *"Ho, I had the recent pleasure of admitting a very beautiful woman into the ARVN Officer Academy at Thu Duc. She is outstanding and she originally comes from Phuoc Tan village which I understand is relatively close to Long Binh! The instructional staff at the Thu Duc academy tell me that they are thrilled at the way she always does things very competently and that they all admire her!"*

Sergeant Ho Anh Sang replied, *"Brother, very early in the year, I and four American soldiers who are part of an American supply unit known as the US 3rd Ordnance Battalion Group at Long Binh, were at Phuoc Tan and we saw a very beautiful girl. She just ignored all five of us and that infuriated me and the Americans! So, we followed her and then the American master sergeant who was with us ran up behind her and threw her onto the ground.*

After that, she was held down by two of us while we all took turns in raping her after the master sergeant had torn her clothes off her. I had the presence of mind to take her photograph before the five of us all fucked her. We did not just rape her; we also fucked her up her arsehole! I have the photo of the girl we raped with me, and I will now show it to you."

With that said, Ho showed his brother the photo of the lovely Hoa. Duy immediately recognised Hoa and spoke to his brother. He said, *"Is this the girl you and your American companions raped near her home at Phuoc Tan? She is this the woman who is about to become an aspirant officer in the AVRN!"* Because Lieutenant Duy Nguyen Sang confirmed that it was Hoa, it caused his brother, sergeant Ho Ahn Sang to say, *"Well, we have a major problem! We must somehow make sure that she can never bear witness against me the or the Americans! Please use your considerable influence to have her promoted to 2ⁿᵈ lieutenant and then posted Bien Hoa or Long Binh areas! Make sure that she is posted to a unit which is active against the patriots we now call Viet Cong. That way, the Viet Cong may wipe her out for us! In the meantime, take whatever action is necessary to have her killed by one of our ARVN assassins if the Viet Cong do not kill her!"*

Ten days later, Hoa presented herself once again the Recruiting Office in Ho Thi Ky Street and was admitted to the office where Lieutenant Duy Nguyen Sang was sitting at his desk. Hoa walked in and saluted him. Then she said, *"Sir, I have been told that you wish to see me urgently!"* Duy replied, *"Yes Hoa, you have completed your training and many things have changed since we last spoke to each other.*

If you now pay me US$100.00, I can get you promoted to 2ⁿᵈ lieutenant now, without all of the other *stuff normally associated with that rank! So, do you have US$100.00, or can you get it? If so, when?"* Ho replied, *"Yes, Duy, I can get it because I have it in my bank account. I can have it here in about twenty minutes from now!"* The greedy recruiting officer said, *"Fine Hoa, now go and get the money and then return here with it. Upon you giving it to me, I shall give you your rank insignia and the paperwork confirming your posting to your new unit based at Long Binh!"*

Hoa left the recruiting office and returned with US$100.00 which she gave to Duy. He reacted by giving her the rank insignia of 2nd Lieutenant, which she immediately put on. He then gave her a large manilla envelope and said, *"Hoa, you have been chosen for the awesome task of being liaison officer to the 173rd Airborne Brigade (US Unit), based at Bien Hoa. Be prepared for constant action, because that is what you are likely to be involved in as of now!"* Hoa said, *"Thank Duy"*, saluted him, and then she left.

As soon as she had gone through the door, Duy picked up the telephone and spoke to his brother, sergeant Ho Anh Sang. Ho answered and was told, *"Hey brother, it is Duy, I have some good news for you. The great embarrassment to you, called 2nd Lieutenant Hoa Lan Xuan has been posted to the 173rd Airborne Brigade as liaison officer. That means that she will accompany them on their missions, and she should die from that soon enough. In case she does not, you must organise her murder in let's say two months from now. I say to wait two months, because the Viet Cong might do the job for us by then!"*

That resulted in Ho saying, *"That is good to hear! If we can have the bitch sent to forward areas, we*

*could find that the Viet Cong will kill her for us. That
will stop her from being such an embarrassment to us!
In the meantime, I shall look around for a hitman to kill
her if the Viet Cong do not do so!"*

The telephone conversation was being held
between the brothers at a sergeants' mess where it was
overheard by a female cleaner. Unknown to her ARVN
and American employers, she was an active agent of the
local Viet Cong patriot units serving the Long Binh
area. Fearing for 2nd Lt Hoa Lan Xuan, she decided to
tell her of what she had overheard. She looked for her
and having found her, she spoke to the lovely Hoa.

She said, *"My name is Dung Cai Diep Ly, Hoa,
I have some bad news for you! I just overheard some
sergeants and officers of the ARVN speaking on the
telephone. They were saying that you are an
embarrassment to them, and they want you dead! I
heard that one of the leaders of that group of ARVN
plotters is the ARVN sergeant who took part in your
rape with four American soldiers also taking part.*

*Apparently, the reason that you have been
posted to the Long Binh area is because of the
likelihood that you may be killed by the Viet Cong. That
is why those in authority of the ARVN have sent you
here! As well, if the Viet Cong units do not kill you by
next month, the ARVN will, and they have already
ordered your assassination!"*

Hoa was shocked into silence for a moment and
then she said to her informant, *"Thank you for telling
me this, Dung, from what you have said, I now have to
defect and become a member of the resistance! Very*

well then, do you know how I can do that?" Dung replied, *"Hoa, I am an active Viet Cong agent.*

I can take you to meet the Commanding Officer of the D440 Viet Cong Battalion from Long Kanh Province who is visiting Long Binh if you would like to become part of that unit! However, if all of that works out, you will have to leave here and go to the Long Khanh area! D440 Battalion is currently recruiting, and I am sure that they would welcome a woman who has been an ARVN officer. So, how do you feel about that?"

Hoa replied, *"It saddens me that I must now fight against my former comrades of the ARVN with whom I became a combat Veteran in my own right! However, as you have pointed out, my enemies are in the ARVN, and I now must flee in order to remain alive! By being a part of the resistance, it may give me the opportunity to confront the ARVN sergeant who took part in my rape and then I shall cut out his balls and so have appropriate revenge! So, please organise this meeting. I have to do this!"* Dung said, *"Be ready tonight by 7pm. By then it will becoming dark, and we shall get you into the meeting with Comrade Nguyen Van Tan the CO of D440 Viet Cong Battalion!"*

At seven pm of that night, Dung, and Hoa waited for darkness to fall before they went into the forested regions surrounding the ARVN/American base at Long Binh. After skirting the outskirts of Long Binh, they melted into the forest with Dung leading the way. After another hour of walking, Dung said to Hoa, *"Hoa, I am sorry, but I now have to apply a bind fold to you so that our forward bases near Long Binh are not compromised by you if you happen to not want to join the patriot movement!"*

With Hoa's blindfold in place, Dung guided her to the headquarters on the Viet Cong of the Long Binh area. Upon reaching there, she removed the blindfold from Hoa and introduced her to others. She asked about the where-abouts of Comrade Nguyen Van Tan of the D440 Battalion from Long Khanh.

She was told, *"That is him over there, about twenty metres away from us. He is still wearing the insignia of the 'People's Army of the Democratic Republic of Vietnam! That is because D440 had been a unit of the north before it was sent down south in order to strengthen the patriot presence in Long Khanh and to help D445 which is Ba Ria's own battalion after it was badly mauled by actions against it by the soldiers of the Uc da Loi during the 'Battle of Long Tan!'"*

Dung walked over to where Comrade Nguyen Van Tan was speaking to another patriot, and she spoke to him. She said, *"Comrade Van Tan, please allow me to introduce to you, Hoa Lan Xuan. She was formerly a lieutenant with the ARVN; however, she was pack-raped repeatedly by diseased members of the ARVN and American soldiers. Because those who raped her now fear that she will bring them undone, she has been marked for death by the ARVN killers! I have spoken to her, and she is happy to join us against the ARVN and the American oppressors!"*

Colonel Van Tan replied, *"Hoa, I have immediate vacancies for medical orderlies that must be filled immediately. After you have proved your worth in the role of medical orderly in my battalion, we shall consider your promotion and training to become an officer. Until that time, you shall be a medical orderly with the duties of going out while under enemy fire and bringing out our wounded after which you shall treat them and give them their first aid. After that you may be required to help with the relocation of wounded D440 members to our treatment areas and hospitals for their continued treatment. Will you accept this awesome responsibility?"*

Hoa said, *"Yes Comrade Colonel, I do accept that, and I am happy to start at the bottom. I shall perform whatever role that you place me into to the best of my ability, sir!"* Colonel Van Tan replied, *"Very well then Hoa, be ready to move out of here and we shall walk to Long Khanh where my D440 battalion is located. Once we are there, your training as a medical orderly shall commence and after your training, you shall be put into action saving the lives of wounded members of D440 Battalion!"* They moved out and returned to Long Khanh that night.

Finally arriving at Long Khanh, Hoa was immediately put into training. During that time, she learned to apply dressings, how to stop the bleeding of her patients, evacuation procedures, and also how to use the favoured weapon of the Viet Cong, the AK-47 assault rifle. That night, all members of D440 were called in to attend an "O" group during which they were told, *"D440 is moving toward Ba Ria to help out D445 which has been badly damaged from coming under sustained attack by Uc da Loi (Australian) forces.*

These men are a much more serious threat than the Americans, because they fight like we do! If we were fighting the Americans, we would receive ample warnings of their actions against us. The is because American attacks are always preceded by firstly a devasting B52 air strike, followed by airstrikes from fighter-bombers, followed by massive artillery strikes, which are in turn followed by a chemical strike involving the saturated used of chemical sprays and other means of poisoning. Also, our agents have infiltrated the American bases at Long Binh and Bien Hoa, and we know what the Americans are planning before their men know it.

Compare that with the Uc da Loi. They do not allow any Vietnamese people into their base areas, and so, we do not have any intelligence about what Australians are planning. Add that to the fact that Australians work quietly, and they do not announce their intentions to us through firstly using massive artillery strikes and massive air strikes before going into an area, and they go looking for us in the jungles, swamps, and marshes!

That means there will be no warning if they find our camps. They will just move into our positions and attack us. Also, these men do in fact call down their own artillery very close to their positions and even include their own position if they feel that is required to win! For that reason, we shall double our on-duty sentries at all times. As much as it is possible, we shall avoid contact with the Uc da Loi forces!

The entire battalion is to take part in the "Stand-to drills" because we cannot take the chance of these soldiers appearing among us and killing us all!" Next, came the announcement, *"After you have checked your weapons and ammunition and other equipment, tonight you should, eat, drink and be merry! Those of you who are on duty as our sentries, shall not drink any alcohol! For starting in the morning, we travel to the areas near Ba Ria and Nui Dat where we shall make war upon the AVRN outposts in those areas!"* (Uc da Loi means big red rat, the name was applied to mean Australians because Vietnamese people saw the red kangaroos painted on the sides and bonnets of Australian vehicles. They did not know what a kangaroo was, and so, they thought that the symbol on Australian vehicles was a large red rat.)

Next the entire battalion practised 'Fire and movement' drills until those in charge were happy with the progress of their soldiers. The soldiers of D440 were easily identified from other Viet Cong units because that unit was originally part of the North Vietnamese Army. They wore green uniforms like the Australians did as well as floppy hats and they were armed with current model AK-47 assault rifles as well as RPG 7 rocket launchers.

At 16:00 hours of the twenty-first of April 1968, The Commanding Officer of D440 Battalion, colonel Nguyen Van Tan, called for an "O" group to be held with all NCOs and medical orderlies attending. When all of these people were in attendance, the colonel began to speak.

He said, *"Ladies and Gentlemen, D440 battalion has been chosen to help strike a blow against the American imperialist aggressor! We shall move out of this locality and go to where we are needed to reinforce the forces of our Fatherland which have been attacking Saigon! We have had reports that American forces are occupying areas near and around the Bien Hoa-Long Binh areas in great numbers. I have been told that we are to bring the hated Yankee to battle as he moves out of the Saigon area and moves towards Bien Hoa and Long Binh areas.*

Apparently, the Yankee aggressor wishes to draw Vietnamese patriot units into a large-scale fire-fight which we cannot hope to win! Very well then! The Yankee aggressor shall have the fire-fight that he wants, but it shall be on our terms, and it shall take place at sites of our choosing! Is what I have just told you clear, or are there things that you still need to know?"

Hoa's commanding officer, called 2nd Lieutenant Hanh Kiên Danh spoke. She said, *"Sir, where are we going to set up our base areas and are they far enough away from the Uc da Loi to ensure that we are not bothered by those soldiers?"* The colonel answered, *"Lieutenant, so far, our information is saying that the Uc da Loi are currently still within the Phuc Tuy and Long Khanh areas. Although that is the case, they can be very quickly put into action against us through the use of helicopters. If that happens and the Australians do in fact operate in the Long Binh and Bien Hoa areas, we shall avoid contact with them unless we and other patriot units find ourselves in the position where we can grab the Uc da Loi by their belt buckles and so render their artillery useless to them!*

We are going to establish a base camp in the area of the town of Tan Uyen. We have superior AK-47 assault rifles, our mortars are new, and we have plentiful supplies of ammunition for them, and we have recoilless rifles and other anti-tank weapons. It is my information that one of the hated Yankee units we could be facing is the First Infantry Division, better known as the 'Big Red One' and possibly the 402 Airborne which is also known as 'Screaming Eagles', does that answer your questions, Lieutenant?" 2nd Lt. Danh said, *"Thank you sir, what is the probability that we will be in direct battle with enemy forces?"*

The colonel replied, *"That depends upon our enemies! I have just been handed intelligence that the Australians appear to be setting up two fire-support bases located about seven kilometres from Tan Uyen, so it appears that the Uc da Loi soldiers shall be within our areas of operations against the hated Yankee after all! The intelligence says that the names of the Uc da Loi Fire Support Bases are 'Coral' and 'Balmoral' That again makes me stress what I have ordered before! Avoid contact with the Uc da Loi units unless we outnumber them by at least three to one and we can get so close to them that we can grab them by their own belt buckles! If we depart from these principles, we shall face a blood bath which our soldiers will lose!*

I find that most disturbing because of how closely the Uc da Loi match our own forces. As you know, D440 was originally a part of the 'Peoples Liberation Army of the Democratic Republic of Vietnam' (North Vietnam). Our unit has the green uniform of the People's Liberation Army and that could cause some problems as to identity. The Uc da Loi also wear olive green uniforms and soft shapeless hats as we do. Therefore, it is vital that all of our soldiers check the identity of any other soldiers whom they may see. We do not want to fire upon, and kill own soldiers, so identify any other soldiers who you may happen to see before you engage them in combat!"

Heroine Hoa

Hoa was in the role of medical orderly, which in other armies would have been called 'stretcher bearer'. Her supervising officer called 2nd Lt Hanh Kiên Danh. As reports of casualties of D440 were coming in, the officer who was a nurse before joining the Viet Cong forces, went to Hoa, and said, *"Hoa, we need you to get out there and rescue our wounded from the Uc da Loi soldiers! They are only at the strength of one company,* (possibly 'B' Coy, 1RAR) *yet, they have successfully held off the entire regiment, and they have killed many patriots!*

They do not seem to have any fear of anything. They are calling their artillery upon their own positions. It is so effective that our soldiers cannot even get close enough to them to kill them! We are losing many comrades in this fight! So go and rescue our wounded soldiers!"

Hoa immediately moved out toward the sounds of battle towards her front. She had only moved forward for two-hundred metres when she noticed a patriot wearing an olive-green uniform lying on the ground and under the cover of some bushes. His AK-47 assault rifle was lying on the ground near him and he was bleeding from wounds to his left knee and his left shoulder.

Hoa went to him and spoke. She said, *"Comrade, I am Hoa Lan Xuan, and I shall help you to get out of this area. So, I first need to know how bad your wounds to the knee and leg are.* The wounded man replied, *"I am Bao Chien Quang. My knee hurts like crazy and I cannot put any weight upon my left leg because of the wounded knee."* Hoa said, *"I am here to help you to get away. You have already told me that you*

71

find it too painful to walk, so how about we arrange things so that you are on my right-hand side and put your right arm around my shoulders. You could then lift your left leg while you put your weight upon my shoulders. As I move forward, you can move your right leg forward and by keeping your weight upon my shoulders, we should be able to get you back to the rear of the fighting!"

Bao did as she had instructed him and then he became concerned about his AK-47 and he asked, *"Hoa, could you please pick up my AK-47 and give it to me?"* Hoa did what she was asked to do and then she said, *"Here you go Bao, now look after your weapon! For now, raise your left leg and put your weight upon my shoulders by placing your arm over my right shoulder and spreading your weight evenly across my back. This is the only way a lightly built person like me can carry someone of your weight and build!"* Bao did as he was asked, and eventually both of them made it back to the rear areas where treatment could be provided to Bao.

Hoa proved her worth over and over again by constantly going out while under fire and returning with wounded members of the battalion during the 'Battle of Fire Support Base Coral'. As soon as she had brought these men back to safe areas, she dressed their wounds and comforted them in general. Having done that, she again went out into the battle field and returned with another wounded soldier of the regular Viet Cong Regiments.

Without waiting for orders to do so, Hoa was seen to constantly go back into the contested areas and then return with a wounded man whom she treated by applying the first aid that she had been taught. There is no doubt that she and other patriots like her saved the lives of many of the wounded patriots during the First Battle of Fire Support Base Coral.

As time progressed, Hoa impressed her male and female friends who were in the D440 Battalion with her. In due course, she was selected for training as an officer of the D440 battalion. She applied herself with vigour to this new role and passed all of her training subjects with ease. Her enthusiasm for throwing the foreign forces out of Vietnam was noted as was her efficiency. She was wondering what was happening after having been told that she was required to see her Commanding Officer, Comrade Colonel Nguyen Van Tan.

As she went into the bunker which served as an orderly room, she saluted her commanding officer and said, *"Officer Cadet Hoa Lan Xuan reporting as ordered sir!"* She was told by Colonel Van Tan, *"Relax Hoa, I have the pleasure of informing you that your training is now over and that you are now 2nd Lieutenant Hoa Lan Xuan of the Viet Cong D440 Battalion!"* He reached into his pocket and took out the insignia of rank of a 2nd lieutenant of the Peoples' Liberation Army of the Democratic Republic of Vietnam.

As he handed them to Hoa, he said, *"Here are the new rank insignia that you shall wear from now on until such time as you are either promoted or dead! You shall for now, have command of the seventh Platoon of this battalion. Its present commander has come down with malaria and he can no longer function as a soldier, let alone a commander. This is your big chance to prove yourself, do not let yourself or the rest of us down! Congratulations 2nd Lt Hoa Lan Xuan!"*

Hoa was thrilled by what her commanding officer had told her. Colonel Tan now continued speaking. He said, *"Comrade 2nd Lt Hoa Lan Xuan, I have been told that you were repeatedly raped some time ago by an AVRN sergeant and his four American companions! It may interest you to know that we now have the services of a qualified medical doctor who has been sent to us directly from Hanoi! She has brought with her, anti-biotics such as penicillin and tetracycline. Please go and see our new medical officer for she should be able to help you."*

Hoa was thankful that she now had the opportunity to speak to a qualified medical doctor at last. She went to the medical outpost of the battalion and reported to Captain Bê Bâo Hoang. Entering the battalion's medical centre, Hoa saluted and spoke to the female doctor. She said, *"Doctor, can you help me? I was repeatedly raped by five men when I was seventeen years old and I think that they could infected me with a venereal disease that appears to have run its course, but every now and then, I get the burning sensations whenever I have to urinate. Therefore, I am worried that I either still have the disease or else I am relapsing and getting it all over again. Is that possible, and if so, can you please cure me?"*

The doctor said, *"Hoa, please take off your under clothes, because I need to examine your genitals in order to be able to give an exact diagnosis! If I see a problem, I shall take a biopsy which is a small scraping to use as a sample which can be put under a microscope and then we will be in a position to find out what is bothering you!"* She then examined the genitals of Hoa. Finally, the doctor said, *"Hold yourself very still Hoa, I now must take a scraping from inside your vagina and after that I need to examine the scraping under the microscope. This will hurt, but it must be done in order for me to see what your problem is."*

So, the medical examination of Hoa was completed and after the doctor had examined the sample, she was not yet able to let Hoa know the diagnosis. Having completed that, she sent for Hoa to again see her three days later. Hoa attended the medical centre as ordered. Upon seeing Hoa again, Doctor Hoang spoke to her. She said, *"Hoa, I think that you are suffering from a relapse of gonorrhoea and that you have had that disease for so long that I would be surprised if you can still have children, because that social disease can spell disaster for the ovaries of a woman who has had it for as long as you!*

Three days ago, I took action to grow a culture from the scraping from your vagina! The culture, when it has completed growing, will tell me for sure whether or not you do in fact have gonorrhoea. Return here later today. By then I have been able to accurately observe the culture and make the correct diagnosis! I have spoken to the Battalion Commander, and he has agreed that you are to be sent for treatment at Hanoi for specialist treatment! After which you shall return to this unit and continue to fight the enemies of the people! Do you understand all of this and are you willing to do what must be done?" Hoa replied, *"Yes Doctor, I shall do as you ask!"*

And so, Hoa returned to the doctor later that day. Upon their meeting, Doctor Hoang said, *"Hoa, I have successfully grown the culture from the scraping of your vagina. The results confirm that that you have had gonorrhoea and your burning sensation now is a re-occurrence of that social disease!* Hoa said, *"Thank you, Doctor for diagnosing me correctly! I shall do whatever is required of me to both combat the venereal disease and the wage war upon the enemies of my country!"*

Doctor Hoang said, *"Look forward to your stay at a hospital in Hanoi, there you will meet new people and you will be cured of your disease by having crystalline penicillin injections. I am sorry, but we cannot treat you for the disease here, in the field, because we do not have the necessary supplies and facilities to treat you, so you must go to Hanoi!"*

Hoa began walking from Long Khanh to Hanoi. She finally arrived at the hospital at Hanoi where her treatment was carried out. She found that the crystalline penicillin injections were rather painful, and she was relieved when she was told that she had finally been cured of gonorrhoea.

Now that she was cued, she decided to return to D440 Battalion to resume her duties. She went to the base camp area, and she was told to wait for the Battalion Commander. She waited for ten minutes before being invited to see Colonel Van Tan. upon being admitted to the presence of her CO, she saluted him, and he said, *"At ease 2nd Lt Hoa Lan Xuan, I have some news for you. Last week, this battalion was in battle with an ARVN force made up of some infantry mixed with tanks and armoured personnel carriers.*

We managed to destroy all of the armoured vehicles and we took prisoners! One of these prisoners is an ARVN sergeant called Ho Anh Sang and I am led to believe that he was one of the five creeps who raped you. Is that correct? Hoa said, *"Yes sir, that is correct, not only was he one of the five men who did it, he appeared to be their ringleader, at least that was my impression, sir!"* Colonel Van Tan said, *"Hoa, I realise what was done to you was devasting at best. However, I cannot just turn the arsehole over to you. So, we shall give him a fair trial, during which he will be defended by a Vietnamese lawyer. I have already drawn up charges against him!*

These include making various people in the military districts that he was a part of live in misery and always be close to starvation because he and others like him were taking even the food from the mouths of the population. Accordingly, his charges are five counts of rape. Other charges include making the people of the military district where he served come close to starvation. Still other charges are that he forcefully entered the homes of people and removed their belongings!

That is theft and when combined with his love of causing misery to others including your rape and his greed resulting in making people starve in order for him to live very well, he will get the death penalty! If he is found to be guilty of the majority of charges, during the court-martial that I am prosecuting against him, he will be sentenced to die by firing squad.

I now need to know if you would like to command the firing squad that executes him! So, Hoa, do you want command his execution or should I find someone else to do that job?" Hoa replied, *"Comrade Colonel Van Tan, I am honoured that you see fit to have me in command of his execution. I accept that responsibility, Thank you sir!"*

Official Actions Against the People by Government Agencies South Vietnam from 1954

As we have seen, the Americans through the 'Hawks' among them, including Vice President Richard Nixon, Admiral Arthur Radford, and the Chief of staff of the US Air Force Nathan F Twining had managed to get Emperor Boa Dai to appoint Ngo Dinh Diem as his Prime Minister.

In direct violation of the Peace Agreements reached at the Geneva Conference of the First Indochina War, the Americans advised Ngo Dinh Diem to set-up a separate South Vietnamese State with its own National assembly and constitution. At a conference held between the Americans and Diem, it is believed that the discussion went along these lines:

General Daniels said, *"Now look here, Diem, you are only in power in South Vietnam because we, the Americans decided that you could help America to remain dominant in the south east of Asia! Our OSS, which has been re-organised and renamed as the Central Intelligence Agency played a major part in organising the Coup d' état against Emperor Boa Dai on your behalf! So, my boy, you are now moving from being our installed Prime Minister to the President of the Republic of Vietnam who has been placed into that position by Americans. I urge you to remember that just as America has put you into power in South Vietnam,*

78

we can also wipe you and your government out if we want to do so!

So, in order to legitimise your presidency of the Republic of Vietnam, there are some things that must be done by you and your ministers! First and foremost is our requirement that you immediately hold a fake referendum about the future of Vietnam. It does not matter what the people of South Vietnam think, in time they will bow to the might of the USA! We do not care how you rig the referendums and elections, just do as we Americans tell you and your country shall keep on receiving American support in both military and civilian terms! Remember to do the things that we want done when we want you to do it!

So, get the fake referendum going and when it is over just say to the World Press, the following statement, "At the referendum held to determine if the people wish to join their northern neighbours in freedom, the people of South Vietnam have overwhelmingly opted to remain independent of the North and to continue with their American relationship!"

And so, a fake referendum was held, and that enabled the Americans to get rid of Bao Dai and install Ngo Dinh Diem into power after he had led a coup d' ĕtat against Emperor Bâo Dai.

By 1954, the main policies of the American neo-colonialist policy became very clear. These were (1) to do away with the French presence, (2) take over South Vietnam, (3) set-up a puppet dictatorship that was entirely dependent on Washington, (4) liquidate the national revolutionary movement in Vietnam, (5) eventually invade and conquer North Vietnam. (Vien, 2009)

The Diem regime applied systematic terror with the help of US advisors, almost as soon as it was in power. Using the fascist methods of the Nazis and the medieval methods of Vietnamese landowners and mandarins, terror was applied in order to eliminate opposition.

Diem called for a conference with his sub-ordinates. That was held and Diem addressed the vassals before him. He said, *"I want a repressive machine controlling the whole country from the capital down to the most remote villages! You shall apply massacres, torture, deportations mass imprisonment and constant raids! You shall make the population so fearful of this government, that no-one will ever dare to become a revolutionary or other kind of outlaw!"*

Not content with this, Diem said, *"As of now, we shall have an apparatus of depression using strong-armed forces and police. The Police shall wear starched white shirts, grey trousers, and a grey peaked cap. They shall be armed with colt 45 pistols, and they shall have whistles for sounding alarms and calling for help. They shall hunt down all of those who were formerly opposed the French Colonial presence. Any person who has played even a minor part against the French shall be termed "A communist". All charges of communism shall be punishable by prison, deportation, and death by torture and/or firing squad.*

Also, I want to have the communists "Re-educated" by placing them into small 'tiger cages' and for them to be kept under those conditions for as long as is necessary to change the minds of these terrorists who call themselves patriots of Vietnam or Viet Minh! After they have had a lot of this done to them and have seen their people and towns wiped out by my police and army, they shall not have the will to fight me anymore!"

Diem was praised by Richard Williams, an agent of the American CIA operating in Vietnam. He spoke to Diem by saying, *"Sir, I have authority from the government of the USA to help you set up a prison system for use against anyone at all who can be shown to have even just sympathy for the communist or socialist causes!*

I can offer you full funding if you were to set up a system of 'Tiger Cages' measuring five (5) feet high by 9 feet in length. Those who are imprisoned in the 'tiger Cages' will not be able to stand up because of the low height of the 'Tiger cages'. By incarcerating the socialists, freedom fighters and all communists, including those who only have sympathy with the Viet Minh, you shall become very feared and that is what the USA wants to happen. We want you to establish the system of imprisoning communists in these 'Tiger Cages' and we want that to take place at the site of the old French prison on Con Son Island.

We want the prisoners to be miserable, not have enough food to sustain themselves and we want the guards to splash caustic substances onto the skin of the prisoners on a regular basis. We want word about that prison to get out to the communists so that they will know that there shall be no mercy for all for those who have communist, socialist or any other viewpoints which could result in them becoming rebels sir!"

Diem answered, *"Excellent Mister Williams of the CIA, please inform you superiors at Langley in Virginia USA, that I have authorised you to establish this 'Communist Detainment System' you have told me about. The 'Tiger Cages' shall be put on Con Son Island as you have suggested and there shall be at least three hundred men in the cages as well as at least two hundred women constrained within the 'Tiger Cages'. I shall even put children into the 'Tiger Cages' and I shall tell the newspapers in Vietnam about it so that the Viet Mihn shall be informed. That way, terror will spread though Vietnamese society, and no-one shall ever dare to cross my government because of what could happen to the person caught being a socialist or communist!"*

So it was that the American presence in Vietnam was beginning, and right from the start, the Yankee and his South Vietnamese puppet officials were guilty of inflicting war crimes upon the people of southern Vietnam and later, also the upon people in the north of the country. The war crimes were committed by the government agencies of the South Vietnamese, the American Forces in particular, and even the Australians[3].

Attitudes of Many Americans and Politicians

---

[3] Australian "War Crimes mainly relate to the apparent deliberate shelling of South Vietnamese civilians who were herding their cattle between Hao Long and other places such as Long Phuoc. Australian artillery shelled these people a total of twelve (12) times. Officially, the Aussie army said that the shelling was 'accidental'. (Ham, 2007) Due to the amount of preparation and planning that goes into artillery strikes, I know that claim to be pure bunkum! If these shellings had happened only once or twice, they may have been accidental, but for that to happen twelve times cannot be accidental!

Many Americans believed that it was fair to deny the people of foreign countries their freedom on the basis of these people were communists and that it somehow made them evil people because of the American hysteria about socialism or communism. The simple fact is that Americans tend to be completely paranoid about the rights of anyone who has the political outlook of socialism or can be said to be different from American ideals. The US President Nixon had inherited the war from Johnston who had inherited it from John F Kennedy.

In the case of the US President Richard Nixon, it was said that he was heard to say, in 1969, *"Fucking Gooks, they have liberated their own country and they have gotten rid of the French colonial masters who were oppressing them! They shall not continue to have freedom because they are communists and therefore, they are the enemies of the United States of America! I shall work against the communists of Asia, and we shall bring them down! I have been working upon this glorious quest to wipe out socialism in Vietnam since 1950 when I was the Vice-president!"*

Richard Nixon's War

Prior to his election as President of the USA in 1964, Johnston used a line which promised peace, within this, had a policy of war. Nixon also used that tactic. In fact, as early as 1950, Nixon was calling for direct intervention by American ground troops which was aimed at helping out the French colonialists and inflicting more suffering upon the people of Indochina. In 1969, he was the USA President and so, he assumed that he was now fully in control of the situation. He was determined to win the war!

However, as he entered the White House, he found that he was not able to reinforce the American Expeditionary Forces because American public opinion about the Second Indochina War was demanding that American soldiers be sent back to the USA. The major reason for this was the fact that the casualty rate and war death rate of US service personnel was too high for acceptance by the public.

The cost of the war had now gone beyond US$30 billion per year and American social welfare and school developments were being denied funding so that the money could be spent on the Indochina War. As a result, public opposition to the war markedly increased and the USA woke up! (Vien, 2009)

Attitudes Towards the Vietnam War by Soldiers of the USA

Although most soldiers continued with their duties without complaint and did them to the best of their abilities, there appeared to be an undercurrent of feelings of approaching doom within some US infantry units. This manifested itself as soldiers having a feeling of not being able to return to the USA alive.

Private John Eggleston was talking to Private David Brown in Vietnam during January of 1969. Both men were from the First Infantry Division (Big Red One). John said, *"David, as you know, I have recently returned from 'R and R⁴' in Bangkok! While I was there, at my hotel, I spoke to an Aussie Special*

---

⁴ Rest and Recreation Leave

Forces soldier. We compared Aussie and American casualty figures, including the American KIA.

I told him that in the week prior to me going on R and R, America had lost eighty men KIA! That appalled him. He said that most Aussie soldiers did not support the war and considered it to be both immoral and unwinnable! He even told me something that I did not know." He said, *"Oh you poor Yank! Please realise that out of the 500,000 men you have in Vietnam, only about 48,900 participate in direct combat duties.*

The rest are in support. Now then, considering that you only have about 48,900 men involved in direct combat duties, and you have just told me that America lost another eighty men KIA last week[5], does that do not scare the fucking shit out of you?" I replied with, *"Yes Aussie, it does scare the fuck out of me. I get the impression that we Americans are simply cannon fodder and that we do not matter at all!"*

David Brown answered, *"John, I did not know that, and it worries me that neither one of us may get back Stateside alive if what the Aussie told you is correct! Like you, I have for a long time thought that our generals are morons who know nothing about anything and who will get us all killed and that it will all be for nothing in the end! It really bothers me that if the average KIA figures for Americans is at or near one hundred per week, so, in one year, we shall have lost 5,200 men KIA for that year! To me that means*

---

[5] During 1969, it was known that the US was losing 100 men KIA a week. At the end of American involvement, there were over 52,000 Americans KIA.

we are losing at least ten percent of our forces every year!

To my way of thinking, that casualty figure is miles too high! Another problem is the morality of this war! I think that it is not right for us to be here, trying to impose American values upon a sovereign country just so the American arms manufacturers such as Boeing, Lockheed, Colt just to name a few, can make millions of dollars from this fucking bullshit war!" Soon afterwards, both men were dead.

The American public had been wearied by the constantly high casualty figures. The number of soldiers KIA were bad enough, but there were also the wounded, and these outnumbered those who were KIA by at least three to one. For the Nixon Administration the main question was to work out how to continue the war and to win it as well as reducing the number of American casualties. The casualty figures and expenditure on the war had to be reduced to levels which were acceptable to the American public.

So, Nixon called in his advisors and a conference about Indochina was held. Starting the discussions, Richard Nixon said, *"Come on people, do not be shy and help me to arrive at a workable solution to continue the Vietnam War and to bloody well win it despite the anti-war outlook of the American public. Somehow, we must 'Vietnamise the War' and it would be marvelous if we can make the God-damned Gooks pay for it as well!"*

Nixon was in the company of his advisors and general staff. An American general spoke. He said,

"Sir, in order for that to occur, there are some requirements that must be met! Our puppet army, (ARVN) must be strengthened in terms of men and equipment to make it the main fighting force conducting the War in Vietnam! The ARVN Forces must become capable of providing the protection for the Saigon administration and that administration must be entirely committed to the interests of Americans and our arms dealers! We should continue the war in Vietnam by providing continuous air support and naval support for the AVRN forces while they gradually take over the fighting in Vietnam!

We must maintain our presence for as long as it is necessary, but we can increasingly make the Gookers responsible for the conduct of the war! That way, we shall avoid more clashes with large sections of the American public!"

The Harvard professor called Samuel P. Huntington said, *"I am advocating the forced 'Urbanisation' of all of the South Vietnamese population by turning all areas not controlled by the US Forces into deserts pockmarked by bomb craters, where no vegetation grows and where no birds and therefore no revolutionary forces will ever go!"* (Vien, 2009)

Soon, many others were discussing what Nixon had started and agreement was reached that suggestion of Professor Huntington be adopted. It was thought that millions of Vietnamese would therefore be forced to seek the shelter of towns and that they could not support themselves if they did not join forces with army of South Vietnam (ARVN) or else, the Police Force of South Vietnam. (Vien, 2009)

In areas controlled by the Americans, programmes were put into place to intensify the so-called pacification by the use of incessant raids, the killing of activists and patriots. As well, a programme involving the imprisonment and deportation of thousands of Vietnamese People was initiated. The South Vietnamese military forces and their police, set about intimidating the people without respite and the use of terror was stepped up using forty thousand especially trained pacification agents. (Vien, 2009)

President Nixon applied that policy at the same time as he was forced to begin withdrawing American soldiers because of worsening American casualty figures and increased home-based opposition to the Vietnam War. (Vien, 2009)

As the US Presidential elections drew nearer, Nixon unleashed his own version of total war. While the Democratic Republic of Vietnam (North Vietnam) was being bombed[6], the weight of bombs dropped on Laos and South Vietnam reached 1,389,000 tons. (Statistics from US Departments of Defence and State) These figures do not include the use of artillery to shell areas or the use of saturated spaying of defoliants and other poisonous chemicals. (Vien, 2009)

The defoliants were sprayed upon several millions of hectares, and it can best be described as biocide! According to the figures by the Americans themselves, ten million Vietnamese people were forced to move to the cities because of what the Americans and their allies had done. (Vien, 2009)

---

[6] This was yet another war crime because no war was declared against North Vietnam by the USA or its allies.

The Expansion of Nixon's War

No matter how much he wanted it to succeed, the intensified bombing, the increased strength of numbers of soldiers or the continual modernisation and re-arming of the puppet ARVN army, could never be successful in crushing the patriots of Vietnam, no matter which part of Vietnam they came from.

Nixon wanted to continue propping up of the unpopular and extremely corrupt Saigon Regime because he wanted to be seen as doing something to lower the extremely high casualty rate being suffered by American forces. His 'Vietnamisation' programme clearly meant prolonging the war in Vietnam. It directly led to the expansion of the war to the point where it involved action by the Americans or their allies against all of the countries making up Indochina. (Cambodia, Laos, and Vietnam).

It appeared that Nixon thought that his policy of 'Vietnamisation' would be easily achieved and result in turning the entire war over to the Indochinese people while ensuring that Asians would fight Asians for the benefit of the USA. By doing so, it would have ensured that the USA remained dominant in the South East of Asia!

The Americans intensified the bombing of entire regions of Laos which were controlled by the Pathet Lao Forces. The Americans used up to six hundred sorties per day of all types of aircraft, including their B52s. for their part, the Laotians were aghast to find that many of their villages had their populations forcibly removed and then rehoused in heavily guarded 'Refugee Camps' under tight control.

Nixon spoke to his generals and advisors. He said, *"I do not care how you do it, I want a decisive strike to take place against the communist foe! I do not want excuses of how it cannot be done, just fucking well do it and show the slope headed Gooks that America is still the boss and that all low-grade slope headed Gooks will obey the United States of America!"*

That next resulted in fifty (50) ARVN battalions which were under the command of twelve thousand (12,000) American advisors. These units were provided with overwhelming US air support invaded Cambodia and launched attacks upon the Plain of Jars in the Xieng Khouang area. The fighting there and other parts of Laos lasted until February 1970. (Vien, 2009)

That was followed by the Laotian Forces obtaining aid from the Vietnamese Forces and together, they launched a major offensive that was successful in driving the hated Yankee enemy out of the region. Many people were joyful that the offensive had killed so many American enemies. Now it became the standard American tactic to use especially trained mercenaries, many American advisors and large-scale air support. However, it was also doomed to failure!

Meanwhile, back in Saigon, the American Ambassador to South Vietnam was holding an emergency meeting with the leading CIA commanders and top agents. The ambassador called out to his US Marines guards to escort in the director of operations in S.E. Asia, called Richard Williams. The US Marine guards escorted him and fifteen (15) other CIA agents into the conference area of the American embassy in

Saigon. The CIA agents were all given refreshments and they were talking among themselves when the ambassador walked into the conference room.

The ambassador said, *"Gentlemen, we Americans have some severe problems in both the Vietnam and Laos areas as well as in Cambodia! Come on someone, please let me have constructive suggestions of controlling these monkeys who think that they are really human!"* No-one said anything, and the ambassador now saw Richard Williams standing among the men near the bar.

He said, *"Richard Williams, it seems to me that you are the CIA director of operations in the S.E. Asia region now and I remember how you helped to solve the Diem problem. Please put your mind to work and help me solve these problems of the Vietnamese, Laotians and Cambodians not doing what America tells them to do!"*

Richard Williams replied, *"Nice to be working with you again sir, I remember how we fixed the problem of Diem becoming too cruel a dictator and how he was an embarrassment for the USA! Therefore, it was decided that instead of simply organising removing him from power, that we did in fact kill the cruel bastard and that solved the problem of him becoming an embarrassment! What is it that you now want the CIA to do?"*

The ambassador replied, *"Richard, we have a situation where the American public wants our country to get the fuck out of Asia and at the same time, the Vietnamese are becoming alarming powerful and assertive! Our president Nixon wants to get his way in Asia and so, we shall need to organise a coup d' état against the neutral government of Cambodia. For that to work, we must get rid of King Norodom Sihanouk who is standing in our way. He has overwhelming support from his people, and I think that we must eliminate him in order to install our own puppets into the government of Cambodia! Our agents and puppets are known as Lon Nol and Sirik Matak. Once they are in power, America will have complete control of the Asian area other than China!"*

Richard Williams replied, *"Sir, you do not have to worry! I have already drawn up the plans for my CIA operatives to take over in Cambodia and even in Saigon, if need be! My units are going to topple King Sihanouk and either arrest him or else, kill him. That way American interests in South Eastern Asia shall be preserved. However, I feel that you should realise that when we successfully carry this uprising against the King and remove him, there will be many Location people who will join with their Vietnamese brothers and help then engage Americans in combat! So, if that is still what you want, I will launch the uprisings against the prince now!"*

The ambassador said, *"Richard, just do it and be quick about it!"* So it was that the King and his government were toppled, and the American puppet government of Lon Nol was installed in his place. In the face of stiff opposition from the people of Cambodia. In order to save their Lon Nol puppet government, the USA launched an offensive against Cambodia by American and ARVN soldiers.

The coup organised against King Norodom Sirhanouk had unexpected consequences for the

Americans. Many Laotian people joined their Vietnamese brothers in fighting the new American/ARVN enemy. That was followed by the reaction of American and world opinion which forced Nixon to slowly begin to withdraw American ground forces after June.

Results of the war against the people of Indochina included: 26 million bomb craters. Fourteen (14) million tons of bombs and shells dropped; three quarters upon the villages of the south and one quarter in the north. All of the cities of the north were intensely bombed, and all bridges were destroyed. Ten million people were driven out of their villages or towns. (Vien, 2009)

There are no precise figures for the number of soldiers killed (North Vietnamese army and patriots) or the number of civilian deaths and maiming by US air strikes. Also, social evils of such as drugs and prostitution became rife. We must not forget the ecological and genetic effects of the chemical warfare unleashed upon Indochina through the Yankee use of defoliants like "Agent Orange" This was, the most disgusting of the war crimes committed by the USA and its allies!

After a war such as the Second Indochina War or the Vietnam War if you wish to call it that, a gradual return to a normal life is usually possible if the people have security and if there is no civil war. After Nixon's disastrous and war-like policies in Vietnam and his continual lying to the American People about Americans not bombing the villages and cities of Vietnam or Cambodia, Gerald Ford succeeded him.

Ford stated, *"There will be a bloodbath in South East Asia when all American Forces leave."* That did not happen. Ford knew that his intelligence services had prepared for just that and all conditions were in place for a Vietnamese civil war to take place. (Vien, 2009)

On the 22nd of January 1975, one thousand and five hundred people who made up fifteen different organisations and who were from various areas around Saigon went to Ân Quy Pagoda in order to celebrate the signing of the Paris agreement. These organisations circulated a petition which demanded that the USA immediately stop sending aid to Saigon and called for the immediate resignation of the South Vietnamese puppet government of President Nguyen Van Thieu.

On the 7th of April 1975, General Vo Nguyen Giap, the Minister of Defence and General Commander of the People's Army, ordered, *"All fighting units are to fight faster and more boldly in order to take advantage of this hour and remove the American enemy from the Fatherland of Vietnam!"*

These things together resulted in the Americans and their puppet forces being defeated and the Americans then leaving Vietnam. Saigon was renamed as Ho Chi Minh city. The Australian infantry battalions and their supporting units left Vietnam in 1972. (Vien, 2009).

Re-unification and Rediscovery

The re-unification of Vietnam was conducted with drums beating and dancing in the streets of towns and cities. It included the rebuilding of all interzonal communications, in particular, the Hanoi to Ho Chi Minh City Railway. Elections to the National Assembly were held in April of 1976. That resulted in the setting up of a single government for the entire country. New administrative structures were put into place at all levels down to the remotest rural communes and isolated villages.

Unlike the situation in Europe after the defeat of the Nazis, Vietnam did not resort to revenge killings of those who happened to be on the wrong side during the years of war against the foreign capitalists. There was tension among some of the ethnic minorities. The two main ones being the Hoa and the Khmer.

Many Hoa were shrewd traders and they often served as intermediaries between large French, then US companies and the Vietnamese population. (Vien, 2009)

Several hundred thousand Khmer acquired Vietnamese nationality and lived in a number of districts in the Mekong delta, keeping their mother tongue and their religions. Some problems arose which were made worse by both direct and indirect intervention of the USA and China. America tried to get the people to revolt by calling upon them to do so using 'The Voice of America' the US propaganda radio stations.

Meanwhile, the Democratic Republic of Vietnam helped the Khmer Rouge to take over Phnom Penh and other parts of Cambodia. After the take-over, Pol Pot and his subordinates drew up and implemented a programme of self-destruction and brutal police state the likes of which had never been seen before in either the western countries or the eastern communist ones.

They instituted a programme which forced the Cambodian city dwellers to live in rural areas and just leave their city homes. That in fact emptied the cities and the people were forced to live in the country. The mismanagement of the country by the Pol Pot regime led directly to hundreds of thousands of deaths from famine.

The Third Indochina War

In 1976, the Democratic Republic of Kampuchea was founded with Pol Pot as its leader. The main force of this new country was the Khmer Rouge. This organisation became well known for its cruelty when the Pol Pot Government decided to make the city dwellers of Cambodia live in rural communes. However, things were mismanaged from the beginning and finally resulted in mass deaths from hunger. The backer of the Pol Pot regime and the Khmer Rouge was the government of China.

The joy of the Vietnamese people of finally obtaining their freedom was replaced by shock as the fraternal communist country of Kampuchea proved itself to be the new menace. That resulted in a shock for the generations of Vietnamese enthusiastic militants who had sacrificed everything to ensure final victory over the American bully! That led to the majority of cadres and combatants returning from the forests to their people and communities.

These people refrained from abusing property of the population, and they were affable with their communities. However, some of them, took for themselves, apartments, cars, and other property left behind by those who had fled, and they became so greedy that they were involved in the same levels of corruption as the previous officials of the ARVN republic.

On the 14th of May in 1978, Cung Whyat was on guard duty at a Vietnamese outpost located near the Ba Chuc hamlet, in Ân Giang Province. After long periods of boredom due to inaction, he was surprised to hear the sound of armoured vehicles and the voices of Kampuchean soldiers of the Pol Pot regime.

He went to his section commander and said to Corporal Binh Chien Bui, *"Binh, come quickly, there is something strange going on!"* Binh said, *"What appears to be the problem Cung?"* That made Cung answer with, *"Binh, just be still for a few moments and tell me what you can hear!"*

The Vietnamese corporal complied with Cung's request, and soon, both men could plainly hear the sound of the engines of large trucks and armoured vehicles. After some time spent in listening to the new sounds, Binh said, *"Cung, do you know of any movements by our army involving the use of armour? I am now getting the feeling that something is not right, just like you have said!"*

Cung said, *"Binh, I am getting the strong impression that Vietnam could right now be getting invaded by the Kampuchean army and that murderous bastard known as Pol Pot! If you authorise me to do so, I shall run the five hundred metres distance to the headquarters of our company and report this suspected invasion of our country by Kampuchea!"*

Nguyen said, *"I would normally have told you to simply report what we are suspecting to company headquarters using the field telephone we have. However, I see that the telephone is no longer working and therefore I suspect that there is a cut somewhere in the line! So, off you go and make sure that you report this suspected invasion of our country by Kampuchea directly to the company commander. May heaven be with you, Cung!"*

As Cung prepared by strapping on his pistol and a water bottle and checking his ammunition, Binh roused the rest of his section and placed all of his men on high alert by yelling *"Stand-to! We are under attack from units of the Pol Pot army of Kampuchea!"* Soon, the first of the Kampuchean infantry and sapper units approached the forward positions of the Vietnamese outpost manned by Binh and his section. Meanwhile, Cung was running with all of his ability and speed toward the Vietnamese battalion's company headquarter outpost.

Finally arriving, he reported to the company commander. He saluted his superior officer and said, *"Sir, I have just run from our outpost at Ba Chuc hamlet in order to warn our people that Vietnam is under attack from the Kampuchean Army. They have cut our telephone lines and therefore the only way to get the word out about what is happening, is to run here and verbally tell you the situation, sir!"*

The company commander said, *"Cung, you have done well in bringing the news of this invasion of our country by murderous Kampuchean Army! Were you able to identify the units the Kampucheans are using?"* Cung replied, *"No sir, I do not know which units the Kampucheans are using. I only know that we are being attacked by the Kampucheans and that they are using infantry, sappers, and armoured units against us!"*

That made the Company Commander say, *"Cung, I want you to run back to your unit and to rejoin it. Tell your comrades to resist the Kampucheans using mainly our AK47s and our RPG7s. Make sure that your section commander knows to use the RPGs against the armour of the Kampuchean Army and also, tell him to use the anti-tank mines he has!"* Cung now ran back to the Ba Chuc hamlet and rejoined his section.

Having arrived there, he went to see his section commander. Upon finding him he said, *"Binh, the company commander wants us to stop these new invaders of Vietnam! We are to use our issued RPG7 rocket launchers and the anti-tank mines which we have with us to hinder and stop this invasion!"*

That resulted in Binh ordering, *"Nine Section of Nine Platoon, we are going to save our country! The enemy outnumbers us, and we are outgunned by the enemy. That does not matter as we shall not let invaders again harass the people of Vietnam! We are only at the strength of a section of ten men. We shall now deploy our anti-tank mines upon the slopes in front of us where the armoured enemy attack is coming from! We shall give our lives so that the*

Fatherland of Vietnam shall live! Today is a good day to die and we will take many Kampuchean soldiers with us before we are all dead!" With that having been said, the section moved out to engage the enemy!

Ten days had passed and there still were six Vietnamese soldiers left alive on the 24th of May 1978. The now understrength infantry section was following the progress of the Kampuchean attack on their portable radios. They followed the news on Radio Hanoi and other stations. The sloping battlefield in front of their position was the scene of four destroyed Kampuchean tanks and the hillside was littered with the corpses of Kampuchean soldiers. Binh grimly spoke to his remaining men.

He said, *"Comrades, we are now understrength due to casualties! Our strength is down to five men, but we have successfully defended our position here in Ba Chuc! I shall now call the roll and make sure that those of us who are left, can still fight. When I call your names, answer with 'Corporal!'"* He then called the roll.

Next, he yelled, *"Private Hanh Liem Tru!"* That was answered by him calling out, *"Corporal".* Again, he called the roll saying, *"Private Duong Duc Phan"* He answered *"Corporal'* Binh continued with *Duc Duong Kim"'* who answered *"Corporal".* Binh continued calling the roll, and he next said, *Cung Whyat?"* Cung answered with, *"Corporal".* That allowed him to say, *"Including myself, this means we have five men out of our original ten-man section!"*

The corporal continued with *Those who can no longer fight will be sent to the rear for treatment! I think that we cannot last much longer, for the enemy is bringing ever more soldiers into this area. I have heard a radio broadcast which stated that the soldiers of Pol Pot are using two divisions of Kampuchean armour and infantry to try to kidnap as many as twenty thousand people who have Khmer ancestry. It is known that the murderous Kampucheans want the people to go into camps set up in remote rural areas and they want all people to leave all cities!*

According to the news, the followers of Pol Pot have so far killed an estimated two thousand and five hundred Vietnamese people! Also, it has been reported that that the invasion in the Ba Chuc region has been followed up with another invasion into the Vietnamese region of Tay Ninh Province by three more Kampuchean divisions and that they shall be used to attack Ho Chi Mihn City! Comrades, we shall hold out or die in defending our Fatherland to our last drop of blood! I am hoping that we shall soon see a more favourable set of circumstances for Vietnam!"

Binh now called for two volunteers! He said, *"My comrades of Nine Section, we again have before us the Kampuchean enemy moving against us with their armoured units! I need two of you to volunteer to stop the armour and sappers of the Pol Pot Army before they can overwhelm us! If no-one volunteers, I shall select the two men use the use of drawing lengths of straws! So, please volunteer for the glorious mission of defending Vietnam now!"*

He had barely finished speaking when both Cung Whyat and Phuc Nguyen Quang yelled their decision to volunteer to take on the Kampucheans. Cung said, *"Hey Binh, both Phuc and I hereby volunteer to take the invading Kampucheans to task! What is it that you want us to do?"*

The Vietnamese corporal said, *"Thank you for volunteering for this vital mission Cung and Phuc! I need both of you to go forth in front of our positions here and I need to take with you, the last twenty-five anti-tank mines that we have here! That shall result in you making several trips in order to lay all of the twenty-five mines successfully! When you get to the where you need to plant the mines, I want you to arrange the land mines in an arrow head shape with the mines being laid fifteen metres apart. The locality where they should be laid is sixty metres west of our position here at Ba Chuc!*

Now come with me to the map and be sure that both of you understand exactly where and how to lay the mines in order to achieve the best outcome for us all!" And so, the two men went with the corporal to where the large map of the position was being kept. After they had examined the map, they indicated to their corporal that they understood completely, where and how they were to lay the twenty-five anti-tank mines, and then they moved out to do so.

As the two men moved out towards the perimeter of the Vietnamese defences, their corporal ordered, *"Nine Section, stand to! Cung and Phuc are moving out to lay the anti-tank mines and perhaps save those of us who are left! If any of you see Kampuchean soldiers trying to intercept either one of our heroic men, shoot the Kampucheans and protect our heroes!"* That resulted in the remaining rest of the section being on high alert and giving covering fire to both Cung and Phuc as they were going towards a gap in the barbed wire entanglements.

After the twenty-five anti-tank mines were successfully laid, Cung and Phuc began to return to the Vietnamese Ba Chuc position. As they were walking towards the defended one-metre-wide gap in barbed wire entanglements, Cung stopped and looked at Phuc while he put his index finger to is lips and then patted himself on the top of his head. That was the signal saying, *"In silence, come to me!"* Having seen and understood, Phuc quietly walked over to Cung and whispered to him, *"Cung, what is wrong?"* Cung also whispered saying, *"I fear that there are four enemy soldiers just ahead of us!*

I get the impression that they are a reconnaissance group that is gathering information about our positions at Ba Chuc in order to launch an attack later! It is now becoming dark, and I want to ambush those four enemies! They are coming this way and they have no idea that we are here, so, we should be able to kill all four of them easily! We shall both move to the left had side of the track and when the four of them come, I want you to wait until I fire before you also fire!"

Phuc understood what was required and he said, *"Very well, Cung, let's do it!"* That resulted in both Vietnamese firing upon the Kampucheans and killing all four of them after which they both made their way back to their own positions and then they reported to their corporal. Corporal Binh Chien Bui told them that he was recommending to the company commander that both men be given decorations for their actions which did much to secure the Vietnamese positions at Ba Chuc.

On the 26th of December 1978, the revolution army Headquarters of the Cambodian United Front for National Salvation (Kampuchea) launched a movement to fight the Pol Pot army and appealed to Vietnam for help. The help was granted, and it resulted in the Vietnamese army invading Kampuchea. After that, the Vietnamese army wiped out the forces of Pol Pot using a multi-divisional invasion of Cambodia supported by Vietnamese air power, armour, and naval forces.

General Nguyen Vo Giap had been kept informed of the situation, and the thought that another country which had a socialist government was making its people starve and letting many people die from famine was completely irresponsible to him. The news that the Khmer Rouge Forces were actually invading parts of Vietnam was distressing to him and many of his officers.

At an "O" group meeting of the Vietnamese general staff, it was decided to invade Kampuchea using Vietnamese armour and to simply race the tanks along the three highways, all of which led to Phnom Penh.

Vo Giap said, *"Ladies and Gentlemen, these days, I often read and attend to gardening which helps to keep the mind and body of this old man well and alive! Many of you here at this 'Orders Group' wish to do something quick and startling to end the invasion by the armies of Pol Pot! Well, ladies and gentlemen, we now have one of the largest armies in the southern region of Asia. Our infantry forces are effective and feared by many others. As well, we now have much modern armour in the form of modern Russian T54 and T59 tanks! We shall end this war very quickly! You have asked me for a quick victory against our Cambodian brothers and I shall do that for you!"*

General Giap now went to the large map displayed on the vertical board on the wall in front of him. While pointing to parts of the map he said, *"Comrades, there are three highways in Kampuchea, and all three of them lead to the capital, Phnom Penh! By having all of our tank units race up these three highways we will be able to launch a three-pronged attack from three different directions at once! That will put an end to Pol Pot and all of his armed units! After that the Vietnamese occupation of Cambodia shall begin!"*

On the 7th of January 1979, the Vietnamese army using its Russian built T-54 and T-59 tanks and assisted by some Cambodian patriots liberated Phnom Penh while the Pol Pot administration fled into the jungle. A new government of Cambodia with Hun Sen as its foreign minister, was installed and nine days later, there was a naval battle between the Vietnamese Navy and the Kampuchean navy. That resulted in twenty-two Kampuchean ships being sunk.

No matter how the Americans try to interpret the situation in Cambodia in 1978 and 1979, it was the Vietnamese armed forces that put an end to the murderous Pol Pot regime and not the Americans!

Michael G Kramer OMIEAust.

Vietnam's War in Cambodia Forgotten in the West

On the 30th of April 1975, the American helicopters flew out of Saigon in an ignominious retreat as the tanks of the Vietnamese Liberation Army (some people call it the North Vietnamese Army) rumbled into the grounds of the American embassy in Saigon. The rotten and clearly very corrupt Saigon Government of the south was removed, and the new national government of the Democratic Republic of Vietnam took over.

The victory against the hated Yankee aggressor is now remembered each year as Vietnamese triumph over foreign aggression. The entire Second Indochina War or Vietnam War is now popularly called the 'American War' by the Vietnamese people.

Although the Vietnamese victory over the invaders and occupiers of their country is celebrated as a great achievement, the Vietnamese occupation of Kampuchea or Cambodia is not.

Vietnam's occupation of Cambodia lasted from 1979 to September 1989 and which resulted in the loss of thirty thousand (30,000) Vietnamese soldiers killed in action.(KIA). Like many of the foreign occupiers of Vietnam during the Second Indochina War, the Vietnamese soldiers in Cambodia thought that they were there to liberate and help the people of Cambodia escape from the brutal Pol Pot regime.

Like the allied soldiers during the Vietnam War, the Vietnamese Veterans of the war against Kampuchea and the following occupation of Cambodia suffered hardships caused by there being camaraderie among the soldiers while they were trying to survive among a population which played host to them by day but was the enemy at night!

That resulted in many of the Vietnamese Veterans of the war against Pol Pot's Kampuchea and the later occupation of Cambodia by Vietnam's forces having symptoms similar to the PTSD suffer by allied veterans of the Vietnam War. Many of the veterans could not understand why the local Khmer people appeared to hate them after the Vietnamese forces had set them free from the brutal camps and other injustices of the Pol Pot Government of Kampuchea.

Hanh Liem Tru was in bed, and he had closed his eyes. He was almost totally relaxed and about to fall into a deep sleep, when he began to relive his role as a member of the 2nd Battalion of the 31st Infantry Division in liberating a very large commune that was being starved to death by Khmer Rouge Guards of Pol Pot! As his dreams started, he was reliving the times when he was in action against the Khmer Rouge as of September of 1979.

His dream was reliving his unit travelling by truck behind the Vietnamese armour which was spearheading the attack on Phnom Penh. The soldiers were expecting much resistance and were puzzled that the whole city appeared to be lifeless and empty. That resulted in the 2nd Battalion receiving order to fan out into the countryside and to locate the Khmer population.

In his recurring nightmares, he saw Corporal Binh Chien Bui who was the leader of his section and who had just returned from receiving his orders. He called his section together and when they were all present, he explained the new orders of the section. He said, *"Listen in, our entire battalion is to move toward staging areas that have been assigned to us as you can see on the map of the border area around Ba Chuc here"* as he was pointing to an area shown on the map.

He continued speaking and said, *"What you may find interesting is that we will hit back at the murderous Kampucheans who invaded Vietnam near the Ba Chuc area and killed more than three thousand of our people! We have the opportunity to obtain revenge for what has been done to our people by the Khmer Rouge Forces of Pol Pot! We shall move out of here today at 10:00 hours, when we shall all board trucks which will transport us to the staging area. Once we get there, we will form up as the 2nd Battalion, of the 31st Infantry Division and we will take part in the glorious invasion of Kampuchea!*

Firstly, we shall be following the tanks of our army and we will move into the towns and cities before taking them over and occupying them! After defeating the forces making up the Khmer Rouge of Pol Pot, we are going to look for the Khmer people, they have all left the cities and towns and our leaders have been getting reports that the people of Kampuchea have been herded into camps where they are being systematically starved to death by the Khmer Rouge! Our attack shall begin at 06:00 hours, Hanoi time, while it is still dark on the 25th of December 1978! All of our battalion shall be advancing by truck transport behind the tanks of the Peoples' Army of the Democratic Republic of Vietnam!"

As all three major highways in Cambodia led to the capital of Phnom Penh, the Vietnamese tanks raced up the highways until the capital was entered and occupied. The Vietnamese soldiers found it hard to believe that the large towns and cities, including Phnom Penh to be deserted!

The men who made up Nine Section of Nine Platoon, Charlie Company of the Ninth Section of the Ninth Platoon of the Second Battalion of the 31st Infantry Division were shocked vast numbers of corpses and human bones all over the countryside, away the from the cities and towns, where the communes had been set up!

PTSD and Finding Hun Sen

Two days later, Corporal Binh Chien Bui explained new orders. He said, *"We have also been handed the additional task of finding Hun Sen, whom Vietnamese Intelligence reports as possibly being held in a commune somewhere against his will! Apparently, he came into this as part of a Vietnamese army group, and he has disappeared! I have been issued with ten photos of Hun Sen and each of you are to take one of these with you. It is important for us to find him, be he alive or dead!*

You may not know it, but when the American agents of the Central Intelligence Agency organised the ousting of King Norodom Sirhanouk in 1970, Hun Sen backed his constitutional monarch by following

Sihanouk's call for the Khmer population to join the Khmer Rouge and so set up the insurgency for use against all foreign powers, in particular the Americans who still were interfering in Cambodian affairs as well as in Vietnam!

Since those times, the American CIA has had its agents move in and they removed King Norodom Sirhanouk from power and helped to install the Khmer Rouge, who have proved themselves to be a major problem for everyone in Indochina! We now have to undo what the hated Yankee oppressors have done to Indochinese people!

We have the task of finding these people and feeding them when we find them! However, do not expect them to be grateful for us delivering them from their tormentors, because the propaganda of the Khmer Rouge is so effective that the population will continue to regard us as invaders instead of liberators! That will place us into a similar situation to the Allied Soldiers of the American War back home during the time of the 1960s and 1970s!"

He was answered by Duong Duc Phan. He said, *"I do not understand why the Khmers would not greet us as liberators, for that is what we are! The Khmer Rouge are the ones who are killing the Kampucheans, not us! So, why would they hate us?"*

Binh answered, *"It is because of ancient traditional rivalry between the Khmers and Vietnamese as well as the Khmer Rouge propaganda! Remember that it is only our camaraderie keeps us going! By day, the Khmers smile at us, but at night, they try to make war upon us! So, while we move*

110

forward and help these people as we find the camps and communes deep in cleared jungle areas, we must be ready for armed attacks upon us by the Khmer Rouge as well as the general population!

A major tragedy from all of this is that the Khmer Rouge started as a liberation force protecting the people of Kampuchea from the ugly Americans! However, since that time a small hard core of amazingly stupid people has taken over the leadership of the Khmer Rouge and that resulted in them moving from being protectors of their people to being the occupiers and enslavers of Cambodia!

We are moving out towards the south-east where our intelligence says there is a very large commune with many of the people from Phnom Penh in it." Later that day a convoy of trucks preceded by Vietnamese armour went into the commune that Binh had described. Upon arrival, the Vietnamese soldiers disembarked from the trucks and took defensive positions before they actively began patrolling and reconnaissance work.

As they were going towards a large area of newly cleared jungle, Binh called out in alarm! He shouted, *"Fucking hell! Look at what those Khmer Rouge arseholes have done to their own people! There appears to be thousands of bodies as far as my eyes can see!"* Ahead of the Vietnamese soldiers were many corpses. Most of these people had died from hunger inflicted upon them by the Khmer Rouge who were the new Communist Government of Kampuchea (Cambodia) and who were backed by the Chinese Government.

Next, he dreamed about moving into the commune living areas and finding more skeletons and corpses. He and Binh cautiously advanced further when they plainly heard the cry of a teenage Khmer girl. Although she was skinny and suffering from malnutrition, she was also attractive.

Hanh could not help but to be impressed by her. As he was attracted to her, he said, *"Beautiful lady, I am Hanh Liem Tru and I hereby offer you my assistance for life, if you will have me!"* She answered, *"I can never be with a Vietnamese man! Vietnamese are the most useless of all males and you are all the enemies of the people of Kampuchea! So do not bother me, just fuck off you Vietnamese aggressor!"*

Hanh was very puzzled by what had happened, and he did not understand it at all. He therefore spoke to his section corporal about it. He said, *"Binh, I am now very confused because I spoke to an attractive but skinny Cambodian girl, and she told me to fuck off! After she had told me that, she said that Vietnamese men are the most useless in the world! Before I spoke to her, I had given her a cooked ration of rice. Instead of her being grateful for the meal, she abused me! So, what gives with these Kampuchean people?"*

After listening to Hahn's story, Binh said, *"This is what I was trying to warn you and the other section members about when I told you all of the probability that we would not be welcomed here as liberators or heroes! We are in a situation similar to the Allied soldier veterans of the Second Indochina War! In time, we will all have symptoms similar the allied Veterans! We have all been in action for some time now!*

I want to know how you are affected Hanh, so that I can put in a report to my superiors about the general well-being of the men under my command. I therefore need to know how you are coping! I have been asked by Hanoi to ask my men if you have flash-backs to actions carried out in the war against Kampuchea! Well Hanh? Do you have them?"

Hanh answered, *"Yes, I do have the flash-backs. Not only that, but I usually find that I am constantly fatigued because of not being able to sleep. During the nights, I find that I wake up in a cold sweat and that I am hyper-alert! That stops me from sleeping as do the nightmares which I get from having killed people due to being in action against our Kampuchean brothers!"* Soon after that conversation, a dirty and mud-splattered man emerged from the edges of the forest and walked towards Binh.

When he finally got to within close distance from Nine Section of Nine Platoon Charlie Company of the 2nd Battalion of the 31st Infantry Division, he spoke to Binh. He said, *Good day corporal, I am Hun Sen! I became separated from my Vietnamese Army unit just as we were giving out food to the people who we managed to rescue from Pol Pot. Then we were attacked by the Khmer Rouge who had active assistance from other Khmer people! Together, they managed to wipe out most of my unit!*

As the Khmer Rouge were attacking us, the people of the commune also attacked us, even though we were giving them food which the Khmer Rouge denied them! Now I need to be rescued myself and I shall be most thankful for the opportunity to wash and to have a meal!" Corporal Binh Chien Bui immediately gave him food from his own ration pack. Hun Sen said, *"Thank you, corporal!"*

Hun Sen's Story

I spoke to Hun Sen many years later and we talked about his origins and the time between 1968 and 1990 as well as up to the present time. After we had exchanged pleasantries, we proceeded to relax with a cup of tea. Being the first to speak and wanting to complete an interview with the   leader of Kampuchea (Cambodia), I spoke first.

I said to Hun Sen, *"Sir, my name is Michael Kramer, and it is my fondest wish to hold an interview with you which I hope to be able to market to the news services on a world-wide basis! I am an investigative author and journalist. I have completed some limited research into your background, and so, far, I find what I know about you to be fascinating to say the least! Other factors about me which you may find of interest or otherwise, are that I am both a qualified engineer and also an ex-infantry soldier. My unit was the First Battalion, Royal Australian Regiment (1RAR) and I served in the Vietnam War during 1968 – 1969!"*

Hun Sen Hun replied, *"I hereby grant you permission to hold an interview with me! It seems to me that this interview should contain details of my personal and family history including my own military history and the reasons for various parts of it! I also believe that your interview shall benefit me and my people!*

One of the reasons that I am granting you this interview is because my own father, called Hun Neang often told me about a German engineer called Fritz Kramer who, I was told was important in helping to design and build the railway line between Shanghai and Northern Vietnam. You have told me that your surname is Kramer, so, I must ask you if you are related to that German engineer?"

My reply was, *"Yes Hun, he was my Grandfather! After he completed his work in China and Vietnam, he was sent by the German colonial organisation, to German South-West Africa. There he built the port city of Swakopmund and various other things. In 1927, my Grandfather, and his family, which included my father, left what is now called Namibia and returned to Germany. In 1953, my parents, my brother and I left Germany, and we settled in Australia!*

Australia has been good to me overall, and I thought that I should display my loyalty to my country by volunteering to be part of its defence and that included going to war for it. And so, I joined the Australian Army in 1967, and I found myself in the First Battalion Royal Australian Regiment (1RAR). In 1968 to 1969, I was serving in South Vietnam. However, I think that we should now concentrate on you and your achievements and how these will benefit your country of Cambodia and Indochina in general, so let us get going with you interview!"

I asked, Hun Sen, *"Let's get started with when you were born and where that happened."* Hun Sen replied, *"Michael, I was born on the 5th of August 1952 in Peam Kaoh Sna Kampong Cham. My father was Hun Neang and he had been a resident monk in the local Wat at Kampong Cham before he decided to defrock himself so that he could join the local resistance against the French. My father did not talk about his time as a resistance fighter very much, but I wish that he had done so, because I would dearly like to know more about what he did!"*

I replied, *"So, Hun Sen, when you became a revolutionary, you were in fact following a precedent established by your father, Hun Neang! I feel that is impressive!"* Hun Sen said, *"Thank you, Michael! As we have already discussed, I do not know much of what my father did during the time of revolution against the French, because he did not talk about those times unless a close friend who had been fighting the French with him happened to visit.*

Since those days, I learned about PTSD, and I think that my father had a severe case of it! I am also sure that I also am suffering from PTSD, even though I have never been diagnosed as such by qualified psychiatrists. I think that will be the case because of the fact that virtually all combat veterans suffer that condition sooner or later!

We continued with the interview. I said, *"Thank you, please tell me more about both your father and your mother"* Hun Sen said, *"While doing that, he met my mother called Dee Yon during the 1940s, and he married her.* I said, *"Thank you, Hun, now, let us cover your immediate family. You and your wife Bun Rany have produced six children. Is that correct?"*

Hun Sen replied, *"Yes Michael that is right! My children are Kamsot, who has unfortunately died, Manet, Mana, Manith, Mani, and Mali. In 1988, we also adopted a daughter She was a very bad disappointment for us! I caught her several times using a dildo to fuck another woman! That is intolerable, and we legally disowned her for being a lesbian!"*

I was surprised at that and so I said, *"My goodness Hun, getting rid of your own adoptive daughter on the grounds of her being a lesbian is rather extreme, is it not?"* He replied, *"No, Michael, it is not extreme! It is a matter of one's own morals! Sexual deviation in the various forms of male or female homosexuality cannot and must not be tolerated! Even the western religions such as the Catholic Church used to campaign against that!"*

We continued the interview, with me asking, *"What can you tell me about your parents' background?"* Hun Sen replied, *"My paternal Grandparents were wealthy landowners of the Teochew Chinese lineage! My father, called Hun Neang inherited some family assets which included several hectares of land, and we had comfortable lives until a kidnapping incident caused my family to sell off many of our assets. These things combined and I left the family home at the age of thirteen years in order to attend a monastic school in Phnom Penh. That move caused me to change my name to Ritthi Sen."*

That surprised me, and I said, *"That is very interesting Hun, can you tell me more about the kidnapping incident and what followed? I am sure that the world press will want to know about this hidden aspect of your life!"* Hun Sen replied, *"Certainly, Michael, let us firstly look at where I fit into my family of brothers and sisters. I have six siblings. In order of age, they are my eldest brother, Hun San, a second brother called Hun Neng who was followed by myself and then, my eldest sister, Hun Senny, my next sister, Hun Sinath and the youngest sister called Hun Buntheoen."*

I was gathering my thoughts as Hun Sen again sated speaking. He said, *"Michael, I thought that you may like some more information about my children and my siblings. Manet was promoted to Major General of Royal Cambodian Armed Forces during 2010! His two other brothers also play big and important roles in the government of Cambodia! Of my siblings, my older brother called Hun Neng is a former governor of Kampong Cham and a current member of the Parliament.*

Something about myself that your readers may find interesting if my ability to speak different languages! I am fluent in my native tongue of Khmer and Vietnamese! I also speak English well enough to be understood by other people, as is evidenced by the fact that both of us are conversing in the English language! I must admit though, that I prefer to use either Khmer or Vietnamese as my speaking languages!

Hun Sen looked weary, and I asked him if he was fit to continue with the interview. He told me,

"Very observant of you, Michael! The wound that resulted in the loss of one of my eyes is bothering me at the moment and I think that it will be wise for me to rest now. I would like to continue this interview at 10:00 hours of the next day. Can you do that for me , Michael?" I replied, saying, *"Thank you, Hun, continuing this interview at 10:00 hours tomorrow is a good idea!"*

Family Member Kidnapping Incident

When the interview resumed at 10:00 hours of the next day, I had been busy making notes of the conversation and I said, *"Thank you, Hun, you have also told me that that there was a kidnapping which almost bankrupted your family! Can you elaborate upon that?"* Hun Sen replied, *"When I was just a boy, there was a kidnapping incident which resulted in which my parents having to raise large amounts of money in order in order for my brother to remain unharmed and to get returned to us. That resulted in my father selling most of his land holdings and after that the family became a lot poorer, but we were still better off than many other families!"*

I could not help being impressed by this man. I said, *"So, because of necessity, you became a monk for a time, I think that there will be a lot of interest in that!"* He continued his story with, *"As you may know, My original name was Hun Bunal, I had no interest in politics until the Americans bombed my home located in the town of Memot and that destroyed my family home! The bombing instilled within me, a growing resentment towards Americans who were constantly taking things without asking and simply telling people what to do, even within their own country!*

As well, the God-Damned-Yankee was placing his puppets into all positions of power and systematically taking things belonging to our people! Although they preach democracy and freedom, what the Americans do to their own people has to be seen to be believed!"

Attitudes Towards the USA by Hun Sen

That prompted me to ask, *"What is it that you mean by saying that? I admit that many Australians think of Americans as being strange people, but I do not know about them preaching democracy and freedom while doing something else!"* Hun Sen replied, *"Really Michael? Just think back to your own service in the Vietnam War! Now ask yourself what it was about the Americans that really struck you!"*

I was silent for a short time and responded by saying, *"Yes, they were often overbearing and arrogant! Often, they made statements without any basis of fact and I at times thought that they did not know shit from clay! Is that what you mean?"* Hun Sen replied, *"No, Michael, it is not! I am referring to how the Americans treat their own people!*

In particular how they treat both their own indigenous people and their African Americans! During the 1800s, they had a civil war which they say was fought to ensure the end of slavery! Since that time, they have made the African American and the indigenous Americans live in squalor and what are third-world conditions! They make those people work

120

for mere pittances and constantly practise racial discriminations against them! In my view, they are using an extension of slavery to keep those people in line! So much for the 'Freedom Loving' USA!

Those people are still living as third class citizens within their own country! Since the end of World War Two, the American administrations have consistently supported right-wing dictatorships around the world! That had had the effect of making millions of dollars for the American arms manufacturers and denying freedom to down-trodden people! Not only that, but the God damned Yankee has since the end of World War Two gone to other countries where he has systematically thrown his weight around and either tried to make or has made the people of that country obey the USA! That is intolerable interference by a bullying super power in the legal running of sovereign countries, no matter what the Yankee Capitalist may say!"

I was silent for a moment while I thought over what Hun Sen had said. Much to my own amazement, I found myself sympathising with him. I said, *"I do not think that the average American person is bad or immoral. However, I cannot say the same for the American administrations! What is your view about it all?"*

Hun Sen replied, *"Now, please do not get me wrong about the American people! They are not evil; They have been lied to by various continuing American administrations now for over one hundred years! It is because of that, that the American people actually believe that all people who are called either socialist or communist are evil!*

121

Answering the Call to Arms

When I left the monastery, I changed my name to Hun Smarach, in order to conceal my identity! I changed my name to Hun Sen in 1972, which was two years after I had joined the Khmer Rouge in answer to the pleas from King Norodom Sirhanouk to help safeguard the country of Cambodia. I joined the Khmer Rouge as a soldier and rose through the ranks. Within two years of service in the Khmer Rouge, I had become a commander of a battalion! By now, the Khmer Rouge Government of Pol Pot had started to empty the towns and cities, and then forced the Cambodian people to live in rural communes!

It was during the purges by Pol Pot of the Khmer Rouge that I and many other patriots decided to flee because it was likely that we would be next in line for that sort of treatment. I saw what I could only think of as criminal mismanagement of the welfare of my people. That happened while the Khmer Rouge were implementing their programme of self-destruction and it so affected me that I defected to the Vietnamese Army. I was active in fighting the Chinese at the Sino-Vietnamese border regions for the Vietnamese Army and later, I took part in the invasion of Kampuchea as part of the Vietnamese Force!

After that, I eventually ended up in the region around the Capital of Phnom Penh. During a military action against the forces of Pol Pot, near the capital called Phnom Penh, I was hit in my eye by a piece of shrapnel from an artillery shell. That resulted in me only having one eye! After which I was found to be wandering around aimlessly by a Vietnamese Infantry Section after my Vietnamese Army unit was attacked by both the Khmer Rouge and the Kampuchean civilians. Many of my comrades were killed by that and it left me wandering around in a daze!

I finally found my way to a large commune in Kampuchea located about fifty kilometres from Phnom Penh. I was found there by the men of the 31st Vietnamese Infantry Division. I was found by Corporal Binh Chieu Bui of Nine Section, Nine Platoon, Charlie Company of the 2nd Battalion of the 31st Infantry Division.

He organised my rescue and I was transported to the Vietnamese Army Headquarters, and I then joined with my Vietnamese friends to act against the Khmer Rouge who by now were guilty of mass genocide of my people! After more service with the Vietnamese forces, I was installed as the Foreign Minister of Cambodia by the Victorious Vietnamese Army! At the age of twenty-six, I was the youngest Foreign Minister in the World!

Leading Cambodia (Kampuchea)

Continuing with his interview, I asked Hun Sen, *"And can you tell me about becoming the premier of Cambodia?"* Hun Sen answered, *"Yes Michael, I shall be glad to relate that story to you! I rose the leadership of my country in January of 1985 when the one-party National Assembly appointed me to succeed Chan Sy, who died in office during December 1984. I held the position of Prime Minister of Cambodia or Kampuchea, is that is what you wish to call it, from 1984 until the 1993 UN-backed elections. They resulted in a hung parliament with the opposition party called FUNINPEC winning most of the votes.*

I looked at the result and I did not like what I saw, therefore, I refused to accept the result. After many long days of negotiating with FUNINPEC, Norodom Ranariddh and myself, I agreed to serve as both First and Second Prime Minister (For some years there were two serving Prime Ministers of Kampuchea) *until the coalition broke down and instability became rife! That left me no alternative but to stage a coup d'état in 1997 which got rid of Ranariddh. Since that time, I have led my Cambodian Peoples' Party to consecutive election victories. We oversaw rapid economic growth and development.*

I did in fact inherit the results of an administration which had practiced human rights violations and deforestation as well as being guilty of a very great amount of corruption! (Khmer Rouge). *Please remember Michael, that the governments before me were the Khmer Rouge followed by the Chan Sy Governments. Many of the problems of Cambodia were put into place by the Khmer Rouge and their leader, Pol Pot. In 2018, I was elected to a sixth term after the collapse of the opposition party! That in turn allowed my CPP* (Cambodian People's Party) *to win every seat in the National Assembly!"*

Kidnaping of an Opposition Leader

Hun Sen continued with the story of his country and incidents that occurred. Relating to newspaper articles appearing on the 10th of October 1999 he said, *"A National Assembly member of the Sam Rainsy Party called Lon Phon was relaxing*

124

outside of his home when four gunmen who were wearing military uniforms came into view. Their leader was a man who wore the insignia of a corporal of the Royal Cambodian Army.

Earlier that night, there had been a break-in at the clothing stores of the Royal Cambodian Army Base at Phnom Penh. Anyway, these four men four men were such heroes that they beat him and smashed rifle butts into his head before they bundled him in to the trunk of a waiting car. At this point, my interest was aroused, and I asked Hun Sen, *"So, Hun, please tell me more about this man called Lon Phon!"*

Hun Sen replied, *"Lon Phon was well as being an opposition party member, was also a successful hotel owner and business man! Dozens of wealthy and successful people such as him have been attacked over recent years, often by actual serving members of the armed services and the police force! A direct result of his abduction was that I and my government were blamed for somehow being involved in his abduction! That is not correct! I would never stoop so low as to do something that is so shameful!"*

At first, I did not know how to answer him, and then I said, *"Very well then, Hun, was he rescued or released by his captors?"* Hun Sen replied, *"To my knowledge, he was released by his captors after his family and my government together paid the demanded ransom of US$140,000.00. My agents have told me that he is currently resting at the home of a friend. Apparently, his head still hurts him where he was smashed by the rifle butt! This type of kidnapping crime is very common in my country at the moment,* *and I must do something to stop such crimes them from happening!"*

On the 10th of June 2014, Hun Sen made a public announcement. He said, *"I do not have any health problems! Now be warned, my people, that if I were to die prematurely, our country of Cambodia shall spin out of control and the opposition should expect a lot of trouble from the armed forces. The fact is that I am the only person in the world who can control the armed forces!"*

Later, during November 2016, Hun Sen said in public, *"Fellow citizens of Cambodia, I hereby endorse the US Republican candidate called Donald Trump to become the next president of the United States of America!"* finding that to be strange, I asked Hun Sen, *"Why did you endorse Donald Trump as a future President of the USA in November of 2016?"*

Hun Sen replied, *"I did that because it became apparent that I need the support of countries other than China in order to remain successful and for my country to progress at very high speed towards becoming both more highly developed and fairer to our people! Also, by there being better relationships between myself and the Trump administration, I may be able to better manage the activities of the American CIA in my country!"*

I said to Hun Sen, *"I have information which says that upon your orders, on the 31st of January 2017, the National Assembly voted unanimously to abolish the Minority Leader and the Majority Leader positions to lessen the opposition party's influence. Can you elaborate upon that?"*

Hun Sen replied, *"On the 2nd of February 2017, I bared the opposition party from questioning some of my government ministers! I bought in a constitutional amendment which dissolved the Cambodian National Rescue Party! For some reason, that led to the surprise resignation of Sam Rainsy. So it was that my Cambodian Peoples' Party (CCP) obtained the right to dissolve opposition political parties. That also resulted in the opposition leader Kem Sokha being arrested for treason!"*

I was somewhat distressed by what he had said. Still, I had a major interview to complete, and so, I continued. Time appeared to be going past me at an increasing speed, things were happening too fast, and I wanted to slow down. However, that was not possible, and I asked him on the 30th of June 2018, which was one week before the parliamentary elections, Hun, *"I have been getting information that there are moves afoot to appoint your eldest son, called Hun Manet to higher military positions! Is that correct?"*

Hun Sen said, *"Yes Michael, that is correct! I hereby affirm that my son could become Prime Minister assuming that he gets elected rather than through a direct hand-over."* However, the fact remains that the 2018 elections of Cambodia were dismissed as sham election by the international community because the opposition party had been dissolved!

Continuing with the interview, I replied, *"Hun, that is fine, now may we go on to what your foreign policies may be?* Hun Sen answered with, *"In foreign policy, I have strengthened diplomatic ties with China and formed a close economic alliance with them. I am inviting capitalistic countries to invest here in an effort to bring secondary industry to my country. Once that happens, it will provide employment for my people.*

Continuing the interview, I said, *"Hun, I was told that you intend to govern until you turn 74. Is that correct?* He replied with, *"Yes Michael! On the 6th of May in 2013, I made the announcement that I shall continue as Prime Minister of Cambodia until I reach the age of seventy-four! That means that I shall rule until 2026!"*

I must admit that I was taken aback by much of what he had told me! Some Australian newspapers described him as being, *"An authoritarian leader who has assumed highly centralised power in Cambodia."* These newspapers criticised him by saying that he was guilty of gaining considerable wealth by the use of violence and corruption.

They even accused him of having a personal bodyguard unit that rivals the Cambodia's regular army in size. It appears to me that no matter what it is that he does, someone will criticise him for doing so! I Therefore understand his attitude of, *'To hell with them!'"* Having said that, I must admit that I like his idea of inviting foreign capitalists to bring secondary industry to his country, thereby lifting both employment and wealth of the people.

Since those times, I have been informed that Hun Sen used his influence to block the return to Cambodia of the exiled Cambodia Rescue Party leaders, including Sam Rainsy and Mu Sochua in

2019. It is said that Hun Sen ordered the military to take action and attack them both on sight if they return . Also, airlines have been threatened with legal actions if they allow them on board their aircraft! As well, many soldiers have been sent to the Thai and Vietnamese borders. Other actions against them include requests to other leaders of ASEAN nations to arrest them and deport them to Cambodia.

PTSD Among Vietnamese Veterans of the War in Kampuchea

A close friend of Cung Whyat was Duc Duong Kim. He was with Cung during the attempted incursion by Pol Pot's forces at Ba Chuc and then later he was part of the Vietnamese occupation force of Cambodia. He spoke to me when I was part of the ANZAC Day parade in Sydney, Australia, on the 25th of April in 2018.

I had been marching with the other veterans of my former unit, the First Battalion Royal Australian Regiment or 1RAR in abbreviated form. At the following reception and celebration activities, Duc Duong Kim came to me and spoke.

He said, *"Uc da Loi, I am Duc Duong Kim, and I am a veteran of the Vietnamese army fighting firstly with the American First Infantry Division (Big Red One), against elements of the Viet Cong. That was followed by fighting for other foreign units until they all left Vietnam during April 1975. After they left, I was put into the new "Peoples' Liberation Army of Vietnam and after more training, I was sent to the Ba Chuc area near the border with Kampuchea, and I was part of the defence against the invaders of Pol Pot's Khmer Rouge Forces.*

Much like the Americans and Uc da Loi forces that invaded Vietnam, we believed ourselves to be the heroes who delivered the Khmer people from the scourge of the Khmer Rouge. However, soon after we had liberated them, the Khmer people were making war upon us using the same tactics that the Vietcong used against you and the Americans. That has left many of us with deep psychological scars which give me constant nightmares and the daytime equivalent of them. Combined, they always drag me back into the terror of battle!

I found that when your companions die in battle, it is a great loss. During the war, the battles do not really stop, because you always have to be ready for the next military engagement and could happen a second later. We had no time to reflect, and we had to remain strong and continue. Most of us found that the injuries to the body could be bad, but much heavier was the mental injuries we all suffered from. Many of my fellow soldiers, who returned to Vietnam one or even six years later, went mad soon after they returned!

During the 'American War' I was member of the ARVN 308 Ranger Battalion. We sometimes conducted joint operations against the patriots of Vietnam with the First Infantry Division of the USA (Big Red One). After the defeat of the Americans in 1975, I was 'Re-educated'. The 'Re-education lasted for three weeks, and we learned things that did not interest me then and they still do not interest me. We were taught about the Capitalist politics as well as

Communist politics and then put into the 'Peoples' Liberation Army of the Democratic Republic of Vietnam. Then, I was sent to Ba Chuc and served there against the Kampuchean Army of Pol Pot."

I was astounded that even our former enemies of the Second Indochina War (Vietnam War) were having experiences that closely matched what Australian Veterans of the Vietnam war were experiencing.

I said, *"Duc, what you have told me sounds a lot like the symptoms of the PTSD suffered by Australian Vietnam Veterans. The main difference I can see is that at least you and others in the Vietnamese army were protecting your own country. We, in the Australian army, mostly did not like what we were asked to do in Vietnam. Most of us were against the thought of simply 'Doing the bidding of the God Damned Yankee!*

In my own case, that manifests itself as flashbacks and nightmares which sometimes happen during the day time as well. Overwhelmingly, I have this horrible sense of guilt which is always with me. I regret having killed some of your countrymen, but I was in a situation where either I killed them, or they killed me. All the same, it continually bothers me that I was part of the Yankee attempt to keep Vietnam enslaved!"

Duc said, *"My friend from Uc da Loi, I think that we have both done our duties to the best of our abilities in spite of not wanting to do so at times. Let us now just celebrate that we are both still alive and hopefully we can talk to others and inform them of the folly of war. After all, it does no-one any good!"*

Running Afoul of the New Vietnamese National Government.

Both Duc and Cung managed to stay alive throughout the war against the forces of Pol Pot. After the Pol Pot threat had been dealt with, Duc worked for Cung in his farm machinery and fertiliser business.

For his services, Cung was both promoted and decorated. After his honourable discharge from the Vietnamese Army, he lived among the Hoa People at Cho Lon, near Ho Chi Minh City. These were ethnic Chinese people originally and they formed a compact group located in a Chinatown in Cho Lon. This area had its own administration, schools, and hospitals. The Hoa People are shrewd business people and that caused many of the ethnic Vietnamese to both envy and to hate them.

Daiyu Chan was a Hoa woman of striking appearance, and she was courageous as well as highly intelligent. Cung was introduced to her after her father had bought a tractor and agricultural implements from Cung.

On a Friday evening, Cung was introduced to Daiyu. The name of Daiyu has the meaning of Black Jade, and her parents named her as such because of her dark complexion. Cung found that he was instantly attracted to Daiyu, and he wanted to continue to see her after the introduction.

Cung Courts Daiyu

He spoke to Daiyu's father called Aiguo. Cung said, *"Aiguo sir, I am strongly attracted to your daughter, Daiyu, and I wish to keep on seeing her. Sir, may I continue to court Daiyu and to make her my wife if she will have me?"* Aiguo said, *"Cung, it is the tradition in my family for the entire family to be introduced to any suitor of our womenfolk!*

What happens is that the suitor is invited to a large family dinner during which time he is asked many questions and all of his answers are considered before any judgement regarding the proposed marriage is made! While the suitor is speaking to the head of the household or to his wife, other more junior family members are behind the bead curtains from where they also observe the suitor.

You have asked me to give you permission to go on seeing Daiyu and in order for that to happen, you must attend a dinner at my house in Cho Lon next Sunday afternoon. I shall expect you to arrive at my house by two thirty pm, so that we can chat and get to know each other before the dinner begins.

While we are chatting, I shall be asking you a series of questions which will tell me if you are a worthwhile and hardworking man with the right morals as set out by Confucius or not! If so, and if the rest of the family likes you, you shall be welcomed into my family, and you may go on seeing my daughter. If not, then you shall never see her again!"

Cung knew that he had to attend that dinner and he knew that he had to make a good impression on everyone in the family. So, he arrived on time and was greeted by Aiguo who warmly welcomed him.

They both went into the house and behind the bead curtains were the small two sisters of Daiyu. The two young girls were quietly talking and giggling.

From where the girls were, they had a perfect view of Cung. Baozhai said to Chyou, *"Ooh, this suitor of our beloved sister Daiyu, I really like him! If my sister does not take him as husband, perhaps I will!"* Chyou said, *"I like him as well, and if Daiyu does not take him I shall have him because I am older than you, and therefore I outrank you in all matters!"*

As the afternoon turned into evening and then night, Cung was invited to stay the night in the home of Daiyu's parents. Then came the break that Cung was hoping for. His prospective father-in-law said, *"Cung you are operating a fertilizer and farm machinery business near Cho Lon. You have impressed my wife, her brother, my other daughters, and me. We are making you an offer to become part of this family. That shall mean that you must work tirelessly to further all family businesses and in return, your own business shall be looked after by all family members. You have the blessing of this family to join with you and your family and so, make things better for all of us.*

There are also responsibilities that we require you to undertake. So, are you willing to undertake them?" Cung answered, *"Yes Aiguo, I am deeply honoured to become part of your family! I agree to work tirelessly towards the establishment and betterment of all family businesses that we singly or jointly own, including my own fertilizer and farm machinery business!"* That was followed by celebration and drinking until well into the night.

So it was that the engagement of Cung and Daiyu was announced, and a celebration was held at the home of Aiguo Chan in Cho Lon. Many people attended the celebration at which Cung Whyat announced, *"My friends and comrades, as you know, I operate a fertiliser and farm machinery business close to Cho Lon. The business is doing well, and mainly, it is being run when I am not there, by my associate, and friend, please allow me to introduce Duc Duong Kim to you and I am sure that he can answer your questions.*

My father-in-law, Aiguo Chan has given financial aid to my business, and it is now a part of the family businesses run by the Aiguo Chan/Cung Whyat group! In due course, Daiyu shall also work in the business with the two of us. I am sure that together, we shall be of great service to the Cho Lon and even Ho Chi Minh City areas!"

A few months later, he married the Hoa woman and together, they worked in his already successful business supplying fertilisers and farm machinery to those who had the money to pay for it and wanted to do business with him.

In post-Vietnam War times until 1980, there were some people who were from the old ruling class of the oppressive South Vietnamese Diem and other despot regimes and who had managed to install themselves into the new Vietnamese society. These people often denounced others who were in fact good and reliable patriots of Vietnam. Cung was walking though Ho Chi Minh City when he heard the loud blast of a police whistle!

He stopped and was wondering what was happening when the policeman had blown the whistle came to him and announced, *"Cung Whyat? You are under arrest for crimes against the people of Vietnam!"* Cung could not believe what he was hearing, but he decided to go along with what was being said to him by the policeman until he could find out what all of this was about and then he could take action as it was needed.

Therefore, he said, *"Yes officer, I am Cung Whyat, what appears to be the trouble?"* Nguyen Phan Lam replied, *"Cung Whyat, you have been denounced as a traitor and an enemy of the people by Sauget et Sang! You are now under arrest!"* Cung was incredulous by this accusation and said, *"Sauget et Sang, you must be joking! That man is an ex-policeman from the old Diem days of super corrupt police and officials of South Vietnam! I cannot believe that I am being charged on the word of such an arsehole! I am a hero of the war against Pol Pot and yet, here you are charging me!"*

Nguyen Phan Lam said, *"It does not matter what the true circumstances are. I have orders to arrest you and to take you to the Central Police Station in Ho Chi Minh City! Once you have been processed there, we may be able to work out why this is happening to you. For now, come along and do not resist or make my job harder than what it is!"* So it was that Cung Wyatt arrived at the Central Police Station in Ho Chi Minh City in the company of his arresting officer.

Nguyen Phan Lam said, *"Cung, I shall now try to find out more about the charges against you. As you have already said, you are a proven hero of the Vietnamese struggle against foreign invasion and therefore, you are much more valuable than is someone who has the background of being in the corrupt Diem administration as police officer! I am taking you to your cell now. When we get there, you will see your wife, who was arrested as soon as the allegations against you were made."* With that said, the Police officer of the Democratic Republic of Vietnam called Nguyen Phan Lam opened the door of Cung's cell.

As soon as he entered the cell, Cung saw his wife, and she called out, *"It is nice to see you, Cung my husband! That grasping old police official of the Diem years called Sauget et Sang has been casting envious eyes upon your business of supplying fertilisers and farm machinery to those who want it. More and more people are moving into the cities and soon, farm machines shall have to do the work of the peasant! Sauget et Sang knows that and he can see big profits for him if he can get you and other people like you out of the way! That is why he has borne false witness against you!"*

Cung took his wife into his arms and kissed her as he was saying, *"Daiyu, my dear wife, I am so glad that you are well! As for these charges, the sooner we can have a hearing and get to the bottom of this mess, the better!"* However, Sauget et Sang had done his work of blackening the names of his rivals well. As a result, it was another two days before Cung, and his wife were released from their confinement and allowed a hearing.

Meanwhile, both Cung and his wife called Daiyu, were sharing their cell with another prisoner, called Nguyen Thiourea. He had been both a tax collector for both the Diem and the Thieu governments of South Vietnam. He did his work efficiently, but he had no scruples about calling in the South Vietnamese Police to make people hand over their hard-earned money and goods as taxes to the corrupt South Vietnamese Governments. He had been arrested prior to him being sent to a re-education camp for the purpose of being re-educated into what was considered to be acceptable behavior towards the public by government officials.

So, it was that the three inmates of the prison cell began to talk to each other. Liking the look of Cung and his wife, Nguyen Thiourea introduced himself by saying, *"Good day comrades, my name is Nguyen Thiourea and I have been arrested prior to being sent to a "Re-education camp for ex-officials of the previous South Vietnamese Governments. I used to work as a tax collector for the governments of South Vietnam and that is why I am being sent to the camp for re-education purposes. Will you also please introduce yourselves to me and let me know what you are doing and why you are here?"*

Cung instantly liked the former tax collector of south Vietnam and he said, *"It is good to know you, Nguyen, my name is Cung Wyatt, and I am a business man dealing in fertilizer and farm machinery. This is my wife Daiyu. She is a from the Hoa Community of Cho Long, near Ho Chi Minh City"* (Formerly Saigon)."

Two days had passed, and the trio were then joined by Nguyen Phan Lam who was the arresting police officer who had arrested Cung. As he walked into their cell, he talked to the trio.

He said, *"Cung, Nguyen and Daiyu, it is my opinion that you have all been falsely accused and other people have much to gain from your being turned into outlaws and therefore your business shall be taken over by the state and that will in turn end up going directly to your accuser, Cung.*

Cung, I have investigated your record and it clearly shows that you are indeed a hero of the military action against the forces of Pol Pot when two Kampuchean divisions invaded the area near Ba Chuc, and they killed two and a half thousand Vietnamese citizens before going after the three thousand descendants of the Khmers living in the area! Your record also shows that you have mastered a sea navigation course and that will make you a very valuable man to know in later times!"

He then spoke to Cung's wife called Daiyu. He said, *"Daiyu Whyat, as well as investigating your husband, I have also investigated you because of the fact that you are born of the ethnic Chinese Hoa people and that your original home was the Cho Long area of Saigon. (Now called Ho Chi Mihn City) It is a matter of record that you are a loyal citizen of the Democratic Republic of Vietnam and that you have never acted against the state! Now then, ordinarily, there would never be a problem regarding you and your activities.*

However, jealous people have accused your husband Cung because they want Cung's fertiliser and farm machinery business! These people are the low-lifes who made the war years under the Japanese and Vichy French administrations such a misery for our people. However, some of them hold power in our new county called the Democratic Republic of Vietnam! Therefore, we must be careful!"

Nguyen the policeman now spoke directly to Nguyen Thiourea, he said, *"Nguyen, I have also investigated your activities. Apart from the fact that you appear to have applied yourself very well to your position of being a government tax collector, you have done nothing wrong. However, there are many who want to take revenge upon the likes of you because of suffering caused by the puppet governments' tax collections! The people of this country are wanting to take revenge against all those whom they think may have had a part to play in their miseries under the successive South Vietnamese governments of Diem right down to Thieu!*

So, here you are, a man who only served his overlords well and other than that, you were not a threat to my people. You are scheduled for transport to a re-education camp in two days from now! You need to form part of a group seeking to escape from Vietnam by boat. You are invited to join my group. More about that later.

That brings us to my own case. My father was a founding member of the Viet Mihn, and I was a lieutenant of the Vietcong. Like Cung, I have been decorated for valour while in action against the

140

enemy. Like Cung, I have had jealous people accuse me of things that I have never done!

That means that the four of us would be far better off if we could start a new life in a new country, I have researched that and after speaking to people who have done it, I am of the opinion that it would be for the best if all of us were to obtain a boat and sail to the land of the Uc da Loi (Australia.) Many Vietnamese have sailed their boats to the land of the Uc da Loi, and I have been in contact with some of these people.

They have all told me that although things were difficult at first, once things had settled down and they were accepted by the Uc da Loi community, they were able to have successful businesses and they are now part of the vibrant and thriving Uc da Loi community! I cannot be seen to simply release the three of you immediately, so that must wait until tonight. Our boat is prepared, and I shall silently release you after dark tonight. Cung, brush up on your navigation skills because we sail for Uc da Loi tonight after we travel to where the boat is!

There will also be another fifteen people coming with us who are desperate to leave Vietnam! Oh, how silly of me, I forgot to introduce myself! I am Nguyen Pham Lam, now rest and do not say a word to anyone or else we are all dead! I shall come for you at eighteen hundred hours tonight Vietnam time!" Having spoken those words, Nguyen the policeman left and went about his business. Meanwhile Cung, Daiyu and Nguyen Thiourea ate their meals and drank their water after which they rested.

Meanwhile, Nguyen Phan Lam, the policeman, was in a conversation with people who also wanted to leave Vietnam and possibly live in Australia. These new arrivals were at the home of the policeman, and they had elected an elder of theirs to negotiate a place with the policeman's group of refugees.

Accordingly, a forty-eight (48) year old man called Ho Hiep approached Nguyen and said, *"Good day to you, sir! I am Ho Hiep and the fifteen people in my group have asked me to help them obtain a passage to the land of the Uc da Loi with your group of people. We shall pay for everything we need or eat! As part of the deal to take us with you on your journey to Uc da Loi across the sea, I have been authorised to pay you US $20,000.00. that should help to grease the palms of the greedy and corrupt Vietnamese police, customs and port officials and also buy us the diesel that is required as fuel for the journey!"*

Nguyen though the matter over for a while, and then he said, *"Very well, Ho, you wish to add another fifteen people and yourself to the sixteen people we already have to take to Uc da Loi (Australia) across the sea! There are some things about this proposed trip that you and your group of people should consider. (1) It is now the middle of October 1979 and (2) soon, there shall be storms and tempests which we shall encounter along the way.*

Our boat is a traditional Vietnamese sea-going fishing boat of the junk style design. It is fitted with twin diesel engines and a two-way radio. By listening to it continuously, we should get warning of any pirates who may try to ambush boats and shipping traffic passing through the Malacca Straits and further south to the Indonesian coast. We will maintain a total radio silence. We shall only listen in order to be warned of possible threats!

It is because of probable interest of pirates that I am asking you about the ages and sex of these additional passengers. Also, it will help us all greatly if the passengers can fight and in particular if they have had combat experience with Vietnamese, Vietcong, or other military forces! Also, it will help if your people are armed, and have ammunition for their arms and are able and willing to fight if the need for that arises!"

Ho said, *"Do not worry about my people! They number fifteen and their ages vary between fourteen and fifty years! Some of the adult men and women have combat experience gained while they were fighting for the Vietcong and in some cases, for the ARVN army of presidents Diem and Thieu! As well, we have with us a cache of sixteen new Kalashnikov AK 47 assault rifles together with two thousand and eight hundred rounds of the necessary 7.62 mm ammunition! Also, we have two RPG7s and three rounds of ammunition for each one of them!*

I should also explain that I am a former member of the ARVN 302 Ranger battalion. Other than having been a member of the former South Vietnamese forces, I have always been a good citizen of Vietnam. You will find that due to my military background, I know how to organise and defend. That could benefit you.

Let me introduce you to some other members of my group. This is Hanh Liem Tru. He has been a peasant and always was loyal to the former puppet regimes, but he always had sympathy for the Vietcong! Over there, is Anh Hong Khanh, he is a very good chef, and he is now twenty-two years old. (in1978)

Here is Ngoc Nguyen Tran, he is 24 (in 1979) and he is a peasant who grows food for the people. Like many others in Vietnam, he is loyal to the Vietcong and the puppet governments of South Vietnam. He never would have lifted a finger against the puppet governments or the patriot Vietcong if he had not been forced to do so.

This woman is Hoa Lan Xuan she is a veteran of both the ARVN and Vietcong forces. This amazing person was always a patriot of Vietnam. As a young girl she volunteered to serve after she was infected with gonorrhea when she was raped by both AVRN and American soldiers. She found that medical help was difficult to obtain.

In time, she became a member of Long Khanh's own D440 battalion and she did so well, that she was promoted to Platoon Commander in D440 Battalion. While serving with D440 battalion, she received the medical attention that she needed, and she was finally cured of the social disease called gonorrhea.

After the Vietnamese victory over the cruel foreign occupiers of Vietnam, she has embarrassed some junior officials of the new government of the Democratic Republic of Vietnam. They have outlawed her because of that. Her only crime was that others have become jealous of her, and they denounced her because of that! The rest of my group are similar people and all of them need to escape from Vietnam for now!"

Travelling Through Waters Infected by Pirates

Although Nguyen still did not completely trust Ho, he welcomed the additional weapons and ammunition to take on the journey ahead of them all. Nguyen said, *"Very well, Ho, you and your people may accompany us on our journey! However, be advised that the area near the engine and steering equipment is out of bounds for yourself and your people! Those areas are for myself and my people only! Either accept what I am telling you or go and find passage to Uc da Loi across the sea with someone else!"*

And so, it was agreed that Ho and his additional fifteen people became part of the group of refugees trying to escape Vietnam and journey to Australia. That satisfied the policeman called Nguyen Phan Lam, who now prepared and provisioned the sea going fishing boat with water and food items such as rice for the journey ahead. Looking at his wristwatch, Nguyen noted that it was now time for him to organise the release of Daiyu, Cung and Nguyen Thiourea and to bring them to the sea fishing boat.

Having released the trio from their cell, Nguyen said, *"Daiyu, Cung and Nguyen, our group of people has been joined by an additional sixteen others. Some of them are ex-soldiers and ex-patriots of Vietnam. They have bought with them, seventeen new AK-47 assault rifles and more than two thousand rounds of ammunition! That shall prove to be very handy if we run into trouble with the pirates of the Malacca Straights!*

Cung, here are the charts that you shall need to plot our course through the Malacca Straits past the Indonesian Islands and onwards to Christmas Island which is Australian territory. Here are also the China-graph pencils and plastic covers for the maps to keep them dry during the storms that we shall be facing.

Use the China-graph pencils and draw our course upon the plastic sleeve containing the map. By so doing, we will be able to see through the plastic casing and be able to see the course in relation to the straits of Malacca and other areas as we pass through them. It is critical that you keep these maps and the course marked upon the plastic protectors current and up-date!

I have decided that only Cung, myself and Daiyu shall be allowed to enter the wheelhouse and be anywhere near the radio. We shall maintain total radio silence until such time as we approach Christmas Island and successfully contact the Uc da Loi authorities!

I have researched Vietnamese people fleeing to Uc da Loi. On the 26th of April 1976, the first boat of Vietnamese refugees arrived in Darwin Uc da Loi. Over the past few years, another two thousand Vietnamese people have gone to Uc da Loi and made that place their home! Although the land of the Uc da Loi has given refuge to about two thousand Vietnamese people, we must remember that they are

146

from all walks of life in Vietnam. Some of them would have been former patriots such as Cung and me, while others have been traitors and those who made life miserable for our peasants!

I have placed all of the AK-47 firearms into the steel locker located in the wheelhouse. If we encounter pirates stay at your post if you are on duty steering the boat and send for me. I shall then come to the wheelhouse and issue the firearms and ammunition to others on board this boat. We will rely upon the training of our companions while they were in the service of the puppets or Vietnamese National Governments."

Meanwhile, Cung had taken the charts and he placed all of them into the water-proof sleeves in such a way as to display the chart clearly. He then took his protractor and ruler and proceeded to plot the course past the straits of Malacca and towards Christmas Island. He had barley finished that task when his wife Daiyu appeared. She had in her hand a streaming hot cup of tea and she proceeded to give that to Cung. He said, *"Thank you, my darling wife, that is just what I need!"*

She looked at the lengthening shadows of the evening sky and she voiced her concerns about the look of the clouds on the darkening horizon. She said, *"Cung, I do not like the looks of that evening sky! The setting sun is making the evening sky appear to be very strange and not red! That makes me remember the words of Vietnamese fishermen and other sailors.*

They all said, *"A red sky at night is a sailor's delight but a red sky in the morning is the sailor's warning! The strange blue and other colours of this night sky, combined with the menacing look of the clouds overhead make me fear the worst! Cung, place all charts that you do not need at this minute into that dry and waterproof chest so that our navigation charts are safe and dry!"*

Cung who was steering the boat had the earphones of the radio on. As well as steering the fishing boat, he was changing radio frequencies in order to pick up possible conversations of shipping around or near the boat load of refugees. Suddenly, Cung called out, *"Daiyu, please go and fetch Nguyen the policeman, I am hearing that there may be some pirate ships in this area. According to what they are saying, they know of our presence in this area, and they are actively looking for us!"*

Without uttering a word, Daiyu left the wheelhouse and went to the deck below to find Nguyen Phan Lam. Having finally found him, she said, *"Nguyen, my husband has been hearing the conversations between different pirate ships. Apparently, they know that we are in this area, and they are currently looking for us!"*

The ex-policeman said, *"Daiyu, return to your husband in the wheelhouse and lock it from the inside. Do not let anyone other than myself into the wheelhouse! That is critical! In the meantime, I shall talk to the members of our group and leader of the new group of sixteen other people on board our boat. After I have talked to Ho, your husband, I, and Ho shall move among the others on board giving out the AK-47s and the ammunition.*

If the pirates do attack us, they shall find this boat to be heavily defended! After Cung and I have given out the firearms and their ammunition, we shall both return to the wheelhouse! I have locked the entrance to the engine room, and I hope that the obstruction to outsiders will hold while we defend our boat!"

With that said, Nguyen Phan Lam walked along the deck to where Ho was talking with some of his people. He said, *"Ho, we are entering areas which can hide many pirates. According to radio voice traffic, they know of our presence, and they are actively looking for us! Please organise your people to come up to the wheelhouse where I shall issue them with the weapons and one hundred rounds of ammunition each. We have to completely trust each other and fight the pirates!* Ho answered, *"It shall be done, Nguyen!"*

Next, Ho could be heard ordering others on the boat. He was saying, *"Listen carefully, each one of you is to go to the wheelhouse in single file and receive your issue of an AK-47 plus three fully loaded thirty round magazines for each of them. That will give each of you ninety rounds and it will leave us with a reserve of ammunition in case of more trouble from pirates at later dates. This boat shall now be made as dark as possible to hide us.*

No lights are to be used and as of now, there shall be no smoking, as that will betray our position! If the pirates do board this vessel, I shall fire a flare into the sky! That will be followed by three long whistle blasts on a football umpire's whistle! When you see the flare or hear my order to fire or three

149

blasts from the whistle, open fire upon the pirates and fucking well kill all of them! Give those murderous creeps no quarter and show them no mercy, for that is what they have in mind for all of us!

For now, quietly move in single file to the wheelhouse and be issued with your AK-47s and your three loaded thirty round magazines! We also have some older carbines of 7.62 mm calibre. In total, there are thirty-one people on board, but we only have seventeen of the most modern AK47s. Those people who are not issued with a current model AK47, will be issued with SKS weapons. We have ten of those. They use the same ammunition as the AK47!

When you have your weapons and ammunition, you are to quietly move back here and take up your defensive positions on the deck! Do any of you have any questions about what you are to do and both when and how to do it?" No-one spoke and so, Nguyen Phan Lam correctly assumed that his men all knew what was required of them and how to perform their assigned tasks.

The black darkness of night was all-enveloping and although all people had been assigned watches and tasks to perform during the watches, everyone only spoke in whispers so as not to alert the pirates to the whereabouts of the fishing boat carrying the refugees.

Back at the wheelhouse, Cung was being uneasy because of vastly increased radio traffic. Much of that was simply maritime conversations between shipping of various nations. However, there were also conversations in Khmer Laotian and Vietnamese.

These did not unduly worry Cung. However, when he heard and understood men speaking in the Thai language, he became worried. He said to Daiyu, *"My darling, please go and find Nguyen Phan Lam and then bring him and Ho here! Please hurry!"* His wife, Daiyu immediately left to find the two men and soon she returned with both of them.

Seeing Nguyen and Ho coming with Daiyu, made Cung relax a little. As they all came into the wheelhouse, Cung spoke to them all. He said, *"Comrades, it is pitch black out there and we cannot even see our own hands if we were to hold them just twenty-five centimetres from our faces. I have been following the radio traffic and most of it is just international ships talking to each other.*

There is a potential problem coming from unidentified sources which is causing me some worry. What is worrying me is the short and infrequent messages in the Thai language saying to others to be on the lookout for a large Vietnamese design sea fishing boat! I am of the opinion that they mean this boat and that they are looking for us! Nguyen, I notice that we have two flare pistols and the flares for them right here.

I would like to keep one here in order for me or Daiyu to use the flare to illuminate the whole fishing boat if we note that there is something wrong. Everyone else on board can then get stuck into the pirates whoever they turn out to be!" Nguyen Phan Lam answered Cung. He said, *"Cung I think that you have read my mind! I was going to suggest that you keep one of the flare pistols up here while Ho and I take the other one down to the deck. So, thank you for doing this, it will give us two flare pistols to use, one the deck and you will still have a flare pistol for use up here in the wheelhouse.*

Ho and I shall now return to our positions on the deck, where we are keeping watches of two men at a time. The reason for it is that if there are two men, and they very quietly speak to each other, they shall find it much easier to stay alert. By the way, Cung, I am giving you this AK-47 and three loaded thirty round magazines of ammunition so that you can fire at any enemy from up here. Being in this elevated wheelhouse should give you an advantage over the pirates if they do come!"

Storms, Tempests, and Pirates

After the quick conference between Cung, Daiyu, Ho and Nguyen, there was a freshening of the wind and the waves rose in height. Recognising the situation, both Nguyen and Ho went to each of their people who were on the deck preparing to fight the pirates, if they came. The wind kept picking speed and soon, the height of the waves were as high as the top of the wheelhouse, which was two metres above the deck.

Meanwhile, Nguyen was busy handing out life jackets. He went from person to person saying, *"Here comrade, is a life jacket. I need you to put it on right now and you must wear it at all times. As well, everyone must either tie themselves or else be tied to the gunwales so that waves cannot sweep you off the deck! Make sure that you tightly hold onto your weapons and ammunition in case we get attacked by pirates. So, put on this life jacket immediately! I shall*

help you put it on, and I will make sure that you are
wearing it correctly and that you have it on at all
times! No-one is allowed to take their life jackets off!"

Suddenly, a large wave broke over the fishing
boat and swept away one the male refugees who was
preparing to fight the pirates. Nguyen and Ho went
among their people and managed to tie all of them
down to the deck so that the tragedy of a man swept
overboard would not happen again. After several
hours, the storm abated, resulting in Nguyen and Ho
again moving among their people, this time untying
them and ensuring that they had complete freedom of
movement in case of attack upon the fishing boat.

Meanwhile, the Thai pirates had a stroke of
luck. The wind now picked up speed and then both
rain and thunder with lightening began. In the
wheelhouse of the Thai boat, Praew (means shining),
was staring into the darkness before him. As the
lightening was flashing about the boat, he was sure
that he could see something in the water. He went to
the bow of his boat and spoke to Arthit (means Sun).

He said, *"Arthit, there is something in the*
water towards the bow and off to the starboard side.
Be on the lookout for whatever it is, and grab hold of
it using our lines with grappling hooks attached. It is
entirely possible that whatever it is has come from the
Vietnamese ocean fishing boat that we are seeking! I
have a feeling in my bones that the Vietnamese cannot
be far away from us!"

Just then, there were another three lightning
strikes, close together and that provided light to both
the pirates and their Vietnamese refugee quarry.

Arthit had performed his work well and he was able to cast a line with a grappling hook attached to it over an object floating in the water on the starboard side near the bow of the Thai boat. As he was pulling the object in towards the Thai boat he *yelled "Got you whatever you are!"* then, he hauled it onboard. Once on board, the Thai pirates found that the object was in fact the dead Vietnamese refugee who had been washed off the deck of the Vietnamese boat.

Arthit went looking for his captain who was called, 'Somchai' meaning 'real man'. Finally locating Somchai, Arthit reported, *"Somchai, the Vietnamese boat we have been looking for cannot be so very far away from us now! I have just pulled the body of a dead Vietnamese who appears to have been washed off the Vietnamese boat in the last squall! I think that if we maintain our present course and keep a sharp lookout towards our front and sides, we should catch sight of the Vietnamese through the aid of the lightning!"*

Somchai said, *"Very good Arthit! Do what you are proposing and when we catch the Vietnamese, we shall rape all of their women, no matter if they are young girls, mature women, or old hags! We shall takeaway everything they may have and kill all of the males!"*

Meanwhile, Ho and Nguyen Phan Lam were talking to their comrades on the deck of the sea-going Vietnamese fishing boat named as the Giang Kien. Talking to others, Ho said, *"Gently feel the AK-47 that you have been issued with. Towards the front of the barrel, you should be able to feel the folding four bladed bayonet that helps to make this such a* formidable weapon. *I want you all to move the bayonet from its folded under the barrel position and into the 'fixed' position so that it is ready for use immediately. That way we shall be an armed force for all to reckon with even after we have run out of ammunition! We shall keep on trying to stay ahead of the Thai pirates, but we shall fight them to the death as soon as that becomes necessary!"*

Meanwhile, Nguyen Phan Lam was having some serious doubts about the current situation of himself and the boatload of people with him. He could not shake off the feeling that something was going wrong, and that everyone was in an approaching dangerous situation. He thought about the situation and decided to discuss it with Ho, who was speaking to other refugees on the deck opposite him.

So, Nguyen went to Ho and spoke to him. He said, *"Ho, I have an alarming feeling that we are being followed by the unseen pirates and that they are in fact fairly close to us. More and more, I am getting the impression that the Thai pirates are following and that they will try to board us as soon as they are in a position to do so and when they think that we are unprepared and an easy target for them!"*

Ho replied, *"Yes Nguyen, I also have that feeling of approaching difficult times ahead of us due to the Thai pirates! It is the main reason that I have asked our people to familiarize themselves completely with our AK-47 assault rifles to the point where they can all use the folding bayonet with ease. I have organised ten of the men to act as riflemen and for them to hold a rear-line of defence if we are boarded.*

Assuming that happens, those men shall remain at the side of the boat furthest away from the invaders while others who are armed with the AK-47s attempt a bayonet charge into the attacking pirates. I think it to best to conserve our ammunition until we are past Indonesia at least, in case of further attacks upon us by pirates of unknown nationality!"

Nguyen Phan Lam thought about what Ho had told him and then, he spoke. He said, *"Ho, I just love what you have done! It gives me the hope that we shall be successful in our attempt to reach the land of the Uc da Loi! Assuming that we make it there, it should result in new lives and opportunities for us all! We must now keep watch and we must stay alert for any signs of trouble. If it comes, we must all act instantly!"*

So it was that Nguyen Phan Lam returned to his position on the other side of the open deck. Like all of the other people on the deck, he was wet from the squalls, and wind driven rain that everyone was experiencing. There was rain water running down his face as he was peering into the darkness towards the bow and the sides of the Giang Kein.

Meanwhile, on board the Thai pirate vessel, Arthit was listening intently to a message on the two-way radio. The message concluded and that resulted in Arthit hurrying to find his captain called Somchai (meaning 'Real Man'). Having found him, he gave him the message. He said, *"Somchai, I have just received a radio message from our spies among the Vietnamese at Ba Chuc hamlet called Sauget et Sang! He said that the name of the Vietnamese boat ahead of us is the Giang Kein. It has a total of thirty-one people on board. It has two modern diesel engines and a two-way radio for communication. Sauget also warned that these people are armed.*

Apparently, they have with them two Russian made RPG7 rocket launchers and ammunition for them. They also have seventeen current model AK-47 assault rifles with folding bayonets. Do not think that they cannot fight, because among this group of people are ex-members of Vietcong and also veterans of the Kampuchean invasion of Vietnam, and even some former members of the former army of South Vietnam Army (AVRN). These are people who can and will fight. One of their fights resulted in Vietnamese occupation of Kampuchea! So, Somchai, what are your orders?"

Somchai considered what he had been told for a while before he spoke. He then said, *"Keep this boat out of the sight of the Giang Kein! We now have no choice but to follow that boat until such time as it has its people go ashore on a nearby island to gather water and fruit such as coconuts for use as additional food for the people on board the boat. They are also likely to try some fishing because up until now, they have been surviving by eating small amounts of rice.*

From what we have been told about them having arms capable of delivering immense firepower for such a small group of people, it will be best if we wait until they are busy resupplying their water and food stocks. If we wait until they are actually on an island looking for water and food, most of them will be busy doing that, and it will make our attack on the Vietnamese boat much easier!" Arthit said, *"As you wish, Somchai, it shall be as you want done!"*

And so, Arthit steered the Thai vessel and adjusted its speed so that it remained out of the sight of the Giang Kein. As the weather settled into much calmer patterns, the Giang Kein was observed to anchor a few hundred metres from the beach of an island. It was observed by the Thai pirates that fifteen people from that boat waded ashore and that they were carrying containers to store water and other items. The pirates did not note that among the fifteen foragers was an escort party of eight people who were armed with AK-47 assault rifles. They also noted that the Giang Kein still had sixteen people on board who were armed and had the disciplined ability to use firearms effectively.

Arthit again spoke to Somchai. He said, *"Somchai, the Vietnamese on board the Giang Kein still have the fire power of the two rocket launchers on the Vietnamese boat and also, there are still at least ten AK-47s on board the Giang Kein. The other seven AK47s could be with the food and water foraging party that has gone ashore for provisions. So, it is highly likely that of the fifteen people ashore, seven are armed with the AK-47 assault rifles while the remainder of those people are acting as porters. They have now been observed leaving the boat and returning to it laden with provisions two times. So, what do you want us to do?"*

The Thai pirate leader called Somchai said, *"Where is the foraging party of the Giang Kein now?"* He was told, *"Somchai, they left again for more foraging about half an hour ago! Based on past observations, they should be returning in about two hours from now."*

Somchai said, *"There shall never be a better time to attack our Vietnamese enemies than now! Ideally, we should wait util twilight or darkness before we attack, but by then, the foraging party shall have returned, and the Giang Kein shall be both fully operational and dangerous for us to attack. Therefore, you are to close with the Vietnamese at full speed and we shall at least manage to catch them with only half of their numbers on board their boat!"*

Arthit, replied, *"Yes, Somchai, it shall be done!"* He then set the Thai vessel into full speed in spite of the fact that visibility was good and the noise from the engines would be clearly heard by the people on the Vietnamese boat.

The Thai vessel was travelling at speed, and soon it anchored in a bay of the same island where the foraging party of the was gathering food and water. Somchai issued new orders to his men. He said, *"Arthit, take ten men and locate the enemy boat! When you have found it, attack it, and kill the Vietnamese. Take care not to put holes into the diesel tanks of the Vietnamese boat because we may need their diesel to make it back to Thailand! Now go and complete you mission!"*

Arthit went to the pirate crew and selected the ten men he wanted, and they all left on their new mission. While they were walking towards the bay where the Giang Kein had anchored. Arthit was experienced enough in attacking vessels and general warfare to know that his party needed to make sure that their silhouettes were not visible as that would warn the defenders of the Vietnamese boat. For that reason, he, and his attacking group of ten men put some vegetation onto the tops and sides of their shirts, thus breaking up their outlines.

As well, the entire attacking group stayed just inside the tree line in order to remain out of sight until the last minute. After another fifteen minutes, they were coming within sight of the Giang Kein. Arthit said, *"Kittsak, you are the best shot in our group, and I want you to take out at least one of the Vietnamese, and so make things better for us when we begin our attack."*

Kittsak could see Cung who was in the wheelhouse checking his equipment for the continuation of the journey towards Australia during the next morning. Kittsak aimed his SKS carbine and fired. As he began to squeeze the trigger, Cung moved and bent down to pick up a chart which had fallen to the floor of the wheelhouse. Suddenly, Cung felt a sharp pain in his left shoulder and then he noticed a bleeding wound on top of the shoulder the pain was now becoming intense and Cung reacted by saying, *"Fuck that hurts! I think that I have been fucking well shot!"*

Cung was seen to be holding his shoulder, by his wife, Daiyu. She went to the wheelhouse and exclaimed to Cung, *"What has happened to you my darling husband?"* He replied, *"Daiyu my dear, I do not know for sure what has happened, but I think that I have been shot in the shoulder!"*

Having heard the swearing of Cung and the expressions of distress from Daiyu, made Nguyen Phan Lam hurry to the wheelhouse. Having reached there he saw the bleeding left shoulder of Cung. That resulted in him speaking. He said, *"Cung and Daiyu, please accompany me down to the deck where you shall be less visible to those who attack this boat! I want to examine Cung to make sure that we do not have to give him more attention and to take a bullet out of his shoulder if that is what has happened here!"* He then closely examined the shoulders of Cung.

After five minutes, he said, *"Cung, I have closely looked at your wounded shoulder and it seems to me that you have a bullet in it! That has to come out and I shall do that for you! We do not have any anesthetic with us, so this will hurt!"* Cung replied, *"Just go ahead and do what must be done Nguyen. If that was a bullet, it means that we are under attack or else we soon will be. Therefore, counter measures must be taken!"*

Nguyen said, *"I have located the bullet. Now hold still while I get it out of your shoulder!"* That was followed by Cung gritting his teeth while Nguyen extracted the bullet from his shoulder and Daiyu washed the blood and dirt in general from the wounded area. As she was doing that, she was praising her husband encouraging him in general. Now that he had his wound dressed and treated, Cung had put on an olive-coloured shirt and returned to the wheelhouse.

Just before he returned to the wheelhouse, he said, *"Nguyen, it seems to me that we should do something about this situation of being attacked before we all end up as corpses!"* Nguyen replied, *"Yes, but you shall not take part in that solution, it is being attended to by Ho and his people right now!"*

Nguyen Van Truc came forward and spoke directly to Cung and Ho. He said, *"I was with the foraging party, and we saw that the pirates have landed a force of about ten armed men upon this island! They have inserted vegetation onto their clothing to break up their outlines and they appear to be headed this way. Their intent appears to be very hostile towards us! Hoa, who is in command of our self-defence section, sent me back here to raise the alarm and to get the defence of our ship ready. I was able to go around the pirates and they have not seen me. Therefore, they will not be expecting an armed resistance from the crew of our ship!"* Cung said, *"Nguyen, you have done well in bringing this vital information to us."*

Meanwhile, Arthit, Kittsack and the eight other Thai pirates were getting ever closer to the Giang Kein. Unknown to the pirates, Ho had organised three sentries who were almost invisible due to the fact that they were located within dense vegetation about one hundred metres from where the Giang Kein was anchoured. Daiyu was one of the sentries, and she saw the pirates sneaking closer towards the ship.

She became alarmed but she remained calm and aimed her AK-47 assault rifle at the closest pirate. She had the ideal sight picture, with the top of foresight post being located on the left side of the chest of the closest pirate, she shot him. She then shot another pirate and that resulted in Arthit yelling, *"Fall back, retreat two hundred metres back towards our own boat!"* The pirates then ran from that area and returned to the pirate ship, where they obtained another five men before again going towards the Giang Kein.

Daiyu had left her cover and she was actively following the pirates, while remaining out of their view. She saw them go back on board their ship and she saw that they now had an additional five men, which brought their number up to fourteen. She noted that and quietly melted into the background before returning to Giang Kein. Upon arrival, she spoke to Cung, Nguyen and Ho. She said, *"We are about to be under attack again from the pirates. The original force against us was ten men, but they lost two who both were shot by me.*

They have retreated back to their ship, where they have added another five men to their group and that now makes their number up to fourteen men. The expanded group of fourteen pirates is now moving toward us and they shall be here soon!" That was followed by the sound of AK-47 assault rifle fire coming from where the sentries were in place. Ho said, *"Daiyu, it seems to me like that the pirates you speak of are now here!"*

That short conversation was followed by Ho calmly and loudly saying, *"Self-defense unit of the Giang Kein, select your targets!"* A few seconds later, he ordered, *"Using the AK-47s only, open fire!"* In front of him, the self defence unit from the Vietnamese boat, was shooting the Thai pirates and they retreated, leaving six of their comrades lying upon the sand of the beach.

Arthit saw that and it so worried him that he now ordered, *"Retreat back to our boat in the next bay! Leave our dead here, we must return to Somchai!"* Ten minutes later, the remaining eight Thai pirates returned to their boat. Seeing them coming, Somchai said, *"I have heard the firefight! I did not want any of you to take on the Vietnamese people because of their superior AK-47 assault rifles. For now, we shall go to one of our Malaysian bases and get some better weapons and more men as well as a re-supply of diesel. After that we shall return to hunting down these Vietnamese dogs who have given us such trouble! I will also get at least one more boat for our use!"*

Leading the foraging party looking water and food, was Hoa Lan Xuan. She was a formidable young woman who had been an officer for the ARVN forces before she defected and joined the D440 Viet Cong Battalion, based at Long Khan, where she was an officer. Ho thought that she was the best person to be in charge of thee foraging party due to her outstanding abilities as an infantry commander. She decided to have at least the seven available AK47 assault rifles with her group, leaving the other ten AK47s on board the boat.

Hoa and the other foragers were on their way back to the Giang Kein when they all heard the pirates shoot Cung in his shoulder. Hoa said, *"Ai, I need you and Bian to come with me. We are going to lend aid to our boat which is under attack from the pirates! I want the rest of you to remain here and keep a close watch on things in case the pirates double back here and manage to get past us! This party has a total of seven AK47s. Three of those are going with me while the remaining four shall protect the rest of this foraging party!"* With the said, Hoa and her two companions walked towards the Giang Kein.

As they were going towards the boat, the retreating pirates under the command of Arkit saw them coming. Arkit spoke to his men. He said, *"Look over there, towards the north-east, there is a group of three women! I think that the time has come for us to get revenge upon these Vietnamese bitches! All of you, quietly melt into the undergrowth on the left side of the track here! We shall wait until we have the bitches close to us before we fire upon them and wound them. Don't kill them, just wound them and then we will strip them and rape them!"*

The group of three women was getting closer and one of the pirates could no longer restrain himself. He open fire with his SKS carbine and hit Ai in the left upper arm. She immediately answered his attack by shooting him with her AK47 assault rifle. She had shot him in the chest, and he fell down and was oozing blood from his mouth.

Seeing that happen, caused Arkit to order, *"Retreat, get the hell out of there! We have to retreat back to our ship!"* and so, the pirates led by Arkit left and went back to their own ship.

As that was happening, the Giang Kein had been reprovisioned with both food in the form of fish and coconuts and water. Other than the wound to the shoulder of Cung, all occupants of the Vietnamese boat were unharmed except for Ai. The daylight was transforming into the evening twilight and the tide had risen. Ho, Nguyen and Cung all agreed that the Giang Kein should immediately continue its journey towards the south. Nguyen hauled up the anchor and the Vietnamese fishing boat got under way.

In the wheelhouse of the Giang Kein, Cung was steering whilst also listening to radio traffic in case he could once again be informed of the probable actions of Thai and other pirates. This time, there was only the normal maritime conversation between shipping and their companies. Although there was nothing to suggest that an attack was imminent or of approaching danger, all people on the Vietnamese boat remained awake and alert.

After a short time, Nguyen, Cung and Ho held a conference to discuss the rest of their journey. Cung started the conversation with, *"I cannot speak for other people, but it seems to me that if we only travel during daylight hours, then at least we have the chance of seeing pirates and other probable enemies before they can close with our boat and either raid or sink us! The only reason that we were travelling by night is because we had to get away from the pirates who want to harm us!*

We still have two thousand rounds of ammunition for the AK-47s, and we still have the fully armed RPG 7s from Russia complete with three rockets for each of the two RPGs. The RPGs have a range of about two hundred metres, but I propose that we let intruders come to within twenty-five metres of our boat before we open fire using the RPGs! All of the AK-47s have four-bladed folding long bayonets attached to them. That is good because if we run out of ammunition, we shall still be able to fight! By only sleeping at night and always having rotating "On duty" shifts of no more than two hours, we must all be able to get enough sleep and remain alert."

Ho said, *"Yes Cung, I agree that we should not travel at night if possible. I also agree that we should post sentries on two hour rotating shifts to ensure our safety and only travel during the day time when we can see what is coming towards us! Also, I like the idea of letting the enemy come to within twenty-five metres of this boat or even closer before we open fire with the RPGs. That way, we shall be sure to hit them and sink the low-life creeps!*

As of now, we shall always have most of our people on board this boat to make sure that no-one can steal it from us! We must remain vigilant at all times because of the large number of pirates and others who would harm us, given the chance to do so!"

And so, the Giang Kein continued its southward journey. It only stopped at small uninhabited islands to obtain resupplies of water and some food items like coconuts or fish when these could be had. Inhabited islands were by-passed in case of a hostile repletion which the Vietnamese refugees did not want. Discussing their situation were Nguyen, Cung, Daiyu and Ho.

Nguyen said, *"After paying the necessary bribes to corrupt officials in Vietnam and Malaysia, and paying for the diesel, we now have left US$14,000.00 of the original US$20,000.00 we started off with! That should enable us to detour slightly toward Java, where we can talk to the Indonesian authorities and get some new clothes for our women.*

There is no doubt that we shall have to pay more bribes to the Indonesian officials, but we should be able to handle that with ease. I have spoken to our women on board, and they have said that they would dearly love to be able to spend some time ashore on some islands belonging to Indonesia. Many of them want new clothes! So, what do you think about this, my friends?"

Daiyu answered with, *"Nguyen, I think that a very short stop-over in Java is a marvelous idea! That shall allow the women of our group to speak to Javanese women and to buy some food or clothing items. It will completely refresh us all and even perhaps allow us to make contact with the government of the Uc da Loi!"* Nguyen said, *"As usual Daiyu and Cung, your wife is making perfect sense. We shall have a one-night stop-over at Java before continuing our journey.*

While ashore in Java, I shall try to make contact with the Uc da Loi officials. The only problem with that is that it is bound to be put onto the international news and broadcast all over the world. It is almost certain that the Thai pirates whom we fought off earlier will redouble their search for us when they hear of this. Still, it is a chance that we have to take, as the well-being of all of us depends upon it!"

Taking on Thai Pirates

At 08:00 hours of the 24th of October 1978, the sea-going Vietnamese fishing boat named as Giang Kein, sailed into a bay on the Indonesian island of Java. After the boat had anchored in the shallow bay, a group of the refugees were organised to go into the nearest settlement for the purpose of trade. It was headed by Daiyu and Nguyen Phan Lam, the former Vietnamese police officer. There were two other women in this group. Everyone else was instructed to remain on board the Giang Kein and to remain on guard in case there was an attempted take-over of the vessel.

Nguyen was on shore mainly to try to contact the Australian authorities in order to have the people on board the Giang Kein accepted as genuine refugees and therefore for them to be permitted to live in Australia. As he walked into a village, he noticed a small post office building. He thought, *"OK, so this appears to be a post office, let's see if I can send a telegram from here to the Department of Immigration in Canberra!"*

He walked into the post office building and said in his broken Malay speech, *"I want to send a telegram to the department of immigration in Canberra in Uc da Loi!"* Amazingly, the post office clerk understood what was required and drafted out the telegram before reading it to Nguyen for his approval. Having finished writing out the telegram the clerk now read it to Nguyen.

He said, *"From Java, Indonesia to the Department of Immigration in Canberra, Australia."*

"Dear Madam/Sir, my name is Nguyen Phan Lam, and I am taking a fishing boat loaded with thirty Vietnamese refugees to Australia. We are currently on Java, and we shall leave that place in the morning. We beg you for your kind permission to travel to

Australia and get refuge from the Communist Government of Vietnam. We know that the Australian Prime Minister called Malcomb Fraser has stated 'Australia and Australians have a duty to provide for and to accept the Vietnamese refugees into their country and to keep them safe!" We shall not be a burden upon our new country, and we shall pay for everything we use! Signed Nguyen Phan Lam."

Nguyen was excited by that, and he said, *"Excellent work! How much money do I owe you for this?"* The Indonesian Post Office Clerk said, *"That will be US$30.00, thank you!"* Nguyen thought that the price was a bit high but paid the money using three US ten-dollar notes as soon as the clerk used his Morse code and radio equipment to send the signal. Almost immediately, an answering telegram arrived.

It said, *"Dear Nguyen Phan Lam, when you get clear of the Indonesian islands, head for the Australian territory at Cocas Island or Christmas Island if you can do so. If you come across Australian warships or patrol vessels on the way, do not be alarmed for they shall protect you and your people. If our navy finds you upon the seas, all people will be taken from your vessel and the given clean clothes to wear as well as hot food to eat.*

You shall all be encouraged to use the showers and cleaning facilities on our warships and patrol boats! So, if you see Australian naval vessels, remember to attract them, and let them come to your aid immediately. – signed by Captain Rodgers, Royal Australian Navy."

The thought that the Australian government was officially welcoming the Vietnamese gave Nguyen great heart! Meanwhile, the others in the shore party were shopping and talking to local Javanese people. Of course, there was a language barrier but that was largely overcome, and everyone got on well together. The group in the landing party lost track of time because they were enjoying the intercourse with the locals.

Eventually they returned to the Giang Kein. As they were boarding their fishing boat, Cung heard the following news bulletin from the ABC Service on Radio Australia. *"On the Indonesian island of Java, a Vietnamese fishing boat called Giang Kein is taking on resupplies before continuing its journey to Australia! The boat has thirty people on board it. A message has been sent to the Giang Kein advising them to contact the Australian Navy ships patrolling the areas between Australian waters and Indonesian waters. The prime Minister, Mr. Fraser has said that Australians should welcome these refugees into our country!"*

That worried Cung, who immediately called a conference between himself, Daiyu, Nguyen and Ho. After they arrived at the wheelhouse, Cung said, *"My people, we have a problem in that the world news services are telling everyone about our story. While that in itself is not bad, the problem is that the pirates we beat off in the Straits of Malacca are almost bound to hear that broadcast and to then start looking for us before we can escape to Australian waters! Therefore, I am proposing that there is no letup in being watchful and we must never trust any vessel unless it is the Australian Navy!"*

Resumption of the Journey to Australia

Meanwhile, near the island of Sumatra, Arthit was listening to Radio Australia on the pirate boat. He also heard that broadcast and upon its completion, he said, *"Holy fuck, so you bloody Vietnamese arseholes are really only a few hours away from us!"* He then hurried to where Somchai was resting and said, *"Somchai, the Vietnamese arseholes who gave us such a hard time in the Straits of Malacca appear to be on Java, and that place is only some hours away from here! So, what do you want done?"*

Somchai immediately answered, *"Arthit, in about eight hours from now, another fully crewed vessel is joining our service! Therefore, we wait here until that ship joins us! You have always demonstrated your outstanding abilities to me and therefore, I want to make you the captain of the new ship, which I am calling 'The Sinker of the Vietnamese!', How do you like that, Arthit?"*

Arthit answered, *"How do I like it? I just love it! I love the idea of finally being captain of my own pirate ship! Is it a big ship, and what sized crew does it have?"*

Somchai answered, *"The new ship is bigger than this junk and it has one powerful diesel engine. It also has radar and a very good radio for communications. I have named the ship as 'The Sinker of the Vietnamese'. It has a crew of fifty men, if counting the sea-borne warriors it has on board! Added together, that will give us a total force of one hundred men which outnumbers our enemies by more than three to one in our favour!*

172

We have re-inforce our numbers and we have replaced both weapons and ammunition. Assuming that the original number of Vietnamese aboard the Giang Kein was thirty-one people, and that one of them is now dead, that leaves thirty people whom we shall have to subdue if we again attack the Giang Kein!

Therefore, we shall hunt down the Vietnamese and wipe them from the face of Earth! When we again get under way, we shall have direct conferences between yourself and me, on this ship on a four hourly basis. Our two ships shall remain within sight of each other, and we shall work out attack plans as they are needed when we sight the Vietnamese boat!"

Arthit was delighted to hear his leader say those words! He then asked Somchai, *"Somchai, should I start plotting probable course that the Vietnamese may have taken? After all, if they are trying to reach Australian Waters from Indonesian territory, there are only a few possible courses that they can use!"*

Somchai replied, With that, *"Arthit my friend, go ahead and plot the probable courses. The longer we wait, the harder it shall become to hunt down the Vietnamese killers of our comrades! Also. Remember that we must wait for another eight hours at least before we are joined by 'The Sinker of the Vietnamese'. When you have plotted the three most likely courses available to them, we shall select the one they will be most likely to use and then we begin hunting those killers of our pirate crew after our new additional ship gets here! Soon, revenge shall be ours!"* With that said, Arthit plotted the courses and informed Somchai when that was completed.

He plotted the three courses he thought were available to the 'Vietnamese Boat People.' As he had discussed earlier with Somchai, three possible courses were now marked upon the clear plastic sleeve containing the chart. That allowed easy changes to be made to the proposed courses and also protected the chart being used. He now returned to Somchai and said, *"Somchai, I have plotted the three possible routes available to the Vietnamese arseholes who killed our crew mates! I have used three different colours so that each possible route is easily distinguished from the rest of them. The route in blue marked along here, is perhaps the least likely one that they will take. That leaves the red marked route and the green marked route.*

The Green marked route from southern Sumatra could be a route that they will take if they decide to travel for some distance in a westwardly direction in order to get out of Indonesian Waters.

If I was the navigator or captain of the Giang Kein, I would firstly sail towards the south and then change direction and sail west until this point on the chart is reached, and after that, I would change course in order to travel towards the south east until such time as the boat approaches Ashmore Reef which is Australian territory.

Therefore, this route marked in red, is the one that I feel is most likely to be used by the Vietnamese murderers of our crew. So, do I have your permission to set our course along the route as marked in red?"

Somchai answered, *"Yes Arthit, take us on your favoured route marked in red and may heaven smile upon us as we chase those Vietnamese murderers of our crew members!*

It appears to me that the Vietnamese people still have to be ahead of us. If I was in command of their ship, I would pull into a bay of an uninhabited island and sleep during the night and only travel by day. It is apparent that the Vietnamese are maintaining complete radio silence in order to make sure that we cannot intercept their messages."

Meanwhile, Nguyen Phan Lam was speaking to the people on the deck of the fishing boat. He said, *"We have been travelling now for three days. During that time, we have replenished the water and food supplies of this boat and we have spent two nights ashore. One of these was on an uninhabited island and the other one was on Sumatra, where we also got some new clothes for our women and some fresh food.*

While we were on the uninhabited island, we clashed with, and killed eight of the Thai pirates when they attacked us! We cannot assume that they will abandon their search for us, and therefore we must always remain vigilant. For that reason, the watch of having two people on duty for two hours before they are relived, shall remain in place for twenty-four hours per day!"

Meanwhile, Cung the navigator, had checked the position of the Giang Kein by taking a reading of the position of the sun using a sextant at 09:30 hours Australian Central Time, he then noted the time travelled and the speed of the fishing boat. Using that information, he firstly calculated the distance covered and plotted that upon the chart.

Having done that, he used the information of the angle of the sun in relation to the boat to calculate the exact position of the boat. He was gratified to find that the position calculated using time and velocity travelled broadly agreed with the position of the boat as calculated using the sextant and the angle of the sun in relation to the boat.

He now said to Daiyu, *"My darling wife, here, please take over the steering while I go and have a leak over the side of the boat. Stay on a course of 278 degrees as shown by the boat's compass."* He then went to the deck and relieved himself over the side. On his way back, he asked Nguyen Phan Lam to join him for a conversation in the wheelhouse. He then returned to the wheelhouse and relieved his wife from her duty of steering the boat. He said, *"Thank you for relieving me, Daiyu, you are a blessing!"*

Meanwhile, Ho was addressing the refugees on the deck of the Giang Kein. He said, *"Friends and comrades, we have before us, a long and dangerous journey which will become even more dangerous than it already has been! I am referring to the Thai pirates whom we managed to drive away from us the last time we clashed with them! At our last clash with them, they left eight of their crew behind them as corpses! I am certain that they shall soon attempt to again inflict themselves upon us.*

After all, they are now out to get revenge upon us! I feel that it is certain that the pirates have plotted our probable course and that they shall try to intercept us at all costs! Therefore, we continue with everyone being assigned to watches of two hours before those on watch are relieved! Seventeen of us have been issued the AK-47 assault rifles while others have SKS carbines using the same ammunition.

Those who have been issued firearms are to keep them clean and oiled and to keep them nearby ready for use at all times! Our two RPG7 rocket launchers have three rounds of ammunition each. With such a lower figure of ammunition available, I think it best to only allow the use of these weapons by people whom I know can use them effectively! So, the two operators of the RPG7s are going to be Cung Whyat and Nguyen Phan Lam! Cung will stay in his position in the wheelhouse which will give him an elevated field of fire. Nguyen Phan Lam will take up a position with us on the deck. Both men will let the pirates approach to within twenty-five metres from our ship! That way. They shall be sure to hit the targets of the pirate ships and even sink them!

The first watch is to begin its duty now! I want you to constantly scan the horizon for any sign of the Thai pirates. The scanning must be to the front of us in case the pirates have managed to get in front of us. As well, those on watch must keep on looking to our sides and also, behind us which could be the direction from which further pirate attacks originate from.

There shall always be two people on watch duty, and they shall be relieved every two hours. The idea behind that is to keep those on watch both fresh and alert. If you see an approaching vessel, make sure that you alert this entire boat! All of our lives depend upon that! That is all!" With that speech over, the refugees settled down to the mundane things like resting, sleeping, and eating before completing their assigned watches.

Things continued and some of the refugees became bored and drifted off to sleep. Duong had started his turn on watch thirty minutes earlier. He was keeping a sharp look out towards the north and northeast when he noticed the shape of a Thai junk to the northeast of the Giang Kein.

He silently went to the wheelhouse and told Cung that he had seen the pirates. Cung immediately said to his wife, *"Daiyu, my love, please take over the steering of this boat. My presence is now required on the deck below us!"* Daiyu answered, *"What is the problem Cung?"* He said, *"We have sighted two vessels which are probably the pirates again! I now must speak to Ho and Nguyen about this!"* He then went to the deck and spoke to Nguyen Phan Lam. Cung said, *"Nguyen, two Thai junks have been sighted. They appear to be following us and I think that we must get ready for an assault upon us by the pirates!"*

Nguyen answered, *"We only have six rounds of the RPG7 ammunition! So, it would be a very good idea to catch the pirates in a crossfire of the AK-47s. As well, by you moving to the stern of this boat and me standing guard at its bow, the two of us should be able to blow the fuck out of any attack by using the RPG7 rocket launchers directly against the Thai pirate boat or boats!*

If we run out of ammunition, we can still fight the pirates using the bayonets attached to the AK-47s!

We should wait until the enemy boats are almost alongside of us before we engage them using the RPG7s. that way, we may be able to sink the low-life creeps and then we be safe from them unless there are more of them underway!"

Ho now came to the two men, and he wanted to know what the problem was. He was informed by Cung, and he was silent for a short time. After that, he said, *"So the Thai pirates wish to track us down and do battle with us! Very well! Let them come! In the meantime, we should make everything on this boat appear to be as normal and as harmless looking as possible!*

I, and sixteen others who have the AK-47s shall now remain out of sight! Cung, please let me know how easily you can see us from the wheelhouse!" Cung moved back to the wheelhouse, and he said, *"Ho, I can see you without any problems, but then again, I am in an elevated position!* Ho was quiet for a time and then he spoke! He said, *"I believe it best that we are covered by some tarpaulins in order to make us invisible to other people on other boats or ships! I agree that Cung and Nguyen should be located at the wheelhouse and bow or stern of the boat as that will give them clear lines of fire into the enemy boat or boats and enable us to sink the pirates using the RPG7s!*

When Daiyu sees the enemy boat trying to tie up along our side, have her fire a flare to light up the boat, or make three long whistle blasts upon the football whistle that is in the wheelhouse! If we hear that or see the flare lighting up the boat, Nguyen and

Cung should open fire, using the RPG7s and the rest of us will fire upon the enemy using our firearms!"

Cung went to the wheelhouse and informed Daiyu what was required of her, and she went to where the whistle was hanging on its lead from a hook near the chart cupboard. She reached into the cupboard and took out the football whistle and then she hung it around her neck. Meanwhile, Cung and Nguyen had returned to their positions at the bow and stern of the boat, and everything looked normal about the fishing boat when viewed from a distance greater than ten metres.

By now, the two Thai boats were only twenty metres away from the Giang Kein. Ho had been sitting in the shadow cast by the gunwale of the port side of the Giang Kein. That allowed him to remain unseen. When he noted that the distance between the two vessels was down to twenty metres apart, he blew his football whistle three times. That was the signal for other refugees to remove the tarpaulins covering the self-defense group armed with AK-47s. As soon as the tarpaulins were off them, these men went into action.

Simultaneously, Cung and Nguyen who were in the shadows of the wheelhouse at stern and the bow of the fishing boat, aimed and then fired their RPG7s. That resulted in two massive explosions occurring. That resulted in a large hole in the sides of both the pirate ships. That was followed by Cung reloading his RPG7 rocket launcher and again firing into the pirate ships. While the other explosion resulted in the deaths or wounding of twenty-nine of the pirates as they were attempting to board the Giang Kein.

Arthit had been standing on the gunwale of the starboard side of the pirate vessel and he was about to jump over on to the Giang Kein when a bullet struck him in his throat. The round had missed his larynx, but it damaged his neck near his trachea (wind pipe). That was a painful injury, but he could still swallow food and drink. Even though it hurt like crazy, he could talk to others.

Somchai was near him and saw what had happened to his lieutenant. Concerned about him, he ordered, *"Arthit, for the sake of heaven, get yourself out of the fighting! Make sure that you rest and just recover from what has happened to you! I need you to again be fit enough to navigate our ship back to Thailand! So, get out of the fighting! You have done enough this day!"* Arthit did as he was told and left the fighting as ordered.

He spoke to Somchai as he was going onto a small dingy to escape the fighting. He said, *"Somchai, please accompany me and get away from here, because we have lost this fight! Both of our ships are sinking and unless you and others also get on board this dingy or other escape vessels, you will die!"* Somchai did not have to be asked twice, he immediately joined Arthit in the dingy and the two men got left the area by rowing away from there while their companions were fighting for their lives.

Meanwhile, what was left of Somchai's crew found themselves facing the self-defense team commanded by Ho and also, both Cung at the stern and Nguyen in the bow of their boat! A considerable amount of ammunition had been used in defense of the Vietnamese boat, and Ho could clearly be heard.

He yelled, *"Self Defense Unit of the Giang Kien, using fixed bayonets, kill the Thai Pirates!"*

The men of the self-defense unit moved as a block with their bayonets fixed and held in the 'On guard' position. They moved forward and the remaining Thai pirates either tried to shoot their way out of trouble or else they tried to flee! However, their pirate ships were both now sinking, and they had nowhere to go! Seeing that caused some of them to raise their hands in surrender. By now, the women, men, and even children of the refugees were so furious and had their anger so aroused, that they gave the pirates no mercy and slaughtered all of them.

Help from Royal Australian Navy

A distance of three kilometres to the south, the Australian Patrol Boat, HMAS Derwent could hear the battle between the refugees and the pirates. Commander Rolf Briggle spoke to Lieutenant Brian Jones.

He said, *"Brian, do you think that the flashes of light and the sound of battle to our north could be the refugees we are trying to find? I did hear those pirates could be following them, and it looks to me like they may have found the Vietnamese. I believe that we have a duty to investigate and to render assistance if that is possible! So, full speed to the north until we arrive where that fighting is taking place! I shall decide what action we shall take when we get there and have ascertained the situation!"*

With that, the necessary orders were given and that resulted in the HMAS Derwent travelling at full speed towards the north and where the fight between the refugees from Vietnam and the pirates from Thailand was taking place. When Derwent arrived at the site of the sea battle, Commander Rolf Briggle used the microphone and speaker system of the patrol boat to address the Giang Kein.

He said, *"Attention ... attention, this is Australian Warship Derwent! You are instructed to heave to and receive boarders from the Derwent!"* The message was again read out in the Vietnamese and Chinese languages! Next, the firing completely ceased and loud cheers came from the Giang Kein. The was followed by the boarding party from HMAS Derwent getting on to the Vietnamese fishing boat.

As the Royal Australian Navy boarding team got on to the Giang Kein, Australian Petty Officer John Klein noticed that the wind was gathering strength and that the waves were becoming higher. Now alarmed, he spoke to the HMAS Derwent, using his small radio set that he had with him. The seaman receiving his message wrote it out and took it to Commander Rolf Briggle.

Rolf decided that the Vietnamese fishing boat was barely capable of remaining afloat, and he wanted to remove all of the Vietnamese refugees and the boarding party from the Giang Kein. He sent a radio message to Petty Officer Klein. It read, *"Petty Officer Klein, get all Australian sailors and all of the refugees off the Giang Kein. I have serious doubts if that boat will remain afloat much longer. You and all everyone else are to return to HMAS Derwent immediately!"* - signed Commander R. Briggle.

It then took another thirty minutes before the last refugee and all Australian sailors were on board the Derwent. The Vietnamese people were given clean clothing and shown where to shower. After they had cleaned themselves in the way, they were taken to areas where they were safe, and they were given hot food and hot tea.

Petty Officer Klein was speaking to commander Rolf Briggle. He said, *"Sir, that Vietnamese fishing boat is now barely recognizable as a sea-going ship, and I am of the opinion that it now is a danger to any shipping within this area! I believe that we should blow it out of the water and thereby render the seas in this area safe from the drifting wreckage of that fishing boat, sir!"*

Commander Rolf Briggle agreed with his Petty Officer, and he said, *"Petty Officer Klein, I fully agree with what you have just said! I now want you to take a boarding party onto the Giang Kein. You are to plant explosives on board her and then return here. After you and the boarding party are safely back on board this ship, we shall command detonate the explosives and blow the fuck out of the fishing boat!"*

As the day turned into the evening twilight, the crew of the Derwent was even more alert than usual. Some of the refugees wanted to know why that was happening and Cung explained to them, *"Comrades, what you can see is a highly disciplined military/naval force. Its members are on high alert because it is during the twilight hours that many attacks traditionally take place! Unless we get attacked, the sailors will finish their 'Stand-to' activities and after dark, we shall continue!"*

With calm again being on Derwent, the evening meals for both the crew and the refugees was prepared. Commander R. Briggle took the opportunity to invite four of the refugees to dine with him so that he could speak to them and get to know more about them. He invited those whom he thought were the most impressive of the refugees. That meant that Daiyu, Cung, Nguyen Phan Lam and Ho were seated at his table and dining with him.

Discussion Between the Refugees and Naval Commander

An Australian sailor was acting as a waiter for Commander R. Briggle and the five people at the table with him. Rolf Briggle was speaking to Daiyu and Cung. He said, *"Daiyu and Cung, I do not know for sure how all of this will play out. However, going by past experiences, when we arrive in Australia, you will all be interviewed by personnel from the Department of Immigration, and they shall have people with them who speak Vietnamese fluently. The aims of the Immigration officials will be to make sure that you are indeed refugees and that you do not represent a danger to Australia."*

As he was speaking, the seaman was serving hot meals and drinks to everyone at the table. His name was Able Seaman William Roberts and he enjoyed being near the refugees. He found himself strongly attracted to the beautiful Hoa Lan Xuan. He said, *"Excuse me, lovely lady, my name is William Roberts, what is your name?"* Hoa could understand him because she was able to speak English well as she was often in conversation with Americans before 1979. Therefore, she replied, *"I am Hoa, and I am seeking an UC da Loi husband! Do you want me as your wife?"* He replied, *"Yes, I think that I do!"*

Commander Briggle said, *"I shall not stop you from seeing this woman Roberts, just make sure that this is what you want before you go ahead and marry her! I expect that you shall be honourable and do what is right by her!"* Seaman Roberts replied, *"Sir, I find myself to be strongly attracted to her and I shall be honourable in my dealings with her! As you know from my being a member of your crew, I always do what is honourable and I expect others to do the same, sir!"* Briggle replied *"Very well Roberts, go ahead!"*

The duty watch seaman came from the radio with a printed message for Commander Briggle and gave it to him. Briggle said, *"Ladies and gentlemen, I have been handed a message saying that the destroyer HMAS Adelaide will be coming along side of us in two hours and taking all refugees directly to Darwin, Australia. I have also been informed that the people from immigration will process all of you refugees when you arrive at Darwin."*

Sure enough, two hours later, the HMAS Adelaide was along-side of the Derwent, and the Vietnamese refugees were transferred to the destroyer. With that completed, the HMAS Adelaide set off for Darwin. As the Adelaide was travelling towards Darwin, the refugees became organised, they were both excited and fearful of what was waiting for them ashore in Australia. Ho and Cung moved among the other refugees and re-assured them.

Ho was the most re-assuring person among the refugees. Typically, he was saying, *"Be calm, and do not be afraid! There is nothing to be afraid of! For we are now in the hands of the Uc da Loi Navy, and these men are sworn to look after us and to help us reach the homeland of the Uc da Loi which they call Australia! We call these people the Uc da Loi, because in Vietnamese, it means Large-red-rat. When the Australians came to Vietnam, they had the image of a red kangaroo painted on the sides and the bonnet of their vehicles. Our people had never heard of a kangaroo before, and they all thought that the symbol on the Australian vehicles was in fact a large red rat. That is why we call Australians Uc da Loi!*

The Uc da Loi Officer of Immigration will interview all of us when we reach Darwin and those among us who are considered to not be a threat to the Uc da Loi security or way of life will quickly be released into their community. While we are waiting for our application for refugee status and permanent residence in Australia to be approved, we may end up at secure holding centres in most of the Uc da Loi capital cities.

In Sydney, one such holding, and accommodation centre is known as Villawood! We can in all likelihood expect to be located in one of these places for up to six months while the Uc da Loi authorities check our histories. Some of us will be released into the Australian community a lot more quickly, it will mainly depend upon how much information the Australian authorities get about us and whether they consider us to be a threat to their country or not!"

Meanwhile, HMAS Adelaide was making good progress towards Darwin. After another four hours, places such as Melville Island appeared and that caused some of the Vietnamese refugees on board to talk excitedly among themselves. Ngoc Nguyen Tran was heard to say, *"Look over there, that appears to be a huge and deserted land mass. Is it part of the Uc da Loi homeland or is it something else?"*

As was often the case, Cung knew that what the people could see was in fact Melville Island. He said, *"My friends, what you can see, is Melville Island. It and many more large islands off the Australian coast are the home of the Australian native people, who are called Aboriginals. That name is in fact a Latin name which means 'Original inhabitant'.*

Many of the more lowly educated Uc da Loi people do not know that their native people have the race classification of Australoid. I do not know about the feelings of anyone else, but to me, the name of Australoid shows recognition of the fact that these people were the first people living on the continent of Australia!"

Ngoc Nguyen Tran said, *"Thank Cung my friend, for informing me of all that. I am sure that by us knowing it, it will help us!"* By now Ngoc had noticed a change in the seascape and he said, *"Cung, we appear to be entering a large harbour, do you think that we could be near Darwin?"* Cung answered, *"Yes, I believe so and if not, we shall soon see!"*

Darwin

Suddenly, an announcement was made on the public address system of the destroyer. The captain said, *"This is the captain speaking, we are entering Darwin harbour and I require all Vietnamese refugees to gather their belongings and papers if you have them, and make yourselves ready for transport to Howard Springs where you shall be housed and fed. While you are there, you shall each be interviewed by officials from the Department of Immigration And Citizenship (DIAC) and the Australian Security Intelligence Organisation (ASIO)."*

A short time later, the HMAS Adelaide was tied to a berth on the Darwin wharf and the refugees walked down the gangplank towards a waiting bus that would take the thirty of them to Howard Springs. Cung, who was known for his theatrics fell to his knees and bent over while he kissed the ground.

As he was doing that, he loudly said, *"Thank you Gods in Heaven for delivering us safely to the land of the Uc da Loi! I promise that I will do what is right by others and myself and that I shall live according to the teachings of Confucius!"*

An agent of the Australian Security Intelligence Organisation (ASIO) called Peter Graham was standing near the entrance to Howard Springs had observed Cung's activities. He spoke to Lilly Davies, who was a processing officer from Department of Immigration And Citizenship (DIAC).

He said, *"Cop a look at that man, he appears to be quite a showman and show-off in general! Firstly, he kissed the ground and then he loudly thanked Heaven for being safely delivered to*

Australia! What a show-off!" Lilly replied, *"Yes, Peter, he does appear to be both a show-off and quite an actor, but I like him!"*

Time was approaching the evening twilight at 18:30 hours Central Australian Time. Because of the clouds and the wet season in Darwin the evening sky was a mass of red and yellow colours mingled with blue. The Vietnamese people at Howard springs saw that view and they were very impressed by it. The sunset and twilight quickly passed, and darkness fell. Cung was so impressed that he spoke about his love for this new land to Daiyu.

He said, *"I like it here very much. I hope that the Uc da Loi authorities will let us stay here!"* Daiyu also liked the place and she said, *"Husband, I agree with you, this is the place to for us to establish a business, build our house and to raise our children! I have been told that there is a place for us all to eat at the end of each street. So, my husband, I am very hungry, please take me to where we can eat in Howard Springs!"*

They had their first hot meal in Australia that night. An Australian guide was showing the people around the camp at Howard Springs. He said, *"For entertainment and to obtain information, I would like you all to assemble at the open-air movie theatre located just fifteen metres to your front. Bring chairs with you from your billets and be sure to take the chairs back to your billets when the movies are over."*

Peter Graham and Lilly Davis were also at the open-air movie theatre. They watched as people began to file into the theatre and Peter addressed the people.

He said, *"Ladies and Gentlemen, tonight's movie is "The Jungle Book", which I am sure you will enjoy. Before that starts, I have some announcements which must be made. My name is Peter Graham, and I am from ASIO. My job is checking on security.*

My colleague is Lilly Davis, and she is from DIAC. She will help with processing your immigration status. All of that will take place tomorrow and for the following week, until all of you have been processed. We shall try to place you in the Australian city or country region of your choice, but that is not always possible, so please bear with us. Please assemble at the communal kitchen nearest you in the morning so that we can get things going smoothly!"

Processing the Vietnamese Refugees

Many of the refugees were waiting in an assembly area just outside a mess hall and when the Australian officials appeared. Ho spoke to them on behalf of the other people. He said, *"Mister Graham, my name is Ho Hiep. I am an ex-ranger of the 302 Regiment ARVN, and I am asking you people from Uc da Loi to allow my people and myself to stay among you in this great land. Among us are even former members of the freedom fighters known as Vietcong. I thank all of you for rescuing us all from our boat and saving us. Please let us stay!"*

Peter Graham said, *"Ho, me, and the other colleagues will tomorrow at 09:30 hours of Central Australian Time begin the process of processing your applications for refugee status and to become permanent approved residents in Australia!"*

191

At 09:30 hours of the next morning the number of Australian officials had considerably grown. As expected, Peter Graham of ASIO and Lilly Davies were at the head of these new officials. Peter Graham addressed the Vietnamese refugees in their own language.

He said, *"Welcome to Australia, which you people call Uc da Loi! Please try to say Australia from now on! Those of you who cannot speak English will find that English classes for you to learn our language are available free of cost to you, during the day and also at night! Please go to the public notice board just outside of the mess halls for the timetable of when and where the English classes will be held for you!*

While you are in our camps, you shall be provided with all necessary medical and dental care. Lilly and I shall move among you now and we will interview each one of you in private surroundings so that no-one will become compromised by the interviews. These interviews are necessary before you can be granted refugee and permanent residential status in Australia!

The people whom you can see behind me are the assistants of Lilly and myself! Please co-operate with us and all will be well in the end!"

Having said that, Peter Graham spoke to Lilly. He said, *"Lilly, do you have a list with the names of these people or has there not been enough time to organise such things yet?"*

Lilly said, *"Sorry, Peter, this boatload of thirty Vietnamese refugees only arrived in Darwin on board the HMAS Adelaide yesterday and as a result, there has not been enough time to get the names of these people onto any list! Perhaps the best way forward is to tell them that we want everyone to form up in groups according to the spelling of their names and in alphabetical order. That way a much more orderly processing can take place we will not have to keep the people any longer than necessary!"*

Peter Graham agreed with her, and he again spoke to the refugees. He said, *"Attention, in order to speed up the processing of your applications for recognised refugee status and for permanent Residential Status in Australia, we need you to form up in groups according to the spelling of your names. That should also be in alphabetical order. You all know the Latin alphabet and therefore you can easily comply with my request! So, form up into your name groups according to alphabetical order now! My colleagues and I shall move among you, and we will begin this process now!*

Before we start, I will introduce you to the team which will help Lilly and me to process you all as quickly as possible! This is Nguyen Van Tam; he is a former Vietnamese refugee who now works for the Australian Department of Immigration and Citizenship (DIAC). You can speak to him in Vietnamese if you are uncomfortable using English. Next to him is Peter White, who is Australian born and he speaks Vietnamese due to his service in Vietnam with the Australian army.

Next to him is John Barclay, he is Australian born and also speaks fluent Vietnamese due to him also having been an Australian soldier with Vietnam Service. You shall also find that Lilly and myself are also speakers of the Vietnamese Language and you can speak to us in Vietnamese if English is too difficult for you. I think that you should all try to speak only English if you are serious about staying in Australia!"

So it was that Peter Graham and Lilly Davies moved among the refugees and interviewed them. Speaking to Lilly, Peter said, *"All right, Lilly, let's begin the interviews. We are starting with Anh Hong Khanh, apparently, he is a successful chef and if so, that is good, because we can get him placed into meaningful work almost immediately. That way he will not become a burden for the Australian taxpayer!"*

Interviews with Refugees

Anh Hong Khanh

Lilly replied, *"Yes Peter, let's call him into the interview room!"* Peter went outside the interview room where the refugees were waiting. He loudly said, *"Mr. Anh Hong Khanh, please step into the interview room and let's get this job done!"* so it was that Anh was the first of that group to be interviewed. As he came into the interview room, he saw that Lilly Davis was waiting to speak to him.

Feeling at ease with her presence, he said, *"Miss Davis, I am Anh Hong Khanh, and I was working as a chef in the Grand Hotel in Vung Tau. It*

194

is now the year of 1979, and I am twenty-eight (28) years old." Lilly said, *"Anh, I believe that we can place you into direct employment with a major hotel in Sydney if you would like to go there."* Anh said, *"Yes, of course I would like that, can you arrange it?"* Lilly said, *"Yes"*. And then she picked up her phone and called the Menzies Hotel at Wynyard, Sydney. Her call was answered by Liam Bronze.

He said, *"Menzies Hotel, Liam Bronze the Chef speaking, how can I help?"* Lilly replied, *"This is Lilly Davis of DIAC. I am helping with the processing of Vietnamese refugees at the Howard Springs Centre. I have a young man who is said to be a chef and who would like to work and live in Sydney. His name is Anh Hong Khanh, and he is Twenty-eight years old, can you use him?"*

Liam replied, *"I remember a chef in the Grand Hotel in Vung Tau called Anh Hong Khanh from back in 1972 when I was in the Australian army. If he is the same person, please let me talk to him!"* Lilly said, *"Hold the line, Liam, I will put him on."* She then said to Anh, *"Liam thinks that he remembers you working at the Grand Hotel in Vung Tau, and he wants to speak to you. Is that fine with you?"*

She then handed the phone to Anh, and he spoke. He said, *"Liam, you Uc da Loi, old fart, how the bloody hell are you?"* That was answered by Liam who said, *"Anh, you silly slopehead, how the fuck are you? Would you like to work at the Menzies Hotel in Sydney with me?"* Anh answered, *"That would be fine my friend, but what about accommodation in a huge place like Sydney?"*

Liam replied, *"Don't bother yourself to much about accommodation in Sydney at the moment. When you get here, I will let you stay at my place for a while, until you can get your own place. I shall also speak to the management at the Menzies Hotel about the possibility of you being given a room at this hotel for you to rent. Is that good for you?"*

Anh said, *"Yes."* and Liam said, *"Give the phone back to Lilly, I now need to organise to organise your travel from Darwin to Sydney and that will best be done by her."* And so, Anh handed the phone back to Lilly saying, *"Lilly, Liam wishes to speak to you."* Lilly took the phone and said, *"Yes Liam, what is it?"* He replied, *"How soon can we expect Anh to arrive in Sydney?"* She answered, *"He will be about another four days while he gets inoculated and completes all of his health checks, after all, we do not want to bring possible diseases like bubonic plague or tuberculosis into our country!*

As soon as he is cleared by the medical staff of the immigration team, we can approve him for travel to Sydney. I shall contact you when that happens in up to four days from now. The usual thing is to send these people to destination using Qantas. It appears that we have solved his employment status, but he still needs a place to live. I did overhear you mention to him that you think he may be able to have a room provided for him at the Menzies hotel. Can you put me in touch with whomever I need to speak to in order to make sure that happens?"

Liam answered, *"Lilly, I recommend that you speak to Nigel Forester about this matter. He is the hotel manager, and he likes to be completely up to* date on all matters concerning hotel employees. I have an old number for him, but that may well have changed. You should check for his current phone number by going to either the Sydney white pages or else the Sydney yellow pages phone numbers. Lilly replied, thank you, Liam, I shall do as you have suggested."

Accordingly, she called Nigel Forester on the telephone number that she had been given by Liam. Nigel answered the phone with, "Management of the Menzies Hotel at Wynyard, Nigel Forester speaking, how can I help?" Lilly said, "This is Lilly Davis from DIAC speaking. I have been interviewing a Vietnamese refugee who is aged twenty-eight years and he is a chef. Your own chef call Liam knows this man and he has vouched for him. He wants to have him working at the Menzies hotel. The only problem is that of accommodation. Can the hotel supply a room for him to rent while he is working for you?"

Nigel said, "Not a problem at all, Lilly! I put a great store in what is recommended by Liam! If he wants this man to be working with him and to live at this hotel, then that is what shall happen! Can you please tell me the name of this man and how to spell his name?" Lilly replied, "His name is Anh Hong Khanh. It is spelt as A-n-h H-o-n-g K-h-a-n-h. does that help?" Nigel replied, "Not a problem Lilly, just send him here after you have processed him."

Next Lilly said to Peter Graham, "Peter, that concludes the DIAC requirements for this person, do you and ASIO have questions for him?" Peter answered, "No, Lilly, I think that he is fine, and you *can send him to Sydney as soon as his health checks and inoculations are complete!"*

Duc Duong Kim

Lilly then called for the next person to be interviewed. She walked to the door of the room and said, *"Duc Duong Kim, please come for your interview!"* with that, Duc walked into the room, and he was relieved that the only ones conducting the interview were Peter Graham and Lilly Davis.

Peter Graham said, *"G'Day Duc, as you may recall, I am part of ASIO, and I need you to tell about yourself so that we can be sure that no threat to security of this country will come from you. So, firstly tell me when you were born."* Duc replied, *"Peter Graham, I was born on the 22nd of May in 1952."* Peter asked, *"Duc, were you ever part of the patriot movement against the cruel and corrupt South Vietnamese governments such as those headed by presidents Diem and Thieu?"*

Duc relied, *"No, Peter, I was never in any Patriot fighting force, but I was a member of the ARVN (South Vietnamese Army). I did not take part in the armed uprising against the French colonialists, the Yankee aggressor, or their allies. I was drafted into the ARVN and ended up serving in the 308th Ranger ARVN Battalion. Many times, we were working with and under the direct command of American advisors and other American units.*

The 308th Ranger ARVN battalion killed many Vietnamese people by going into two villages and then just murdering everyone, including women and

198

children, even the very old and infirm people. I am sorry to admit that I was part of that disgusting unit which committed those atrocities and then blamed everything on the Viet Cong freedom fighters!

My platoon leader even managed to call in the newspapers of South Vietnam and the American 'Stars and Stripes' after the 308th Rangers wiped out two villages near the 'Parrot's Beak' area near the Cambodian border. They sent reporters to those villages and took photos. Then they printed stories about the villages being wiped out by the Viet Cong! That was a lie! It was the ARVN 308th Ranger battalion that is guilty of those war crimes! Those actions so sickened me, that I ran away from service to the puppet government of the Yankee aggressor and lived my life as quietly as I could.

I was just a peasant trying to remain alive in a dangerous country during a time of foreign aggression towards the people of Vietnam because the foreigners wanted our resources! I was sympathetic towards the members of the Vietcong, however. After the defeat of the hated Yankee and his lackeys from Australia and other counties, I was willing drafted into the Peoples' Liberation Army of the Democratic Republic of Vietnam and ended up serving at Ba Chuc. We put up a spirited defence against the Kampuchean army of Pol Pot and the cruel bastards that made up the Khmer Rouge! I was serving in the same section as Cung.

Lilly now spoke. She said, *"Duc, you are still a young man, we are trying to stop people from becoming a burden on the Australian taxpayer. Therefore, I need to know what sort of work to place you into and where you would like that to happen. So, tell me what sort of work you are qualified in and what experience you have."* Duc replied, *"Lilly as you already know, I have been a peasant. Therefore, I am skilled at agricultural occupations involving the use of farm machinery and the use of animal power such as oxen and buffalos.*

While living in Vietnam, I took the opportunity to attend night classes and learn welding. That was electric arc welding, MIG (Metal Inert Gas) welding and TIG (Tungsten Inert Gas) welding." Lilly said, *"I see, that means that you are multi-skilled, and you should be able to be of use in either the country or the city areas of Australia. My question is now where do you wish to live and work?"*

He replied, *"I would like to live and work in Sydney because I have Vietnamese friends living at Cabramatta. Will it be OK if I go there to live and work? After all, it will be better for me if I can be near other people whom I already know. However, I will go where you want to send me, and I will do as you require!"*

Lilly said, *"Fine, unless Peter has objections, I will send you to where we consider you will be of the greatest use once your health checks and inculcations are complete. That should happen after the next four days."* Peter now spoke to both Lilly and Duc.

He said, *"Fair enough Lilly, although I think that this man could be better off if he went to an area where rice is widely grown, and he could then apply his knowledge and agricultural skills in that area!"* Peter then spoke directly to Duc.

He said, *"Duc, you say that you are a peasant and that you know agricultural practices and have the necessary skills in that area. I realise that you have already told us that it is your wish to live and work in Sydney, but there is no possibility for you to work in Sydney as a farm worker or peasant as you have put it!*

Therefore, I put it to you that you work in a manufacturing plant making various things from metals such as steel. By you doing that, and applying your knowledge of Manual Metal Arc Welding, Tungsten Inert Gas Welding, Oxy-acetylene Welding, and cutting and Plasma cutting, you should be in a high demand.

Therefore, I propose to send you to the Borg-Warner Transmission and Axle plant at Morebank where you should be able to apply the skills that you say you have. If you decide to do that, you could live at Cabramatta among the people you know and simply commute between there and your workplace at Morebank. How does that sit with you?" Duc Duong Kim was thrilled at Peter's suggestion, and he said, *"Thank you, Peter! Working at the transmission plant will be fine with me! Now then, is there anything else that you need from me?"*

Peter replied, *"Yes, Duc, we have not yet covered the security questions, but given your background of not having been actively involved in the fighting in Vietnam during the country's push for independence from the French and Yanks, that should only be a formality. However, it must still be done, for paperwork rules all people! So, let's get this completed.*

You have already told me that you were in the 308th Ranger ARVN Battalion, and you left that force because you could not stomach the fact that that unit wiped out two entire villages and then blamed the Viet Cong patriots for it! What I need to know now, is if you were ever involved in any military or police force at any time after 1975."

Duc replied, *"Peter, we have already covered my service to the People's Liberation Army and that I was a member of the same section that stopped the Kampuchean forces of Pol Pot at Ba Chuc as was Cung Whyat. So, although we have already covered this subject, let's go over it again in case you do not understand me!*

As you would have heard, Vietnam was invaded by the forces of Pol Pot of Kampuchea. Many people say that was the work of the Yankee CIA stirring the pot in order to destablise the whole of the South-East Asia region in order for America to remain dominant in Asia! I do not know if that is the case or not, however, I do know that a 'State of Emergency' was declared, and I was drafted and put into the Peoples' Army of Vietnam in 1978.

I was sent to help stop the army of Pol Pot at the Ba Chuc area, near the border with Cambodia. There are streams in that area which feed directly into the Mekong river, thus providing a transport route for people with boats. I was serving with another Vietnamese man who served there, and he has also come to Australia onboard the same fishing boat as myself. His name is Cung Whyat, and he used to run a successful fertiliser and farm machinery business at

Cho Lon." Peter replied, *"Oh, I see, that concludes the security interview.*

I do not think that there will be any problems for you, however, I am only a small cog within a large organisation, so things could change because of something that I have not foreseen. All the same, you should be able to work at the plant located at Morebank and there is no problem with you living among the people you know at Cabramatta! That is all for now, but I may have to do some follow-up work with you at later dates!" So, with his interview completed, Duc went outside and rejoined his people.

Cung and Daiyu Whyat

Meanwhile, Lilly went to the waiting area outside the door and said loudly, *"Cung and Daiyu Whyat, please come forward and have your interviews!"* Cung was enthusiastic and said, *"Thank you, Lilly for seeing both of us at once."* That was followed by both Daiyu and Cung following Lilly into the interview room. When they got into the room, Daiyu and Cung could see Peter Graham seated behind a large desk. As Lilly returned, she walked to her large desk and sat down behind it.

Peter opened proceedings by saying, *"Mr. and Mrs. Whyat, please help us to understand everything about you. Daiyu, I have it on record that you are part of a family of Hoa people from Cho Lon near Saigon. Is that correct?"* Daiyu said, *"Yes"* Peter said, *"I see, I also note that your family is typical of the Hoa people of being shrewd business people who are not liked much by the ethnic Vietnamese, is that correct?"* Again, she said, *"Yes."*

Peter continued and said, *"It is my understanding that the Hoa People do not involve themselves with the politics of Vietnam and that they think that to stoop down to such things is beneath their dignity. Is that correct?"* Again, Daiyu said, *"Yes."*

Peter now spoke to Cung. He said, "Cung, it is my understanding that you have been decorated as a Vietnamese soldier for your part in resisting the forces of Pol Pot during their attack upon Ba Chuc, is that correct?" Cung said, *"Yes, it is correct. I was even promoted in the field and led my section to a number of victorious actions against the Khmer Rouge!*

However, all of that is past history because some corrupt elements of the new National Vietnamese Government saw my fertilizer and farm machinery business was doing well, and so they thumped up false charges against me. I had no option but to flee because I am somehow being portrayed as a traitor to my original country. The fact is that I have never acted against Vietnam!" Peter made some notes and said, *"I see! To my mind, that makes you a genuine refugee like you say you are!"*

He then continued. He said, *"Cung, from what you have told me, you appear to be a loyal citizen of Vietnam, yet you are being hunted by the Vietnamese security organisations. Do you know of the names of some of the people who may have been involved in your fall from grace?"*

Cung replied, *"Yes, the main accuser and the one who originally denounced me is known as Sauget et Sang and he is well known as one of the most corrupt South Vietnamese police officials to serve under continuous South Vietnamese Governments from Diem down to Thieu.*

He somehow managed to get himself installed into various government agencies that were setup by the new Government of the People of Vietnam and he always wanted my business! I have been told that he has been successful in getting just that. It is because of actions of jealous people like him, that I have had to flee from Vietnam! I now hope to make it here in Australia! It really bothers me that anyone at all can take the word of that disgusting man such as him, over me, a decorated war hero! Yet here I am, a refugee because I am hunted in my original country because of the likes of him!"

Peter said, *"It may interest you to know that I both know and despise that man! OK then, I am authorizing your release to any part of this country where you may want to go. However, be advised that there are plans afoot to open some market gardens near Adelaide River and to possibly cut up the large grazing property known as Humpty Do Station into smaller privately owned farms. So, if you were to again set up your fertiliser and farm machinery business at for example Adelaide River, Batchelor, or another suitable small town including here at Howard Springs, you will do well as the boom approaches. Government funding shall be on hand to help to get you started."*

Daiyu was almost beside herself with excitement. She said, *"Thank you Peter, what you have said is marvelous news! On behalf of myself and Cung I thank you so much! How long before we can go to places like Adelaide River and begin?"* Peter said, *"You and Cung can leave for Adelaide River as soon as both of you have been cleared of carrying infectious diseases and you have been inoculated.*

I am recommending your immediate release from here and for our government agencies to help you to firstly build a suitable home at Adelaide River or some other place of your choosing and that the government of Australia helps to setup your fertiliser and farm machinery business. Once you are successfully set up in business, you will pay back the Australian Government the money that they invest in you at agreed rates. How does that sound to you both?"

Both Daiyu and Cung were almost overwhelmed by this good fortune. Cung said, *"Thank you Peter, my wife and I shall work long hours to make the business that the Australian Government is helping us with a great success! Thank you again, my friend, and may Heaven watch over you!"*

Daiyu and Cung obtained a Honda agricultural motor bike and used it as their means of transport. Cung said to Daiyu, *"My darling, I have just bought another motor bike. It is also a Honda agricultural bike and I have both of the bikes fueled up and ready for travel. Today, I want both of us to ride to the Humpty do area where the proposed sub-division of that Cattle station in smaller farms is going to take place. What we are looking for is the most ideal place to again set up a thriving fertiliser and agricultural machinery sales and service centre.*

At the moment, I feel that one of the following three locations will be the most suited for our purposes. I think that our most suitable location will turn out to be at or near to Howard Springs! We should check out the possibility of building or obtaining suitable buildings at Bachelor and both Adelaide River and Daly River! Also, we should consider carefully where and when to build our home and what materials to build it with. Here at Howard Springs is an ideal area for building both the business buildings and the home we must have for ourselves and our children when we finally have them."

Daiyu said, *"My dear husband, I am glad that you are serious about building our home! I have now missed two periods and I think that I am pregnant with either your daughter or son! Therefore, it is important that we build our home without delay! With reference to our business site, I get the strong impression that Bachelor is too far from where our business must be located. After all, we are going to supply fertiliser and farm machinery, and therefore, we should be where the demand will be the greatest and that will be at or near Howard Springs!*

I like the area around Howard Springs, and we should take advantage of the fact that there is already a small community here. This is a growing area and soon, there will be many more people taking up land in the newly sub-divided Humpty do area near here. There is land for purchase available near the southern edge of Howard Springs and I have checked it out! I think that it is perfect to locate the business and to build our home behind it!"

Cung was overjoyed at the news that Daiyu may be pregnant. He said, *"Daiyu my darling, what great news it is that you are giving me! It looks to me like things may work out well for us now. We are in a new land, we know new people, and we are building both a new business and home. Now it to make it all even better, you have told me that you are expecting our first child! So, I had better get on with building our house located behind the business buildings!"*

Having said that, he went to Darwin and approached the accountant at the 'Bank-of-New-South-Wales', which was to change its name to Westpac in later years. He was ushered into the presence of the accountant of the bank, called Trinh Van Lam. Seeing the accountant for the first time, Cung was immediately at ease in the presence of the account, who appeared to be of Vietnamese origin as well.

As Cung walked into the accountant's office, Trinh stood up and walked towards him with his hand extended. He said, *"Mr. Cung Whyat? It is my great pleasure to meet you at last! I have heard much about you form both Lilly Davidson and Peter Graham. Both of them bank with the Bank-of-New-South-Wales in both Darwin and Sydney!*

You and your wife Daiyu have greatly impressed both Peter from ASIO and Lilly from DIAC. Peter asked me to organise a housing and business loan to get you started. It is my understanding that you and your wife have previously operated a successful fertiliser and farm machinery businesses at Cho Lon. Peter has told me that your business there was so successful that envious people began to denounce you in order to be able to get your business and that is the main reason that you are here and not still in Vietnam!

Today is the 22nd of December 1979 and I can offer you the following loans. (1) A housing loan of $25,000.00 and (2) a business loan of $88,000.00. both of these are small, and you will need more money as time goes on. As well, there are grants available from churches and other religious groups which can give you another $6,800.00 for things like furniture. I have looked at the paperwork that you submitted via Peter Graham, and I get the impression that you and Daiyu have done your research well. The business and home site you have chosen will in due course, become very sought-after property and its location is ideal to service the agricultural businesses that are bound to be set up as the closer settlement of the Humpty Do Station proceeds.

Also, there are some government loans and grants which may be accessible by you. Lilly Davidson is more than likely the best person to talk to about those and she will be here in about thirty minutes from now in order to help you! Make sure that you repay all loans and fees on time, and you will not have any financial problems! Keep good financial records both for this bank and for the Australian Department of Taxation." Next came the signing of the necessary forms.

After Cung had signed them, Trinh said, *"Thank you, Cung! Now go home and return here quickly with your wife, because in this country, it is good practice for the business and the family home to be in the ownership of both the husband and the wife.*

By setting-up the ownership of the property in this way, there will not be a problem with probate of the property because you both own it already! I want you to do this because in the event of the death of one of you, who-ever is surviving, will be too upset to worry about probate or taxes very much!"

Several moments later, the telephone on Trinh's desk rang. Trinh answered the call. He said, *"Bank-of-New-South-Wales, Darwin Branch, the accountant, Trinh Van Lam speaking! How can I help you?"* The caller said, *"This is Lilly Davison, I have Cung's wife, Daiyu with me and we are travelling to Darwin. We should be at your location in about twenty-five minutes!"*

A Further thirty minutes passed and then both Daiyu and Lilly walked into the office of Trinh at the Bank-of-New-South-Wales. After the necessary introductions were completed, Daiyu signed the papers which had already been signed by Cung.

Lilly then made the announcement, *"Today is a great day! Daiyu and I are late because we were at Daiyu's doctors' surgery, and he has confirmed that she is expecting a child. Therefore, this act of setting up both the home and business could not come at a better time! I now propose a toast to Daiyu and Cung to celebrate their new home, their new business and their first child, all of which is happening for them in their new country of Australia! Long live Daiyu, Cung and their children!*

By the way Cung, I feel that both you and Daiyu should learn about Australian business structures! I suggest that both of you enroll into an external studies programme with the College of External Studies, 322 Wakefield Street, Adelaide, 5000 South Australia." (Post codes were introduced as of Saturday, 1st of July 1967. Some people considered their introduction to be an unnecessary nuisance, but the majority of people supported the introduction of the post codes.) *If you wish to speak to the staff there, just use the telephone. You will find the telephone number in the Adelaide phone book!"*

That prompted Peter Graham to speak. He said, "*Yes, Daiyu and Cung, learning how to keep business books and how to apply Australian income taxation laws will be one of the most beneficial things that you can do for yourselves! The course offered by the College of External Studies in Wakefield Street will be sent to you from the college in Adelaide by mail and you can simply do the lessons at home and send your answers back to the college by mail.*

In the meantime, you will have all of the knowledge that is needed by you. I would like to see both of you involved in the management of your home and business. With regards to your business right now, I suggest that you register a business name that you are both happy with. Make sure that you choose the name wisely, because you shall be required to lodge taxation returns for business done under that name!

That brings me to the next subject, once you have decided upon a business name it must be registered as such with the appropriate Northern Territory Government Office in Darwin. In the meantime, I also advise you to legally setup a business structure called a partnership between the two of you.

That way, any taxable income from the business will be split between the pair of you and you will therefore pay less income tax than a sole trader would pay. After that, and seeing how the business proceeds over time, it may become advantageous to change the business structure from a joint partnership between to a family-owned company.

Cung and Daiyu decided to set up a partnership between the two of them as had been suggested. Cung drew up the housing floorplan of his home and submitted it to the council for approval. He did not have long to wait, for within three weeks, he received a letter from the council which told him that his floor plan design for his home and business at Howard Springs was approved.

By now, Daiyu was showing increasing signs of her pregnancy, but other than having some cravings that amused Cung, and some morning sickness, she was fine! One night, soon after moving into their new home, Daiyu took Cung's hand and paced it upon her abdomen. She said, *"Cung, can you feel your daughter or son kicking? That way this child is kicking me, I get the impression that you could have a son in there!"*

Cung answered, *"My darling Daiyu, I do not care if our child is a daughter or a son. All that I want for her or him is to be a normal and very healthy child who shall have in me, a doting father! Just as in you, the child will have a doting mother! We will jointly do whatever is possible for our children and that also means that we shall make many sacrifices in order for the children to achieve high educational outcomes!*

As our children develop, we can and should always be there for them, we can help out by explaining to them the things from their school work which they may not understand. While our children are under the age of twelve years, we shall read to them on a nightly basis. By so doing, we shall be instilling a love of being read to and of books in general into them. That in turn will make them eager to be able to read themselves.

I would like it if our children can all read and write before they start attending school! I will also teach all of them the times table so that they know instantly that nine multiplied by nine equals eighty-one.

I was speaking to Peter Graham about the education of children, and he agrees that parents should involve themselves in the education of their children by teaching the children things like how to read and write as well as simple arithmetic. By the children knowing the times table up to twelve times twelve equals one-hundred-and forty-four, will give them a great start in their school life!"

Daiyu said, *"Cung, now that our first baby is growing inside of me, can you please let me know what name or names that you would like her or him to be called?"* Cung replied, *"I think that in the event of this child being a son, I would like him to have the name of Nguyen Cung Whyat. If the child is a daughter, I would like her first name to be Nguyet. Either way, the first name of the child will reflect out original Vietnamese traditions! What names would you like for her or him?"*

Michael G Kramer OMIEAust.

Daiyu replied, *"Cung, I agree with you totally about the first name of the child being either Nguyen or Nguyet, depending upon is the child is a boy or a girl. If we have a son, I would like his names to be Nguyen Cung Whyat and if we get a daughter, I think that I will name her as Nguyet Daiyu Whyat. What do you think of that?"* Cung replied, *"Certainly, Daiyu, I fully agree, so let it be done!"*

At midnight, of the 21st of September 1980, Daiyu gently woke up Cung and spoke to him. She said, *"Cung, please get dressed and take me to the 'Royal Darwin Hospital', because our child is coming, and it is not a good idea to wait any longer!"* Cung immediately dressed and took his wife to the hospital in Darwin. Soon after arrival there, Daiyu was made comfortable as possible, and she immediately went into labour.

After a labour lasting for three and a half hours, a baby boy was born. The attending midwife, called Sarah Evens was attending to Daiyu and she said, *"Daiyu, you have done very well, you have a fine and healthy son"*. As she handed the baby over to Daiyu, the baby was making himself heard by all who were close by. Sarah said, *"Here you go, Daiyu! What names for him should be put onto his birth certificate?"* Daiyu replied, *"His names are Nguyen Cung Whyat"*, can you please enter those names onto the birth certificate for me?" Sarah said, *"Certainly Daiyu, but please tell me how I should spell those names."* That was done and the birth certificate was entered as Nguyen Cung Whyat as both parents wanted.

214

Eventually, Daiyu returned from the Royal Darwin Hospital with her son. During the nights, both Cung and Daiyu got up whenever their son was crying and attended to him. That usually meant the person who was with the infant had to feed and clean him up. During the day, either Cung or Daiyu would read to the infant son and a loving relationship between them developed quickly.

The child grew up in a household of love and almost before they were aware of it, the parents found that a year had passed since his birth. Daiyu said to Cung, *"My darling husband, I am doing to the doctor this morning. I think that I am again pregnant because I have now missed two periods and I am once again beginning to experience morning sickness. How do you feel about being an expectant father again?"*

Cung replied, *"My dear wife, I am ecstatic about the possibility of your pregnancy! So, I hope that when you see your doctor, he or she will confirm that you are again expecting a child! If young Nguyen ends up with either a sister or a brother to play with, that would be marvelous!"*

Daiyu rode her Honda motor bike to where the doctor's surgery was located and reported to the receptionist. After waiting for twenty minutes, she was called into see a female doctor. That was doctor Stock. Doctor Stock examined her and confirmed that Daiyu was indeed pregnant. That made Daiyu happy, and she returned to her Howard Springs home.

Cung was at home, looking after baby Nguyen, when Daiyu walked into the home and said, *"My darling husband, my doctor has confirmed that I am expecting a child! In about two months, it may become possible to see if I am carrying a boy or a girl through the use of a device called ultrasound."*

Cung was happy about Daiyu carrying another child. He said, *"Daiyu, my love, thank you for this wonderful opportunity for us to have another child. A new brother or sister for young Nguyen is most welcome! We shall treat this child in the same fashion as our first child. By that I mean that one of us shall read to him or her every night.*

And we shall teach both children to read, write and to perform simple arithmetic as well as teaching our children the times table up to twelve times twelve! That will stand the children in good stead for the rest of their lives! Oh, my darling, I am so excited by all of this, that I forgot to ask when the new baby is due?" Daiyu replied, *"The baby should come on or before the 21ˢᵗ of September 1981!"*

Cung's fertiliser and farmer machinery business was doing well, and Cung was now employing two full time helpers in the business called Cung's Farm Machinery and Fertiliser Supplies Pty Ltd. The latest addition to his staff was called John Jones. He was an Australian who was born in Adelaide and moved to Howard Springs. He was a qualified diesel mechanic and therefore a valuable addition to the staff of Cung's business.

The business had started off selling only small Massey-Ferguson tractors and associated equipment and small machines such as large rotary hoes for use in market gardens. Cung found that he was asked to provide more and more different machinery both for the market gardens being set up at Adelaide River and the Humpty do subdivision into smaller farms near Howard Springs. As well the small grey Massey-Ferguson tractors, he was selling larger tractors of the same brand and people were asking for other brands of tractors as well.

Cung had ordered agricultural implements such as ploughs, scarifiers and seeding machines. These and other machinery were located in the secure compound behind the business building and close to his home. He had also opened agencies for Fiat and John Deere tractors and other agricultural machinery.

Due to this vastly increased business, Cung was in a position to repay his business and housing loans ahead of time and he spoke to the accountant at the Bank-of-New-South-Wales in Darwin, Trinh Van Lam using the telephone. Cung said, *"Hello Trinh, this is Cung Whyat, and I want to completely repay the business and housing loans that my wife and I currently have."*

Trinh was thrilled that Cung had done well in business and was now in a position to pay off his outstanding loans. He said, *"That is great news Cung! By paying off your loans well ahead of time, you will always have a ready line of credit with this bank! I think that what you are doing is perhaps the smartest move possible. I shall be here at the Bank-of-New-South-Wales in Darwin until 6 pm (18:00 hours), so please come in before then and we will finalise all of this!"* That was completed, and the papers were signed and witnessed. The two men shook hands and Cung returned to his business and family at Howard Springs.

Both Cung and Daiyu worked in the business while the children were at school. Daiyu would finish working in the business at three in the afternoons that she could be at home in time to be with her children. Both she and Cung would read to them every night and teach them things about life and the teachings of Confucius. Both children, Nguyen and Nguyet knew the times table up to the twelve times twelve table and they could both read and write before they started school. Nguyen expressed his desire to become a veterinarian while Nguyet wished to become a medical doctor. By now, Nguyen was aged six years and his sister Nguyet was aged five years.

During the times that followed, both Nguyet and Nguyen completed their primary school education and that was followed by their attendance at the Nightcliff High School. They both worked and studied with great enthusiasm and were awarded their respective Higher School Certificates. That allowed both of them to gain entry to the universities which were expert in the respective courses of medical science in the case of Nguyet and in veterinary science in the case of her brother Nguyen. For his initial veterinary studies, Nguyen enrolled at the University of Sydney and Nguyet also studied her medical degree there beginning in the following year.

One night after both children had gone to Sydney to attend their respective courses, Cung and Daiyu were speaking to each other in their lounge room at Howard Springs. Cung said, *"Daiyu my dear, I am most happy that both of our children have made it as far as the first year and the second year their university studies. Thank you very much for supporting the children and me in all of this. I believe that that by our teaching our son and daughter how to read and write as well as the times table up to twelve times twelve equals one hundred and forty-four has stood them both in good stead! Thank you, my darling for your continued support and being the mother of my children. I love you deeply, Daiyu!"*

Hoa Lan Xuan

The next refugee to be interviewed was called Hoa Lan Xuan. She was waiting outside of the interview room while Lilly and Peter refreshed themselves by having a cup of tea and some biscuits. Meanwhile, Cung and Daiyu departed, Leaving Lilly and Peter to enjoy their cup of tea before Lilly opened the door and spoke to the refugees outside. As she went through the door, she spoke to them.

She said, *"Could Hoa Lan Xuan please come into the interview room now?"* Hoa answered, *"Yes, I shall do so, immediately!"* and she stepped through the door. Closing it behind her, she asked, *"What can I do to help?"* Lilly answered, *"Tell us about your time as a Vietcong Veteran but start before then when you were raped by five allied soldiers and infected with gonorrhea. Our information about you is sketchy at best, but what I have read about you so far is fascinating!"*

Hoa began speaking. She said, *"I was just twelve years old when I was raped by an ARVN soldier! On the same day, I was repeatedly pack-raped by his four drunk American soldier companions! There was nothing that my parents or I could do about it because we had no weapons, and the*

219

police and ARVN soldiers always kept a close eye upon my family.

Both the police of the Republic of Vietnam (South Vietnam) and the members of the ARVN (Army Republic of Vietnam or South Vietnam) were present as the Yankee soldiers were pack-raping me. They did nothing to stop these crimes from happening and they were jeering me as they watched me being repeatedly raped by the four American creeps!

About two days afterwards, I began to have burning sensations every time I had to urinate and that told me that I had been infected with a venereal disease such as gonorrhea. However, I did not know from where I could get medical help to eradicate the social disease or where there were any medical people whom I could consult about this distressing aspect of my health. Eventually, I was examined by a female doctor who confirmed that I was suffering from gonorrhea.

What made that even worse is that by that time, it was too late to stop the damage to my reproductive organs and now, I was told that I can no longer have children. I have had that birthright taken away from me by the ARVN and the god-damned Yankee soldiers who pack-raped me!

After some time, word about my fate had spread to Vietcong sympathisers and a meeting was arranged. An elder woman of my village thought that a good way to take revenge upon foreign occupiers of my country was to infect the foreigners with gonorrhea. I already was infected with that disease because I got it from being repeatedly fucked by the four American soldiers!

I know for sure that although one of them infected me, and I in turn infected the other three of them! After I was treated for that social disease and it was cured, I became a member of Long Kahn's own D440 Vietcong Battalion. At first, I served as a medical orderly with my duties being helping to dress the wounds of D440 and D445 soldiers and taking them to places of safety where they could recover from their wounds. I performed these duties to the best of my abilities, and I was selected for officer training as soon as I told my superiors that I had served as a lieutenant in the ARVN army, but I defected and joined the patriots. After that was completed, I became a platoon commander of the D440 Battalion.

After the victory against the Americans in 1975, I was denounced by people whom I do not know, and I do not know why they did so. I only know that instead of being treated as a heroine, I am currently thought of as a traitor!"

At this point, Peter Graham, the ASIO field officer became interested, and he asked, *"Hoa, it seems to me that Vietnam has turned its back towards you! Although your heart may say that you should be loyal to Vietnam, will you now pledge allegiance to Australia instead of Vietnam if we allow you to stay here?"*

Hoa replied, *"As you have said, Peter, Vietnam has turned its back on me and I am branded a traitor, even though I have always been a loyal Vietnamese patriot, other than my service for the*

ARVN, from which I defected in order to help out the revolutionary effort. Therefore, I am left with no choice other than to run to where I can live and develop myself. Whichever country gives me permanent sanctuary therefore shall have my loyalty! If that country offers me full citizenship, I shall take it and I will then volunteer to become part of that country's armed forces. Will that be all right with Australian authorities?"

Peter replied, *"What you have said, sits very well with me. However, I do not make decisions about security matters, I only enforce them. I am sure however, that my superiors will look at your case favorably. Now then Hoa, this will take some time until the security investigations are complete. After they are complete and you have been cleared as to your security status, you will be free to live among Australians. Until you are cleared, you shall be living at the Villawood detention centre in secure facilities! That could easily take up to two years!"*

Hoa replied, *"It disappoints me that I cannot become a part of Australian society immediately, but I see the sense in it! I shall wait as long as is necessary and I do not blame this country for being cautious about who comes here. It is what I also would do! So, detention at Villawood, here I come!"* Peter replied, *"Thank you for your positive outlook, Hoa! I hope that the investigations into your past do not take very long, but this is the only way forward for you!"*

Hoa said, *"After we were rescued by the Australian Navy, I was very strongly attracted to an Australian sailor called William Roberts. Is there any way of getting in touch with him?"* Lilly asked, *"Why would you want to get in touch with him?"*

Hoa answered, *"He told me that he wants to marry me, and I would like that to happen, so can we get in touch with him, or is that not allowed to proceed for some reason?"* Peter said, *"Hoa, I think that the only possible reason, if there is one, could be your past service with the enemy units which were fighting Aussies. However, as I have already told you, I feel that you present no present or future threat to Australia. I believe that a marriage between you and William Roberts, if he will take you for his wife, will be a good idea because that will also make your Australian citizenship a sure thing!"*

At this point, Lilly spoke. She said, *"Hoa, I propose to send a signal to the HMAS Derwent asking Able Seaman William Roberts if he would like to marry you or not. The Port of Darwin is only about one-half hour's travel by car from here, so he should be able to arrive here quickly after his patrol boat has returned to Darwin. Please carefully consider everything about this proposed marriage. Be sure to tell him that you were once infected with gonorrhea by ARVN and American soldiers when you were young. If he still wants you after hearing that, you may have the makings of a good marriage."*

Hoa replied, *"Lilly, I agree that he should be informed. That way it would save future problems. I want you to send him a signal outlining what we have just discussed and offering him my hand in marriage if he wants to have me as his wife. I guarantee that such a union between us will be the best thing that he could ever do for himself."*

And so, a signal was sent to the HMAS Derwent asking Able Seaman William Roberts to consider what Hoa was offering him and to reply immediately with his decision.

His reply was given to Peter Graham one hour later. The signal read. *"Able Seaman William Roberts says, 'Yes' to the proposal stop He will be with Hoa in two days from now stop"* Peter told Hoa about that. He said, *"Hoa, your chosen man has accepted your proposal. He should be here in about two days from now. Something that you may not know about him is the fact that he is about to enter the Naval Services Academy and become an officer.*

By you being married to him, and his new status as an officer of the Royal Australian Navy, it will not only pave the way for your own acceptance into Australian community, but it will also make it easier for your own acceptance into the Australian Defence Force as an army officer." Hoa replied, *"Good, that is what I want to hear!"*

After waiting for another three days, Hoa was finally re-united with William Roberts. She was sitting in the mess hall of the Howard Springs Detention Centre when William was ushered in to see her. She immediately attended to him and after they had made love, she told him of her history in great details, leaving nothing out of her story!

William said to her, *"Hoa, I am glad that you have had the courage to tell me about your past history while you were still in Vietnam. As far as I am concerned, your story changes nothing and I am still crazy about you! I hereby propose to you! I want you to be my wife. Hoa, will you marry me and have my children?"*

Hoa said, *"I am happy to marry you, but I think that cannot have children because when the hateful Americans raped me, they infected me with gonorrhea which in turn has played havoc with my reproductive organs! So.do you still want me as your wife, even though it will be a childless marriage unless we adopt a child?"*

William said, *"The fact that you cannot have children is of no consequence to me, I want you as my wife and that is all that there is to the matter! Assuming that we want children at some time in the future, we can always adopt a child! I just want to be with you! So, I will now again ask you to marry me. Hoa, Will you marry me?"*

William was pleasantly surprised to hear Hoa answer, *"Yes William, I shall take you as my husband! It will be the best decision that you have ever made! I do love you and I know that by working together, we can both be officers in the Australian Defence Force. In your case, the Royal Australian Navy, while I shall become an Australian Army Officer. Peter Graham agrees with me that one of the best ways for me to show my total resolve and determination to be an Australian is to be part of this country's defence!"*

Hoa was finally cleared and released from detention after marrying William Roberts. After Peter Graham investigated and found that she was truthful in what she had told him. She became an Australian citizen. She later entered the Australian Army at the age of twenty-five. She worked hard and obtained her Bachelor of Science and Bachelor of Engineering degrees; she was granted Australian citizenship and entered the Royal Military College of Duntroon in Canberra.

She and William Roberts have married, and they share a house on the army base at Townsville in Queensland. When I last spoke to her in 1999, she had been promoted to the rank of an army captain.

At that meeting, she told me that she had her sights set on achieving the rank of colonel. I wish her the best of luck in achieving her goal! She is childless and she will remain that way because she was badly knocked about when she was infected with gonorrhea while she was repeatedly raped by the American and ARVN soldiers.

Ngoc Nguyen Tran

Lilly was opening the door and she announced, *"Ngoc Nguyen Than, please come in for your interview."* Ngoc immediately went through the door, and he saw that Peter was already seated, while Lilly was still going to her desk.

Lilly asked, *"So, Ngoc Nguyen Tran, let us get the basics over with first. How do you like to be addressed? Do you want people to call you Ngoc or would you like others to call you Nguyen?"* Ngoc replied, *"I think it best if other people call me Ngoc! I think that there are too many men of Vietnamese origin called Nguyen! At times that becomes confusing, even for a Vietnamese man like me!"*

Lilly answered, *"Very well, Ngoc, I totally agree! What do you think about this Peter?"* Peter Graham said, *"I agree that there is no reason why he should not call himself Ngoc, because that is written on his documentation. Also, there is the fact that he is happy with that name, so I am happy for him to use it."*

Peter now started his questions of Ngoc. He said, *"Ngoc, we have you down as being 'Ngoc Nguyen Tran' is that correct?"* Ngoc said, *"Yes."* Peter replied, "Ngoc, we do not have your age. How old are you?" Ngoc replied, *"Twenty-four"*. Peter asked, *"Were you ever a patriot of Vietnam? If so, which unit did you serve in, what rank did you hold and who was your immediate superior?"*

Ngoc replied, *"No, but I was a full-time member of the ARVN army and ended up a regular member of the 21st battalion of the 2nd division! My ARVN army number was A771415678. The A in front of the numbers of my regimental army number indicate that I originally was from the area near Ap Sui Nae, which was the village that Australian soldiers built for us after we were all evicted from our original villages of Hoa Long, Long Tan and Dat Do by Australian soldiers. I do not understand why the ARVN put me into service as a private soldier in a combat unit.*

I wanted simply to please my father called An Bao Cuong. He always said that sooner or later, the foreign forces would leave Vietnam and he told me to work and study hard to become a professional pharmacist. That was because my father thought that such people would be in great demand after the foreigners all left our country. My father sacrificed all in order to get me through the education system in Vietnam followed by study in Paris where I eventually obtained my degree in pharmacy. So, I have a degree in pharmacy, and I believe that I would be much better suited to the role of being a pharmacist. I have no political leaning toward either the South Vietnam governments or to the patriot movements. I just want to be left alone and not to be involved in politics at all!"

Peter said, *"That is very interesting, how do you now feel about Australians?"* Ngoc said, *"I do not feel anything at all. I did not, and still do not have political interests for any side, anywhere! I did of course hear about the Vietnamese patriots whom the Americans call Viet Cong (Vietnamese Communist), no matter if the person they are calling a communist was ever a party member or not! I was just too busy to ever become involved with the patriot movement because I was always studying, either in Vietnam or else in Paris! With reference to Australians, they are perhaps, one of the most highly respected soldiers in the world.*

I have even heard some of the Vietnamese veterans call Australians "The Gracious Enemy", because you do not have a reputation of mutilating the bodies of your enemies. Your reputation states that you just bury your fallen enemies. That is yet another reason for men like me to want to settle among you. You have the reputation of fairness! The same cannot be said of most other countries and in particular, not the French or American bullies! According to both my mother and father, the hated Yankee aggressor should stay on the north American continent"

Peter said, *"I see. If you are allowed to settle here, would you become a citizen of this country and would you help to defend if the need arose?"* Ngoc answered, *"Yes, I would defend it as if I was born here, for this shall be my country as of now! With me, there are no half-measures, and I shall always help to defend the land that I am a part of!*

I pledge myself to the service and defence of Australia, if Australia will have me as one of its citizens!" By now, Peter was impressed with Ngoc, and he said so. He said, *"Ngoc, you earlier told me that you would like to go to Sydney because you feel you may have some friends or relatives in Cabramatta. Do you still want to go there?"* Ngoc said, *"Yes!"*

Peter again spoke to Ngoc, he said, *"Ngoc, you have answered all security questions for now. Unless Lilly has further tasks you other than health checks and inoculations, I think that you can move to the Villawood detention Centre in Sydney. Do not be alarmed by the name of Villawood Detention Centre. It is only called that because it is sometimes used as a detention centre until refugees are fully processed. While you stay there, you will be able to enter and leave the centre as you see fit. You can use it for accommodation until such time as you are able to live among your friends in Cabramatta!"* Ngoc answered, *"Thank you, Peter!"*

Lilly now joined the conversation. She said, *"Ngoc, you have mentioned that you studied for your final pharmacy degree at Paris France. Do you happen to have the degree with you, or can you somehow get hold of it? I ask that because here in Australia, we generally do not take the word of foreign qualifications unless that the person who has them can in fact pass an Australian examination in the subjects concerned for those qualifications. So, firstly, it is important for you to get a copy of your French degree in pharmacy and secondly, you shall have to sit an examination in the pharmacy subjects to ensure that you are fully conversant with the subjects. Are you willing to do more study in pharmacy to obtain your Australian qualifications?"*

Ngoc said, *"Thank you for asking Lilly, the original degree has been destroyed when I fled from Vietnam. I shall apply to the university in Paris for a copy of it and that could take some time to finally arrive here, but it will get here in due course. I can see the need for Australian authorities to make me sit for an examination in my pharmacy subjects and I believe that only good can come from me again studying the subjects in order to be 'Full bottle' about all things to do with pharmacy and the Australian laws relating to pharmacy.*

I therefore welcome the coming examinations. So, if you can organise the pharmacy examinations for me, I shall be eternally grateful." Lilly replied, *"Ngoc, can you be ready for the examinations to be held at the University of Sydney at 09:00 hours,*

Eastern Australian Standard Time on Wednesday 18th of May 1980? It is late December 1979 at the moment, and I think that if you wish to become a pharmacist in Australia, then by studying the pharmacy subjects between now and May, you should be able to pass your examination with ease and then obtain your license to practise pharmacy in Australia."

And so, Ngoc studied for his Australian pharmacy degree and attended the examination for it at Sydney university at 09:00 hours on Wednesday the 18th of May 1980. As the examination progressed, he would at times ask for an explanation of some terms used because they were in English and sometimes, he did not know what was meant. After three and a half hours of examination, the time for it was finally up and he was asked to hand in his paper.

As he handed in his exam papers, he was both relieved that the examination was finally over, and he had the impression that he had done well. I caught up with him at the Student's Bar of the University of Sydney on that day and spoke to him. I said, *"Well Ngoc, how do you think that you did in the exam?"* He replied, *"I think that I have done well! I knew all of the answers, but I did have to ask the supervising staff for explanation of some questions. Now, I must await the results and then I apply for positions in pharmacy in and around Sydney, possibly in Cabramatta and places close to there."* He did that and I am told that he has a successful pharmacy at Cabramatta. I have not been in touch with him since 1980.

Lilly spoke to Peter. She said, *"So far it has been a good day's work! Of the six people processed so far, only Hoa has been put into detention until we can confirm her story. I really like her, and I hope that you ASIO people will clear her soon, Peter!"* Peter replied, *"Yes, Lilly, I like her as well, and I am confident that she will be cleared soon! It should just be a matter of speaking to the people in the area where she was a platoon commander and speaking to both the civilians and the members of the opposing forces of the time. I shall be happy to do that myself! As well, it looks to me like she and her fiancé in the Australian Navy will marry and that will pave the way for her to become an Australian citizen."*

Nguyen Phan Lam

Diep Duyen Hien (meaning A charming, graceful women, beautiful, Gentle, and quiet) was in labour and experiencing discomfort at 14:20 hours Vietnamese time on the 23rd of April 1955. She had put up with some minor pain associated with the birth of her child.

This birth was taking place in the village of Dat Do in the then province of Phuoc Tuy which has now been renamed as Vung Tau-Baria Province. Just outside of the village was an extinct volcano which had the shape of a horseshoe and was named as "The Horseshoe" by Australian soldiers who used it as a base because it over looked the village and surrounding areas. It was found to be an ideal observation post when used by the Australians who arrived in 1966 and stayed until 1971.

This area was totally sympathetic towards the Viet Minh and the following Viet Cong The truth of the matter being that the people had no real political affiliations with any particular political party, the people were simply the true patriots of Vietnam who had been fighting foreign occupation for over one hundred years! One foreign occupier was replaced by another one almost as soon as the existing foreigners were beaten and removed from Vietnam! Into this mess of foreign occupation and constant crimes committed against the people of Vietnam by foreign occupying forces, the baby of Diep Duyen Hien was born at 14:50 hours of the 23rd of April 1955.

The midwife in attendance was Nguyet Cai. As Diep was having her final contraction, she said, *"Good girl Diep, just keep ongoing, and at the next contraction, push as hard as you can, so that we get the baby out of you!"* Diep replied, *"Very well, I shall be glad when this has been completed and I can get some rest!"*

After more intense pushing and straining on the part of Diep, Nguyet said, *"Good girl, Diep, I can see the head of your baby coming out now! Keep on pushing and we will soon have this over with!"* With that, Diep gave a huge push and there was the sound of an infant crying very soon after. Midwife Nguyet came to Diep and said, *"Diep, here is your fine son, what name or names shall you call him?"*

Diep said, *"I name him as Nguyen Phan Lam. I am certain that he shall become a protector of the community of our people, and he will be a fierce warrior who takes the fight right up to the foreign enemy occupiers of Vietnam! I and his father will teach him the history of our people who have been under foreign domination now for about a hundred years and it is high time for Vietnam to be free! Both I and my husband Nguyen will see to it that this child becomes fully knowledgeable in all matters relating to the foreign occupation of our country and he shall be one of those who will lead us to victory over the foreign thieves and murderers!"*

As Nguyen Phan Lam was growing up, he was constantly spoken to by both of his parents about Vietnam, its people, and their history right to the present day. He was taught why the people were living as paupers in a rich land and how that was the fault of the various foreign occupiers of Vietnam and their puppet governments which they installed to keep the people enslaved, yet dependent upon the French, followed by the Americans and others. He was also shown that the wealth of Vietnam was constantly drained by the French and the other occupiers at the expense of the people.

At the age of ten years, young Nguyen Phan Lam was taught about the resistance movement known as Viet Minh and how that was changing things in the north of Vietnam and also, the south. After he had been told that, he said to his father, *"Father, what can I do to help further the cause of our people? I mean what is it that I can do for the resistance now? I do not want to wait until I am eighteen or older, I want to take the invaders to task right now!"*

His father said, *"Nguyen, you are young and very passionate about getting independence for our people and that is good! However, you need to become educated and learn many things such as reading, writing and mathematics. you must learn to navigate and lead our people! You need to learn life's skills, and only then shall you finally be able to master what warriors have to learn but learn it you shall!*

In the meantime, would you like to act as a messenger between units of our Peoples' Liberation movement? It is highly dangerous work, and the French will either just kill you or torture you to death if they catch you!" Young Nguyen replied, *"Father, I shall do what is necessary to do for my people! As far as I am concerned, it is my destiny to be a revolutionary so that my fatherland of Vietnam can be free!"*

It was this kind of attitude of the ten-year-old boy that always was a source of pride for both his mother and father. On young Nguyen's eleventh birthday, his father said, *"Nguyen, there is a vacancy as a messenger for the Viet Mihn unit of the Dat Do area! Do you wish to take it?"* Young Nguyen was beside himself with excitement and he quickly said, *"Yes, my father, how soon can I start working against the occupiers of my country?"* His father said, *"You shall begin by going to the home of our neighbour called Ba. He will introduce you to others and begin your training. Are you sure that you are ready for this and that you want to do it? The work is over long hours, and it can become very dangerous!"*

Young Nguyen said, *"Father, I can handle it! Let me meet with Ba, so that we can begin doing the work of the resistance and lay down the infrastructure for its future!"* Nguyen senior replied, *"Very well, let's go!"* With that, they walked the short distance to Ba's home.

Nguyen senior introduced his son to Ba and told him how the now eleven-year-old boy wanted to work for the resistance by being a messenger. Ba was impressed by what he was told about the boy. He said to both the father and his son, *"Nguyen, I am grateful to be able to train our messengers and future leaders of our resistance movement! Now then young Nguyen Phan Lam, in order to be a successful messenger, you need to know where to hide yourself when the south Vietnamese puppet government and its police or army units come.*

Come with me and I shall show you the entrance to the tunnel which goes all of the way to the next village. Here, under my home is the entrance to the tunnel to Hoa Long. At Hoa Long, the tunnel's exit/entrance is in the home of the village chief! Tunnels are of great concern and benefit to the resistance movement. We first began putting our tunnels into place over most of Vietnam during World War Two, when our country was jointly occupied by French and Japanese! The resistance has been digging many tunnels since we were suffering from being occupied by the French, followed by the dual Vichy French and Japanese, followed by British and then the French again, and then the God-damned Yankee!

Our tunnel systems now include underground hospitals and stores areas where our patriots can recover from their wounds and get resupplies when they are required. We constantly work on improving and increasing the tunnel systems which we have, and they are forming an invisible impediment to the Yankee and his minions who are trying to keep our people enslaved! Therefore, you shall also work in expanding the tunnel system!

You will have to get used to using that tunnel and others like it to travel between various villages without being seen! This afternoon at about 15:00 hours Vietnamese time, come to my home, and I shall get you started! You have a lot to learn including the coding and decoding of messages.

It is now the year of 1965, and you are eleven years old. In another five years from now, you shall know the entire areas between here, Vung Tau, Baria, Long Khanh. Now go and rest, I want you to be fully alert and ready for your instructions and your first mission by the time we retire for tonight. How does that sit with you?" Young Nguyen replied, *"Thank you Ba, it sits with me very well! I shall do my utmost to become the best messenger that you have ever had!"*

And so, the young Nguyen Phan Lam was soon running messages of importance to the resistance on a nightly basis. As that was happening, he was also growing and that made it increasingly difficult for him to keep on using the tunnels, some of which were of too small a diameter, even for him. Therefore, and because he wanted to take part in military actions against the South Vietnamese puppet officials, He began training as a member of the Ba Ria based D445 battalion.

During his interview with Peter Graham of ASIO and Lilly Davis of DIAC, he had been asked about all of that and he told them both the entire story. He said, *"Things did not stop there, as already stated,*

I was running messages for the resistance the Americans call 'Vietcong' which is American slang for Vietnamese Communist. I was not and never have been a member of the Communist Party. I was just a member of the community. All of the people from most communities in Vietnam supported the freedom fighters no matter if they said so or not. It was what General Giap calls 'People's War'.

When I was approaching the age of fifteen in 1970, I had completed training with the D445 Battalion, and I had been in action with that unit six times by the end of July. These actions were against the ARVN forces. During September of 1970, I had been informed by my superiors, that they wanted me to become a member the South Vietnamese Police based at Ba Ria.

Once I was there, I was to then arrange constant information flows about the movements of the police and military units of the puppets and their foreign masters. I did in fact become a police lieutenant at the Ba Ria and other stations. The information flow about the foreign forces in my country was passed to resistance units. After that, I was invited to do an officer training course with the newly formed D440 Battalion based at Long Kanh. Upon completing the course, I was given the rank of Lieutenant and then, sent back to D445 Battalion, from where I led my first action as an officer member of the D445 battalion.

In the meantime, I was firstly a police constable, followed by going through the ranks of the police of the south of Vietnam until I reached the commissioned rank of captain. Although I was a captain of the Police Force of South Vietnam, I was continually providing information and intelligence to the Vietcong patriots.

Things kept up like that until the victory over the foreigners in 1975. After that, I was invited to become a police officer by the new government of The Democratic Republic of Vietnam. It was something that I had always wanted to do and so, I did just that! It was 1976 before my training as a member of the new National Police Force of the Democratic Republic of Vietnam was complete and I was serving as a policeman.

My station was in Ho Chi Minh City, and one day, I went to work as usual and found that my police comrades looking at me in strange ways. One of my friends in the police force told me that I had been denounced by Than Sam Trinh, whom I had proved was a thief and rapist a year before that.

Things became very bad for me and more of my police comrades kept on talking about me behind my back. Finally, my rank was reduced to that of constable and then I was charged with sedition. That should never have happened! So, I now had little choice but to run, therefore, when it became possible to escape and also to help others to do so, I did just that! Now here I am with Cung and his wife and others!"

Both Peter Graham of ASIO and Lilly Davis of DIAC were impressed by the straight-talking former police officer from Vietnam. Peter said, *"Nguyen, what you have told me sounds both creditable and genuine. If I told you that the New-South-Wales Police in Sydney want to have many Vietnamese men join their police force, would you be interested in becoming a policeman and policing places such as Cabramatta in Sydney?"* Nguyen Phan Lam replied, *"If you could put that into place for me it would be marvelous, and I shall be eternally grateful."*

Peter Graham said, *"Well, Nguyen, the fact is that the police in Sydney are in fact setting up a Vietnamese unit to combat crime in the Vietnamese occupied suburbs such as Cabramatta. I have made constant notes about your case, and I expect that you should have your security clearance before long. If we are going to put you into the New-South-Wales Police Force, then we should have you living in Sydney at for example Villawood, and from there, we can organise your release into police academy at Goulburn in New-South-Wales!*

I have no doubts about your security and therefore, you can come and go as you like from Villawood, which also has a more secure holding area. In those areas, other refugees such as Hoa will be living until, she gets her security clearance. So, Nguyen, would you rather go to Sydney, or should I ask those in authority about you becoming a policeman here in the Northern Territory?"

Nguyen said, *"I am sure that I can lend my hand to do whatever is required and where-ever that maybe! I could easily be a policeman here in the Northern Territory, if need be, however, you have mentioned that the New South Wales Police Force is setting up a Vietnamese unit and I am attracted to that idea. So, if Lilly agrees, let us go for the Sydney option!"*

Lilly answered, *"Nguyen, as far as I am concerned, all that you need to do is to complete your health checks and your inoculation against diseases. After that, I am happy to release you into the community dependent upon your security checks proving your worth and that you are not a threat to this country!"*

Lilly now asked, *"So, Nguyen, he have said that would you like to be an Australian policeman in Sydney, or some other place like Cabramatta."* Nguyen replied, *"Lilly, I would like to be part of the NSW Police Force, and operating in the new Vietnamese speaking unit in and around Cabramatta is of particular interest, however, it seems to me that we have already been down this path before when Peter was checking me out, Therefore, I ask "Why are we going through it again?"* Lilly replied, *"The information that I require often duplicates information and it is added to by Peter and his colleagues in ASIO.*

It is just that two different departments are involved, and the departments often do not speak to each other. Peter has already told you that he is satisfied with the answers that you gave him, and I am now also satisfied that all outstanding questions have been answered. I have recommended that you are to have unrestricted movement in and out of the Villawood Centre while you are awaiting entry to the Police Academy at Goulburn. I have also arranged for you to have an interview the Recruiting Section of the New South Wales Police Force. Your interview is with the Asian Unit of NSW Police at Cabramatta, and it is scheduled for 09:30 hours tomorrow morning! Is that good with you, or can you not make it at that time?"

Nguyen replied, *"I shall sleep overnight at a hotel as close as possible to the police station in Cabramatta and I shall be at the interview on time and of good appearance! I thank you and Peter for this wonderful opportunity!"* Nguyen was as good as his word. That resulted in him completing his training at the NSW Police Academy near Goulburn.

Soon after graduating from the academy, he was sent to Cabramatta as a probationary constable. He was taken out on his first official duty by his sergeant and mentor Sergeant Robert Jones. They went to the scene of a motor vehicle accident in which a truck had collided with two small passenger cars. One of them was an older Volkswagen Beetle.

Amazingly, the two people who had been travelling in the Volkswagen Beetle were completely uninjured. The car was only slightly damaged in that its front left mudguard was pushed hard against front left wheel. The other car involved was a Toyota Corolla. This car was almost unrecognizable as a Toyota Corolla because of the amount of damage was imposed upon it. It had a single occupant, and she was a young woman from Liverpool.

When the two policemen arrived, Sergeant Bob Jones spoke to Nguyen. He said, *"Ahead of us is the scene of the accident Nguyen, there are things that we must attend to now. I have been told that you were a serving police officer while you lived in Vietnam. So, I now would like to know what this accident scene suggests to you. And please tell me how you would have handled this problem if it had happened in Vietnam."*

Nguyen replied, *"If I was investigating this kind of accident in Vietnam, I would firstly see to it that all distances between the vehicles involved in the collision are measured as well as exactly where the accident happened. In order to be accurate, we would need the exact distance from the kerb of the roadside to where the impact took place. By gathering the statements of witnesses, we can determine if excessive speed was a factor in the accident. Secondly, I would gather statements from people who witnessed the accident and take their names and addresses.*

The reasons for me to carry out these sorts of actions are (1) the distance between the vehicles must be known in order to be able to calculate the speed of the vehicles involved. (2) to have on record, the names, and addresses of witnesses to the accident so that they can be called upon to give evidence in court at future dates." Bob Jones said, *"Well done Nguyen! That is correct! With your past experience in police matters and your approach to the job, you should do well in the New-South-Wales Police Service!"*

Nguyen went on to say, *"Bob, it is my opinion that this accident was caused by the truck which crossed over the railway line that runs along Railway Parade in Cabramatta to the intersection with Broomfield Street. According to witnesses, the truck did not stop at the traffic lights which were red. The driver of the truck just went through the red light at high speed and that is why he hit the Toyota Corolla so hard that it is now hard to recognise as a Toyota Corolla!*

Mitigating circumstances for the truck driver are that there was fog which may have contributed to the accident by confusing or even temporarily blinding the driver. However, that does not change the fact that the truck hit the Toyota on it left hand side, which indicates to me that the truck did not give way to its right. To my way of thinking, it is clear that the truck caused this accident to happen, and both the drivers of the Toyota Corolla and the Volkswagen Beatle have been compromised by the action of the truck driver who is guilty of causing the accident because he both went through a red light, and he did not give way to the right!"

Bob replied, *"Very well researched and documented my friend! I must now ask you, what other actions have you or will you now carry out in relation to that accident?"* Nguyen replied, *"I shall next charge the driver of the truck with traffic infringements. He is guilty of breaking a few New-South-Wales traffic laws and he must be brought to justice! I have all of this in my note book and after we return to Cabramatta Police station, I shall formerly charge the truck driver called Peter Evans!"* Bob's reaction was to say, *"Well done, Nguyen!"*

Since those times, I have been out of contact with Nguyen, but I spoke to some people in the New-South-Wales Police Force who know him. They have told me that Nguyen applied himself to his work with enthusiasm and that he is currently a senior sergeant in the Cabramatta area.

Nguyen Thiourea

Back at the Refugee Processing area of Howard Springs It was close to 2:30 pm (14:00 hours) when Lilly finally decided to have some afternoon tea and biscuits. Having completed her refreshment, she spoke to her colleague Peter Graham. She said, *"Well Peter, I do not know about you, but I consider what we have achieved so far today to be outstanding! I am very happy with the calibre of the people we have processed to become future Australians!*

Our next interview is with Nguyen Thiourea, whom I believe has the history of being in the public Service of South Vietnam. According to his history he was a tax collector for a number of right-wing and hardline regimes of South Vietnam from Diem through to Thieu! What do you know about him Peter?"

Peter Graham replied, *"Lilly, so far, I cannot see why this man cannot become part of the Australian community! He does not appear to have any connections with any organisation which may present as a threat that ASIO knows of! I have no knowledge of his health or inoculation status, but then again, that is your area, Lilly! I have been investigating him for a while now, but I cannot find anything that would stop him from becoming an Australian permanent resident or an Australian citizen!"*

Lilly said, *"I also think that he may have something to offer Australia! How about we get him to take an entrance examination to join the Commonwealth Public Service? He could well end up in the Australian Tax Office which will be something he is already experienced in!"* Peter replied, *"Yes Lilly, I agree, so let's do that! The less time these people spend in detention, and the more they can live their own lives and earn money, the better!"*

Lilly went to the door and called out, *"Nguyen Thiourea, please come in and let's get your interview under way!"* Nguyen Thiourea left the seat he had been sitting on and walked into the office of Lilly and Peter. Peter began proceedings by asking, *"For the record Nguyen, is Nguyen Thiourea your complete name or are there still other names that should be added but about which we know nothing?"*

Nguyen replied, *"My mother also gave me another name of Cung, but I never use it."* Peter replied, *"That may be so Nguyen, but you have reportedly been a public servant in Vietnam and therefore, you know that paperwork rules all men! You also know that the paperwork must be complete and that all of your names must be recorded, no matter if you use these names or not. Therefore, we are adding the name of Cung to your file."*

Peter was silent for a short time and then he again spoke to Nguyen. He said, *"Nguyen Cung Thiourea, I know that that you have been working as a tax collector for the various governments of southern Vietnam and that you did your duties to the best of your abilities. My information about you says that you were charged by the South Vietnamese Police for their crime of sedition. I want you to tell us about that.*

Nguyen replied, *"Yes, I was charged with sedition after I laid charges of tax evasion against Khuong Lanh Nguyen. He was a Roman Catholic Church Jesuit Priest and when I charged him with tax evasion, he swore that he would get even. He has a history of somehow blaming everyone else for what he does himself! He was also a provincial governor with his own private army.*

He has never done any manual work and he grows two extremely long finger nails on his left hand which shows Vietnamese people that he is high born and above them in life. He is a greedy and cruel prick. I was present when an Australian convoy of two large trucks loaded with food items drove into one of his villages.

The Australian captain in charge of the transport unit went to see him and explained that he had brought in two loads of food for the people. Upon hearing that, this man-of-God demanded to know what was in it all for him. Upon being told that the food was for his people and not for him, he said, "In that case, Australian soldier, I am putting an armed guard upon the food which shall then be sold to the highest bidder!" So, please do not take his word against me or anyone else in the world, for that man is both evil and corrupt!" He then went on to explain how he had uncovered a plot by the priest and provincial governor to never pay any taxes that were owed by him.

That almost stunned Peter Graham of ASIO. He said, *"Nguyen, I find it outrageous that a "Man-of-God" could ever be accused of such things, do you know for sure that this priest did in fact put an armed guard onto the food which was supplied by the Australian army for him to distribute to the people?"* Nguyen answered, *"Yes, Peter, I was present while all of that was happening. I heard and saw everything that happened, he most certainly did put an armed guard which was a section of infantry (ten fully armed infantry soldiers) into place guarding the bags of rice. I saw that with my own eyes!*

The priest was not just a priest, he was a Jesuit Priest, he wore black robes like those of his order, but his clothing was made of the best quality silk. To complete the picture, imagine him as being dressed in black and wearing a large broad brimmed hat which was a brown colour. As well he always wore his rosary beads which had a very large crucifix at the end of them, and which was made of pure silver!

Added that that, he also wore a colt 45 magnum pistol which was in a holster at his right side! As soon as the Australians departed, he did in fact slap an armed guard on the food, and it is well known that he sold it to the Viet Cong battalions. The food was in the form of bags of rice. The priest was an instrument of the terror unleashed upon the population of southern Vietnam by various dictator governments of the south from Diem through to Thieu!"

It was because of my investigations proved that man was systematically robbing the state of the Republic of Vietnam of collected taxes that the Thieu government prosecuted him, and he swore to get revenge upon me! That is among the reasons is why I had to flee from Vietnam after the National Government of Ho Chi Mihn took over the running of all of Vietnam. It was that priest who denounced me! I was never a communist nor a supporter of the right-wing dictator governments of the south. I just hope that you will let me stay here in Australia, where I can be safe from harm!".

Peter was by now very interested in the man he was speaking to. He said, *"I like how you have the courage to make everyone pay their fair share of taxes. From what you have said, I get the impression that you apply the tax laws fairly. Therefore, I put it to you to sit for an entry examination to the Australian Taxation Office. It is my observation that you are ideally suited to an application like that. So, would you be happy to work for the Australian Tax Office?"*

Nguyen replied, *"Yes Peter, I am very interested in becoming an Australian Public servant working for the Australian Tax Office! When I sit for the entrance examination, will there be supervisors on hand who can explain to me what some questions mean? After all, English is not my first language!"*

All of that happened years ago, and the last that I heard of him, Nguyen Cung Thiourea was still working for the Tax Office where he was promoted to the rank of Regional Tax Inspector.

Ho Hiep

After she and Peter had finished processing Nguyen Thiourea, she and peter relaxed for a short time with a cup of tea. That was followed by Lilly going to the door of the interview room and calling for Ho Hiep to come forward and have his interview. Ho had been sitting near the door and he immediately said, *"Miss Davis, I am Ho Hiep, and I think it will benefit everyone to get this interview and other processing completed as quickly as possible!"*

Lilly replied, *"Excellent! I am glad that you have such a positive attitude Ho!"* with that said, she led the way into the interview room. As Ho was entering, he saw Peter Graham and recognised him. He said, *"Good day Peter Graham, how are you?"* Peter replied, *"I am great, thank you Ho, and how are you?"*

Ho said, *"I am good Peter, now let's get this processing over and done with! I have no wish to live a detention centre for even one day if that can be avoided!"*

Lilly now spoke. She said, *"Ho, both Peter and I have some questions for you. As you already know, Peter and his colleagues are mainly concerned with what security risk to Australia you may or may not present, while I am more concerned about your general health, your level of inoculation against diseases and how you will fit into Australian society!"*

Peter Graham now started the security questions. He said, *"Ho, I have information that you served with the South Vietnamese Army (ARVN)unit known as the 302 Ranger Regiment. Is that correct?"* Ho replied, *"Yes, it is correct! I served in that unit or others for close to fifteen years! I entered it as a private soldier and left it as a captain in command of a company! I am now aged forty-eight years, and I feel as if I have wasted my entire life by being Vietnamese born, because things are so difficult for Asian people at the moment.*

Not only that, but things have been difficult now for many years! I keep on getting constant insults and barbs such as "Go away, you little brow monkey" mainly from French and British people. From the Americans, we usually get – "Fuck off you Gook!" While the Australians will often say, "G'Day, Ho, you, silly slope head" if they like you. If not, they also tend to call us Gooks!" However, in the case of the Australians, most of the name calling is usually good natured and that does not worry me. However, the attitudes of the British, French, and American people towards us does worry me and I feel their insults deeply!

I have only ever tried to be honest throughout my working life, but the British, French and Americans do make life hard for Vietnamese people! I believe that here in Australia, I have the chance of a better life and being appreciated for who and what I am!"

Lilly said, *"I see, I do aplogise for the way that others have treated you. However, as you say yourself, that is mainly being done by people outside of Australia. What I want to know is 'Are you willing to forget all about your past, and where you have come from, and will you now strive to become an Australian? That brings me to what you can do for Australia and what you are willing to do for the country. I also want to know what you would now work at in order to support yourself. I ask that because of your age! Regardless, if you are willing to learn new skills and to apply yourself as you have during your earlier life in Vietnam, you will be welcomed as a new Australian!"*

Ho Hiep said, *"I can see why you could feel that I could end up as being a burden upon your social security system, however, that is not me! I am a proud ex-soldier even though I may have been on the wrong side during Vietnam's War of independence! Please take note of the fact that I shall always do what is correct and in line with the teachings of Confucius."*

Peter Graham now soke. He said, *"Ho, I think that you should approach the Australian Department of Veterans' Affairs with your story. It seems to me, that by your outstanding actions when you were in the*

302 Ranger Regiment of ARVN, you could find that you are entitled to what we Australians call the "Service Pension". Check it out, you may even be entitled to back pay from it. Whatever happens, get your application for it into Department of Veterans' Affairs now!

In order to help you with the forms and such things that you will find are in use here, I suggest that you live among other Vietnamese people in places such as Cabramatta and obtain their help to fill out forms! You will also find that the Australian Department of Veterans' Affairs has Vietnamese born people directly working for it and they should be able and willing to help you! So go ahead and see the people at Veterans' Affairs in Sydney when you arrive there and talk to them about the 'Service Pension'."

Lilly said, *"Ho, do not worry about your accommodation. You may live at the centre of Villawood in Sydney until such time as you have your own place!"* Ho departed to have a toilet break as Lilly spoke to Peter. She said, *"Peter, I am happy with what we have done today. I wish that all of the cases we have to handle would be so straight forward as these cases!"*

After Ho returned, she was silent for a short time and them she resumed speaking. She said, *"Ho, with reference to your skills and work preferences, are you willing to attend some short formal courses which will result in you being able to either find employment in fields that you have no experience in yet or even to set-up your own business?*

If we go down that path, I put it to you that you enroll in (1) a vocational course at the Cabramatta College of TAFE. TAFE is not really a word; it is an abbreviation of Technical And Further Education. So, I suggest that firstly, you do as Peter has suggested and go and see the Department of Veterans Affairs in York Street, Sydney about obtaining a Service Pension.

The Service Pension is small, but you will be able to live on it. Only people with 'qualifying Service' are entitled to it. By you having that as a source of income, it will aid you greatly while you are studying courses such as 'Small Business Management, which you will need as well as your requirement to undergo vocational training of your choice. For those courses, I suggest that you go to the Cabramatta TAFE and speak to the administrators and teachers there in order to find the best course for you and the ones which will give you the most interest."

Ho said, *"Thank you, Lilly! I shall do as you and Peter have suggested. First and foremost, I think it best if I do as Peter has suggested and see the people at the Australian Department of Veterans' Affairs. I think it marvelous if my war service in Vietnam can actually give me a small Australian pension of my own! If that actually happens, it will aid me tremendously! Once the Service Pension has been organised, I can go and see the people at the Cabramatta TAFE! How does that sound to you Lilly and Peter?"*

Lilly said, *"Ho, I think that your plan of doing things is the right way for you to proceed. What do you think, Peter?"* Peter answered, *"Lilly, I totally agree that is the way forward for him. Ho, can you please go to the Department of Veterans Affairs in York Street, Sydney and make an appointment to see Richard Clark as quickly as possible? I shall call him and explain the situation to him! The reason that I think you should be able to get the Australian Service pension is that other Vietnamese Veterans of the Vietnam War have already received that pension before you. Some of them are not as deserving as you are!"*

Progress of Ho Hiep

Ho was quickly processed and like many other Vietnamese refugees, he decided to obtain formal qualifications in such things as cooking Asian style meals, an example of which is 'Stir Fry' meals. He opted to live in the area of Cabramatta which already was being called Vietnam-Matta by many Australians living in Sydney.

Some of the Australian residents of Cabramatta were openly jealous of the Vietnamese 'Boat People' and referred to them as 'Bloody undeserving Slope-heads and Gooks!' These Aussies did not understand that the refugees were given aid to settle after they had been processed for security and health problems and that none of them posed a threat to Australia. As well, these Australians were openly hostile towards the refugees, and they would speak against them at every opportunity.

Ho was introduced to the leader of the Vietnamese community at Cabramatta called Nguyen Van Truc. After the introductions had been completed, the two men spoke to each other, Ho told Nguyen about his plans to do vocational and small business management training prior to opening his own restaurant. That impressed Nguyen who said, *"Ho, I am impressed by what you have told me! Just remember that the TAFE course in cooking that you are undertaking will give you formal qualifications but not much experience in cooking. For that you need to actually do the cooking!*

In order for you to both gain that valuable experience and to have a place in Cabramatta to live, I propose that you live in the flat above my restaurant. I will I due course get out of the restaurant business which I am willing to sell to you. If you are interested in that, we can come to arrangements as to how much and when you should pay me for what shall become your own restaurant. I hope that you are interested in this because it is an outstanding opportunity for you!

I have been here in Cabramatta since 1970 when I arrived in this country as a 'Boat Person'. I have become heavily involved in aiding the resettlement of fellow refugees from Vietnam into this country, in particular in the Cabramatta and other Sydney areas. I am leaving the restaurant because I am now the leader of our Vietnamese community in Cabramatta.

As more and more Vietnamese people come into the area, I find that I am extremely busy providing services and shelter to new arrivals. I am standing for election to the council and later on, to the Parliament of New South Wales! So, because I am constantly working for the successful integration of our Vietnamese refugees into the Australian community, I do not have enough time to devote to the successful running of a restaurant. That is the reason that I am offering it and the flat above it to you!"

Ho replied, *"Thank you so very much Nguyen Van Truc, I am most impressed, and I thank you for giving me such an outstanding opportunity to enter my own restaurant business! I shall make this great opportunity work and I shall totally repay you for this outstanding aid and support! In order to make sure that I do things correctly, I will make sure that I apply what I learn in the small business management classes at the Cabramatta TAFE, and I will also learn to prepare meals correctly and hygienically.*

Due to the fact that I cannot be here all of the time and also because there will be many times when things are so busy that I cannot do everything myself, I wish to ask you if you know of trustworthy people from the Vietnamese community of Cabramatta who may like to work for me."

Nguyen replied, *"Ho, I do know some worthy people whom I will speak to on your behalf about them working for you. I shall have some of them with me at this restaurant this evening at eighteen hundred hours in two days from now. Can you be ready to speak to these possible employees at that time?"*

Ho was happy with that. He said, *"Thank you, Nguyen, things are getting better all of the time. I shall be ready to meet these helpers in two days' time at say, 18:00 hours (6 pm)."* Ho agreed to pay Nguyen the sum of one thousand and six hundred and fifty dollars per month. Next, Ho contacted a sign writer called Andy Blake. He said, *"Andy, I want you to change the name of the restaurant from "Nguyen's Vietnamese Cuisine" to "Ho's Vietnamese Restaurant". How long will all of that take and how much do I have to pay you to complete the job?"*

256

Andy replied, *"Nguyen my boy, I think that this job will take about twenty hours. So, multiplying the twenty hours by eighteen dollars per hour, will come to AU$360.00! It is now up to you to decide if you wish to go ahead with this or not! You may think that the price is a bit too steep, but this is year 1980 after all, and even I have to eat!"*

Ho took it all in his stride and said, *"Go ahead and do the job! I do not mind paying, but I demand top quality work! If your writing is not up to my standards, I will not pay. If on the other hand you meet all requirements, you may find that you receive a bonus!"* Andy said, *"Fair enough Ho, I get start immediately!"* He then cleaned the existing sign and then painted over it with a white paint. Next, he said, *"Ho, I have prepared the existing sign for painting, and I can do no more until the paint has set and is completely dry. That has taken one hour so far. I shall return here at ten hundred hours tomorrow morning and then complete the job!"*

At 10:00 hours of the following morning, Andy was at the restaurant he started by using a pencil to draw the outlines of the letters he wanted to paint onto the sign. Before he applied paint to the sign, he checked the pencil outlines of letters in order to ensure that no spelling mistakes were present in the work and that the outlines of the lettering conveyed the correct message. Next, he went to Ho and showed him the pencil outlines of the lettering.

He said, *"Ho, here is the sign with the outlines of the lettering drawn upon it in pencil. I now need you to closely look at it and make sure that everything is the way that you want it to be. This is the last opportunity to change anything! So, please closely look at this before you agree to the final product!"*

Ho inspected the sign with the lettering outlines drawn upon it in pencil and he said, "Andy, you have done well, I look forward to seeing the completed work!" That satisfied Andy and he resumed his work. Andy completed his work and he then put the sign down onto a table top so that it would completely dry and allow other people to handle it without causing damage to it. On the next day, he took the completed work to Ho for approval and payment.

Ho was happy with it, and he said, *"Capital job, Andy, how much do I owe you now?"* Andy replied, *"Three hundred and sixty dollars as we agreed!"* Ho paid AU$450.00 him without further comment. As he was making the payment, he said, *"There you go Andy, you have done such a good job, that I have paid you AU$450.00. Thank you for your work!"*

Time passed quickly, and Ho suddenly found that he had to hurry in order to be ready to again meet Nguyen and the restaurant workers he was going to have with him. So, he quickly cleaned himself up and was enjoying a cup of tea when Nguyen and two attractive Vietnamese girls called in to see him. Nguyen said, *"Ho, these two girls are the help that I have in mind for your restaurant! This is Cai, she is twenty-two years old, she is a chef in her own right, and this girl is her sister, Dieu. Dieu is not a chef, but she is as hard working as her sister, and she is eager to learn. Both girls are happy to work for you at the price of ten Australian dollars per hour."* Ho was very happy with his new work force, and he bought out his drink glasses for special occasions.

He then proceeded to fill each glass with his special wine and gave each person a glass of it. He said, *"Nguyen, I hereby propose a toast to you and these beautiful young helpers who will help my restaurant become successful!"* He then raised his glass and held it toward the girls. That that was followed by the others doing the same thing. Ho concluded by saying *"Welcome to Ho's Vietnamese Restaurant Ladies and Gentlemen! We shall formally open the restaurant at 18:00 hours or 6 pm Eastern Australian Summer Time. Girls, please be here, ready to start work five minutes earlier at 17:55 hours or 5:55 pm."* After that, the four people enjoyed each other's company and chatted before they all went their separate ways.

At 5:30 pm of the next day, Cai arrived and reported to Ho for duty. She was dressed in the traditional cheongsam of Vietnamese women, and she looked lovely in it. Fifteen minutes elapse before Dieu also reported for duty to Ho. She was also dressed in the traditional cheongsam as was Cai. Ho was very impressed with presentation and poise of both of his workers. He said, *"Thank you, girls, when the diners arrive, make them comfortable, and give them a feeling of being at home. Ask them to let you know of anything that you can obtain for them, and we should begin our first night with an outstanding success!"*

After the guests had left and the cleaning up had been finished, Ho counted the takings. The restaurant had been busy all night, with many people of Australian and other nationalities attending. Ho was pleasantly surprised to find that the takings for the night amounted AU$1,885.00.

He thought about his restaurant and the payment for his workers. He began thinking about it all in depth and concluded, *"My waitresses are the hostesses in this restaurant, they are bringing in the money and I am lifting their pay from AU$10.00 per hour to AUS15.00 per hour. I have good staff and I shall pay my workers well! The average wage for the hospitality industry is AU$8.00 per hour at the moment."*

Hanh Liem Tru

While awaiting his turn to be interviewed by the combined ASIO and Department of Immigration and Citizenship team of Lilly Davis and Peter Graham and their staff of helpers, Hanh Liem Tru was once again experiencing the racing heart and anxiety associated with PTSD due to his service against the Khmer Rouge at Ba Chuc in Vietnam. At long last, he was relieved when Lilly walked through the door and said, *"Mister Hanh Liem Tru, please come into the interview room and then we can get these necessary actions out of the way!"* Hanh replied, *"Thank you, Miss Davis, I shall be glad to finally have that over and done with. All of this is playing hell with my nerves!"* Having made that statement, he walked through the door and sat down in front of the two desks manned by Lilly Davis and Peter Graham.

Peter could not help but notice the fact that Hanh appeared to be uncomfortable, and he began to ask why that was. He said to Hanh, *"Hanh, you give the appearance of some-one who is uncomfortable in the presence of officials of the Government of Australia! Please tell Lilly and me why that is so!"*

Hanh did not know about PTSD, but he knew that his war service against the followers of Pol Pot had affected him badly! So, he decided that honesty was the best policy. He said, *"Miss Davis and Mister Graham, I do not know why I am like this! I only know that ever since serving with the 2nd Battalion, of the 31st Infantry Division of the Peoples' Liberation Army of the Republic of Vietnam, against the forces of Pol Pot at Ba Chuc, followed by the Vietnamese invasion and later occupation of Kampuchea, I have been like this!*

Now, I find it difficult to get to sleep, and when I finally manage to do so, I find myself awakening at the slightest sound. Once I am awake, I become hyper-vigilant, and I find that my hearing can detect sounds that I normally cannot hear! One of the results of that is that I am constantly fatigued because I cannot get enough sleep to be able to fulfill the normal duties of a soldier or worker. A major problem is that I do not know what is happening to me or what can be done about it!"

Peter Graham had been following the story of Hanh with interest, and he said, *"Hanh dear boy, I think that you have be suffering from what psychiatrists call Post Traumatic Stress Disorder! If that is the case, it explains why you suffer from the lack of sleep and your hyper-alertness during the night! Your symptoms are like those of many Australian soldiers who served in the Second Indochina War. Many of them suffer from PTSD which in not curable, but it is treatable! With that in mind, would you like to undergo some treatment for PTSD?*

Hanh replied, *"Yes Peter, I would love to be rid of the nightmares, flash-backs, and hyper-alertness! Together these things make my life a misery! So, if you can organise treatment for my psychological condition, I shall be most grateful. However, bear in mind that I have no money! I am a refugee just like the others with whom I am being processed by your ASIO Department and also Lilly's Department of Immigration and Citizenship! I only mention that I have no money in case you want me to pay for the treatment that even you say I should have!"*

Peter Graham replied, *"Hanh, you worry too much! There shall be no cost to you for your treatment of your PTSD. Many people do not realise that the condition was first recognised in about 345 BC, when some Greek heroes appeared to be acting strangely after combat with invading enemies. The ancient Greeks called PTSD 'Soldier's Disease'. During World War One, PTSD was called 'Shell Shock' by British and other allied armies. It was not recognised as a war caused psychological condition during the time of World War One and its sufferers were unjustly accused of being slackers and cowards who were trying to get out of their responsibilities. Some members of the Allied armies were even shot for having what we now know is PTSD!"*

So, please tell about your PTSD, because as a combat Veteran myself, I will understand what is ailing you!" Hanh answered, *"Peter it is a long story, and I am unsure of where to begin!"* Peter Graham said, *"Just begin your story at whatever point you like.*

The main thing is to get it out into the open so that you can recognise your symptoms for what they are. It is only then, that treatment can be applied effectively!"

So, it was the Hanh began his story. He said, *"I find that I constantly have flash-backs to my times in combat against the Kampuchean Army of Pol Pot! I all too often find great difficulty in getting to sleep. As well, once I am asleep, I all too often wake up shaking in terror and then I become hyper-alert and start scanning the areas around me for possible intrusions by enemy forces!"* Peter Graham replied, *"That sure sounds like some of the symptoms of PTSD to me! Please now tell me about your dreams or nightmares, as these also have a direct bearing upon your behaviour and job performance!"*

So it was that Hanh related his nightmares to Peter Graham. He said, *"I have several different nightmares and several different versions of them. Perhaps the most disturbing is the nightmare beginning on the 25th of December 1978, when my unit, the 2nd Battalion of the 31st Infantry Division of the Peoples' Army of the Democratic Republic of Vietnam was mobilised as part of the invasion of Kampuchea by Vietnam!*

Typically, when I close my eyes and begin to relax, I all too often get uptight and begin to stress out due to seeing myself again boarding the trucks which were following the tanks of the Vietnamese Army into Phnom Penh! I relive seeing my section leader, Corporal Binh Chien Bui organising us to board the truck as a section sub unit of the 31st Infantry Division. Once we got to Phnom Penh, we found that it was empty because all of its people had been removed to rural communes by Pol Pot and his cronies!

So, after we had established that there were no enemies or civilian people in the capital city, we moved out into the jungle areas about fifty kilometres out of the city. Eventually, we found a large area of cleared jungle and at the jungle edges were the hastily built homes of people who had been forced to leave the cities and towns in order for them to live in rural communes!

We had been told by our superiors that we were rescuing the Khmer People from Pol Pot and his Khmer Rouge! After we had begun to fan out after discovering the large commune, I could see what looked like hundreds or thousands of corpses or bones of people of both sexes who had been systematically starved to death by the mismanagement of the Khmer Rouge!

We had been warned by those who commanded us, that we would not be received as liberators and even when we found survivors and gave them food, they would regard us as enemies! That turned out to be the case! I came across an attractive but skinny girl whom I then fed by cooking her a portion of rice mixed with some chicken. Instead of her being thankful for the meal, she abused me as an enemy of her people, and she told me that all Vietnamese males are inferior and not to be trusted! I did not and still do not understand why people who have been downtrodden by their own government would hate Vietnamese soldiers when what we did was in fact to liberate them and to feed them! It makes no sense to me at all!"

Peter Graham said, *"What you have just told me is a classic case of PTSD! You really must get help to treat that condition! Otherwise, things will become much worse for you, and you will end up not being able to work because you shall be constantly fatigued from not sleeping! So, let's get your treatment for PTSD under way! Now we go on to other matters concerning security! So far, you have told me that you have been a loyal serving member of the Vietnamese Army in its invasion of Kampuchea and that you were part of the defence at Ba Chuc before that. I now need to know why you felt that you had to leave Vietnam by joining the other refugees on the boat!"*

Hanh said, *"I am sure that by now you would have heard that when the 'American War' finished, many patriots returned from the forests and jungles to reclaim their former lives in their original villages or towns. Most of them were accepted back in to their communities without any problem and they were as one with the people!*

However, some of the people had amassed wealth by the misappropriation of land holdings and by denouncing others as traitors, just so they could have the property that these people or their families owned! A brewing problem was that some people used false accusations and corruption to get what they coveted. Before I was drafted in to the army of the Democratic Republic of Vietnam, I was working the land belonging to my father in the Republic of Vietnam (South Vietnam).

After the defeat of the Americans and the re-unification of Vietnam, a local mandarin wanted the family's property, and he swore out false charges

265

against me! That happened to me after I returned from the war against Kampuchea! I had heard some stories of what happened to those who were accused of treason by such people, so I decided to get the hell out of Vietnam! All of that makes me sad, because I had always been a good citizen of my country and I was part of the Vietnamese army which beat the Kampucheans! I do not understand why I should have to run, but I know that I must, because government officials are taking the word of those who want my family's property over what I, a mere soldier may say! It distresses me!"

Peter Graham was sympathetic, and he said, *"Based upon what you have told me, I cannot see you as presenting a security risk to Australia. I shall therefore recommend that you be given genuine refugee status! Remember that security investigations are ongoing matters and I hope that nothing will come to ASIO attention which could result in a reversal of your refugee status! Now Lilly and her Department of Immigration and Citizenship have questions for you!"*

Lilly began her conversation with Hanh by saying, *"Hanh, my information about you says that you are at the age of twenty-four years. Is that correct?"* Hanh replied, *"Yes, Lilly that is right!"* Next Lilly said, *"I know that you have been a soldier in the army of Vietnam and that you were a peasant farmer working your family's land in southern Vietnam before that. I now need to know what skills you can bring to Australia and where you would like to both work and live."* Hanh replied, *"I have the skills of being an agricultural worker with experience in the use of oxen and machinery such as tractors and rice harvesters.*

My father was progressive in the use of machinery, and he successfully used machinery because more and more people left the country side because they wanted to live in towns and cities. As more and more people left, a shortage of rural workers was experienced because the workers had moved away. Therefore, my father was able to acquire more land and that in turn caused other people to turn upon him in order to obtain what he had secured for the family. That is why I am here!"

Lilly said, *"I understand that Hanh, now let us see what you would like to work at and where you would like that to happen. From what you have said so far, I get the impression that you are suited to live in the rural areas of Australia. Therefore, would you like a position as a farm hand or station worker on an Australian property, or should we look at the possibility of placing you into a factory job in one of our state capital cities?"*

Hanh thought over what had been said by Lilly and he said, *"Lilly, do I have to make that decision now? I must admit that I am experienced in the use of farm machinery, but that experience is now some years old, and it is likely that it is likely to be superseded by the use other machines. Therefore, if I am to go back to rural activities, it would pay for me to have some refresher courses before I do so. For the time being, it may be better for me to go to a state capital city and earn a living as a factory worker! What do you think?"*

Lilly replied, *"Hanh, I think that you must do what you think is best for you! If you want to work and live in rural areas, then I think that we can organise that for you. If on the other hand, you wish to go to the cities, then that can also be organised. I must leave your preference up to you. So, what do you wish to do, and where do you want to do it?"*

Hanh replied, *"Lilly, I am sorry if I have not made myself clear, I wish to go to a capital city in an Australian State. Where does not matter. What matters is for me to have a home that I can rent and work that I can do in order to pay for various things including rent and food. Can you organise these thigs for me?"* Lilly replied, *"Yes Hanh, I can and will do so! First, we need you to complete your medical screening and you must have your inoculations against various diseases. Starting tomorrow morning at 10:00 hours, you are to see the Medical Officer, here. After that you will be notified!"* At 09:45 of the next morning, Hanh was waiting at the surgery for his appointment with the Medical Officer. Doctor Gillian Clarke and said, *"Hanh Liem Tru, please come through to the examination room and we shall get your final medical examinations and inoculations under way!"*

Hanh did as he had been told and followed her into the examination room. After they had reached there, the medical proceeded and then the inoculations were carried out. Finally, having completed all inoculations and medical examinations, Hanh was told that it was over and that he should report to Lilly who was in the office where he had earlier undergone interviews with Department of Immigration and ASIO. Hanh went to see Lilly as instructed and he was finally admitted shown in to see her.

As he went into the office, Lilly said, *"Nice to see that you have passed all of the tests and that you have now had all the necessary inoculations!*

Currently, you are living at a camp located at Howard Springs which is near Darwin. I believe that you know Cung Whyat. He is building up a farm machinery and fertiliser business here at Howard Springs. Should I speak to him on your behalf so that you can work for him if you want to remain in the Darwin areas? Or should I call other possible employers in other major centres on your behalf?

Hanh answered, *"I prefer to work in or near either Adelaide or Sydney, if that is possible, please, Lilly! I also wish to stay in touch with Cung and the others with whom I made the hazardous journey to Australia, if you will kindly allow me to do so!"* Lilly replied, *Very well then, which city do you mostly prefer, Adelaide or Sydney?"* Hanh answered, *"I feel that for now, Adelaide could be better! Can you arrange my accommodation and work in Adelaide?"*

Lilly replied, *"Yes,"* and then she called the Adelaide distributors of John Deere Tractors. Soon after speaking to the manager of that company, she spoke to Hanh. She said, *"Hanh, there is an opening for you with John Deere based in Adelaide. Does that interest you?"* He replied, *"Yes"* and the deal was done. The following day, Hanh boarded a Qantas flight to Adelaide from the Darwin Airport. Before he left for Adelaide, he attended a meeting of all of the refugees who had travelled on the Giang Kein, which had been organised by Ho Hiep. Before he left, he saw Cung and got his address at Howard Springs.

Travel to & from Vietnam & Australia

Meanwhile, back at the Howard Springs camp, Ho spoke to the assembled refugees most of whom had been cleared to continue living in Australia as permanent residents. He said, *"My friends, together we have travelled for some time through waters infested with pirates whom we had to fight! We beat them in the end, and we are now about to embark upon our new lives as permanent residents of Australia!*

I have asked Cung, and his wife called Daiyu to record the names and addresses of each one of us so that we can all keep in touch with each other and even have re-unions at times and various places in the future. I want all of us to stay in touch with each other. Please come forward and you shall all be given the name and address of Cung and Daiyu at Howard Springs where they are settling, and their house will be built!" And so, the other refugees came forward and received the address of Cung and Daiyu as Ho had said.

Time passed quickly for the refugees because there was much that they had to do. Almost before he was aware of it, Cung suddenly released that it was now the year of 1985. He had been reading whatever publication he could in order to obtain news about what was happening in his original home country of Vietnam. As part of that, he came across a newspaper article from the 11th of January 1973.

The headlines said, *"Australia's Governor General, Mr. Paul Hasluck has said that Australia's role in the Vietnam War has ended. The Prime Minister, Mr. Gough Whitlam has recognised the Democratic Republic of Vietnam (North Vietnam) which congratulated him on his success in becoming Australia's Prime Minister! Mr. Whitlam said that Australia shall maintain a platoon of infantry personnel to safe-guard the Australian embassy in Saigon! The platoon, (32 men) shall remain in Saigon to safe-guard the Australian Embassy there for as long as they are required."*

Cung Reads of Australia's Recognition of Vietnam

Having read that, Cung spoke to Daiyu. He said, *"My darling wife, I have been reading old Australian newspapers from the 11th of January 1973, which clearly says that Australia recognises the government of the Democratic Republic of Vietnam and that all Australian forces would be withdrawn from Vietnam as of that date other than a platoon of infantry soldiers who shall remain in Saigon to guard the Australian Embassy there. To me that simply means that in time, when things have settled down a lot more, we can look at the possibility of returning to Vietnam for the purpose of visiting friends and relatives who are still living there. So, my darling, in a few years would you like to visit Vietnam with our children and introduce them to our relatives?"*

Daiyu answered, *"Yes, my husband, I would like to do that when it becomes possible to do so! I think that for us to visit Vietnam would be a marvelous idea, but we must never forget that we are naturalised Australian citizens, and our children are Australian born and therefore they are also Australians! We should speak about visiting Vietnam again and also look at the idea of forming a group of us who travelled to Australia on board the Giang Kein. We have the addresses of the others so I think that we should contact them when the time comes and ask them if they would like to visit Vietnam with us."*

Cung said, *"Thank you, Daiyu, as always, you are right! I shall keep on researching as to when the right time is for people such as us to visit our original homeland."* In 1985, he read a report on the industrialization of Vietnam since 1975. The report stated: *"The socialist industrialisation policy is to have a centrally planned economy! That the Vietnamese Government would overcome the consequences of the war and restore the country's infrastructure network and industrial bases including state-owned enterprises! That Vietnam now concentrates on the setting up of heavy industry."* That formed the basis of the first five-year plan .

That was largely successful, and it was followed by the next five-year plan to be actioned between 1986 and 2005. It stated: *"Vietnam shall, by using the Doi Moi processes transition towards full industrialisation and a free market and open economy. The next five-year plan is below:*

"1991 to 1995 the development of prioritised sectors: These shall include heavy industry (cement and steel) as well as oil exploration and mining. In the South China Sea, our country has vast oil fields which Vietnam must develop and exploit before the Americans or Chinese do so and block us from using our own resources! There shall also be manufacturing for the Vietnamese domestic market as well as items such as footwear for export."

Having read about these five-year plans of the Vietnamese Government, Cung said, *"Daiyu, please get into contact with the Vietnamese Embassy in Canberra for us to be issued visas to visit Vietnam as Australian passport holders sometime in 1987 or*

1988! Also please contact the others with whom we fled Vietnam on board the Giang Kein and invite them all to have a re-union with us firstly here at Howard Springs and then later also in Vietnam as visitors!

I think that is would also be very good if you could make sure that we have our Australian passports and other documentation ready with us when we finally manage to go to Vietnam for a visit." Daiyu answered, *"Yes Cung, I shall do it! However, much will depend now upon how fast the Vietnamese Government gives us the necessary visas and how long it takes for us to receive our Australian passports from the Department of Immigration and Citizenship! Also, we must wait for the others to con tact us about this if they are interested in coming with us! So do not be disappointed if some of them cannot make it!"*

Daiyu wrote the letters to the other refugees and posted them to their last known addresses. Of the thirty letters she sent out, only eight of them remained unanswered. Both she and Cung thought that the response was good, and they continued with planning the visit to their former homeland.

No matter how they tried to organise a re-union of travellers on board the Giang Kein, Cung and Daiyu could not organise the re-union in Vietnam until 2011. It was early in January of 2011 when Daiyu finally received confirmation from most of the other refugees that they would like to attend the re-union in in Howard Springs followed by visiting Vietnam. Things quickly felt into place with the necessary visas from Vietnam and the Australian passports becoming available without undue difficulty.

As usual, Cung did research on what had happened in Vietnam while the refugees were in Australia. He was astounded to read that Vietnam in 2011 was already employing many people in secondary industry and that cottage industry was also alive and well. He read that tourism has become a major in industry which is a prime employer. Heavy industry has been successfully installed and is producing both cement and steel.

Much of Cung's information came from official Vietnamese Government sources. A report which he read is below:

'One of the most important policy decisions made in the Doi Moi process was the shift from using imports to a policy of becoming self-sufficient in the manufacture of many goods. The leaders of Vietnam want to avoid the failures of Latin American countries and to learn from the successes of industrialised nations. That has resulted in Vietnamese industrial output increasing at an average annual rate of fifteen point two per cent (15.2 %) over the past ten years.

Over the past twenty (20) years, industrial performance has increased to the point where the export of manufactured goods have become increasingly important to the well-being of Vietnam's economy! In the earlier years the State-owned enterprises were found to be inefficient and that there was a need for investment in Vietnam by foreign companies. State Owned Enterprises are still in existence, and they shall continue to be part of the industrial and agricultural make-up of our country.

Cung was impressed that the Vietnamese Communist Government was now allowing investment within Vietnam by foreign owned capitalist companies. He decided to discuss the industrialisation of Vietnam with Daiyu. He said, *"Daiyu, I have just read reports about Vietnam that have impressed me! I have been reading about the industrialisation of the country and it appears that Vietnam now has successfully invited foreign capitalist companies to set-up in Vietnam and manufacture items from motor cars and semi-trailers through to food canneries.*

It is very apparent that Vietnam has recognised the value of private enterprise in conjunction with State-owned enterprises. When that is coupled with the Vietnamese tradition of total religious freedom for the people, I can see that things have really changed for the better in our former country. In time, I am sure that life in Vietnam will become as good as it is here in Australia after a lot of time has passed. It is now the year of 2011 and given the improved outlook in Vietnam I think the time has finally come where we can look at visiting there! So, how are your tasks of organising our Vietnamese Visas and Australian passports coming along?"

Daiyu answered, *"Cung, the industrialisation of Vietnam is all very well, but I think that there shall still be the problem of people not having the freedom of speech that we take for granted here in Australia!"* Cung was silent for a while and then he spoke. He said, *"Daiyu, you are correct as usual! Vietnam still has a one-party national government, and that political party is the 'Workers Party of Vietnam' which is also known as the Communist Party!*

All the same, before any country can concentrate upon the political freedom of its citizens, the citizens must firstly have a high standard of living which allows the people to have enough to eat and to have shelter from the elements. The industrial set-up in Vietnam is working so well that Honda has built a third production plant located at Ha Nam Province which is about 40 kilometres from Hanoi.

Since establishment in Vietnam in 1995, Honda has been producing 2,500,000 units from its combined three plants at Ha Nam Province. The work force of Honda is 9500 workers. The workers are well-paid, and the work-force is contented! I think that it will be interesting to watch Vietnam and the changes taking place there, because I expect that in time, Vietnam will allow elections that are completely free of government interference! I think that may happen within the next ten to twenty-five years from now! Oh, how silly of me, we got side-tracked and discussed politics as well as the industrialisation of Vietnam. As a result, we still do not know about our Vietnam visas or our Australian passports! I meat to ask you to let me know about those things! Can you let me know about those things now please Daiyu?"

She replied, "Cung, our Australian Passports have arrived, and they are in the safe under the floor of our home along with other papers. Our Vietnamese visas are not here yet, and it could be advantageous for us if we were to travel to Canberra and actually go and see the Vietnamese Embassy in order to get the visas."

Re-union of the Refugees on Giang Kein

Cung was silent for a short time and then he said, *"Daiyu, please get into contact with as many of the other people from Vietnam with whom we arrived in Australia as refugees for the purpose of having a re-union. I would like the re-union to take place at the Victoria Hotel, located in Smith Street of Darwin, right in the CBD. They must arrange their own accommodation, because there is no way that we can cater for thirty people at our home at Howard Springs! Ask all recipients to RSVP within fourteen days and let them all know that we are looking at returning to Vietnam for a quick visit as Australian citizens.*

Daiyu immediately drafted out a form letter which she wanted to send to out to all of the other refugees from Vietnam. She wrote the letter as appear below:

Dear (insert name), It is now the year of 2011 and my family of Cung, Nguyen, Nguyet, and me, would like you to RSVP within fourteen (14) days to attend a re-union celebration for those of us who arrived in Australia after travelling on board the Giang Kein. We are planning a grand celebration to be held om the upper floor of the Victoria Hotel located in Smith Street Darwin within the CBD. Everyone should arrange their own accommodation which is available from motel/hotels such as the Swan hotel a short distance from the Victoria Hotel.

After the re-union, my family and I shall be travelling to Vietnam to visit friends and relatives we left behind when we fled to Australia. We shall travel using Australian passports as we are Australian citizens. We will be visiting the area around Ho Chi Minh City, with particular emphasis upon seeing my family located at Cho Lon near the main city of Ho Chi Minh City. With reference to air fares, we paid AU$2,168.00 for first class return air fares using Qantas. Malaysian Airlines have similar prices.

It is up to yourselves to provide your own transport costs if you wish to join us in travelling to Vietnam. Hawaiian Airlines also flies to Vietnam, and you may be able to get lower priced return tickets through them. Please note that my family and I only travel using first class these days because we do not want any problems and we travel exclusively by Qantas. Please send me your RSVP within fourteen (14) days. My address is: Daiyu Whyat, PO Box 2014, Darwin 0800, NT, Australia. I hope to read your answering letters very soon! Love from Daiyu.

Five days later, the first of the answers to the proposed re-union and possible travel to Vietnam after that event arrived. Daiyu was thrilled to read, among the people coming to the re-union followed by travel to Vietnam and return were Hoa and her husband, Ngoc Nguyen Tran, Duc Duong Kim, Phuc Nguyen Quang, Nguyen Van Truc, Bian Tran, and Ho Hiep. She spoke to Cung about it.

She said, *"Cung, I have received some of the RSVPs to the re-union at the Victoria Hotel in Smith Street of Darwin. So far, ten people have said that they and their families shall attend. With luck, this list will grow to include more people within the next seven days. The fact that we are travelling to Vietnam during the Christmas is ideal because we would normally shut our business between the 24th of December and the 8th of January. So that time-frame will serve us well and we have our return air tickets already!"*

Cung answered, *"Thank you, Daiyu, now please hop onto the internet and do some research for us! I would like to know if that grasping arsehole called Sauget et Sang is still alive and if he is still running our former business in Cho Lon, which he obtained by falsely accusing us of treason! I realise that we are Australians now, and that we shall have to return here after our visit to Vietnam, but all the same, I cannot forgive that lying and grasping arsehole for what he has done to us!"*

Daiyu answered, *"Cung, I also have problems with the likes of that man! However, please remember that we are Australians who will be visiting Vietnam and therefore, we must obey Vietnamese laws! I therefore urge you to forget everything that happened in the past, because if you confront that man, you shall more than likely find yourself in jail in Vietnam and that is something that we must avoid!*

So, swallow your pride and forget about what happened. If we are to return to Vietnam for a visit, and then return here without problems, we must be seen as law-abiding citizens of Australia who respect Vietnamese laws and customs! Nothing else will do!" Cung immediately agreed with his wife. He said, *"Thank you Daiyu, for pointing that out! I agree that I must not let my sentiments caused by people who have wronged us in the past involve us in possible breaches of Vietnamese law! Therefore, I shall keep my mouth shut and forget about things. All that is important is to introduce our daughter and son to your parents. We cannot introduce our children to my parents because they have died!"*

Investigation of Sauget et Sang

Colonel Nguyen Van Tan was having an evening meal and holding a discussion about the struggle against the Americans and other Allies with his son named as Anh Duong Van Tan. He said, *"Anh, our country was well served by the many patriots it has had and continues to have! During my time as a revolutionary, I had the privilege of serving with a very patriotic woman of striking beauty called Hoa Lan Xuan. After the foreigners were beaten and Vietnam became unified again, she was falsely accused of treason by the family members of those who were guilty of her rape! Because of the lies told about her, she had to escape to Australia because of the actions against her by those who were guilty of base crimes such as rape. What was done to her was a great injustice and I have heard that she now is a lieutenant colonel in the Australia Army!*

That means that that woman is Australia's gain and our loss! I know that would never have happened if she had been given justice and treated fairly here in Vietnam by her own people! Instead of that happening, She felt that she had no option but to flee! My son, it is now the year of 1981, and I want you to launch an investigation to put right the wrongs suffered by her and Also a Vietnamese man called Cung Whyat.

He was never a member of one of my units, but I know of him because of his outstanding reputation in the area of Cho Lon! He was in fact a decorated hero of the attempted Kampuchean incursion into Ba Chuc! After Vietnam became free of the God-Damned Yankee, he was denounced as a traitor by Sauget et Sang who managed to get Cung's successful farm machinery and fertiliser business. Sang was a very corrupt policeman right up to the time the Americans

280

left. My son, you have successfully risen to the rank of divisional director of the Police of the Democratic Republic of Vietnam, and I want you to investigate both of these cases and obtain justice for both of these highly deserving people who are heroes.

The last that I heard of Cung Whyat, he was said to be living at a place called Howard Springs, which is close to Darwin in northern Australia. Currently, I do not know the where-abouts of Hoa Lan Xuan, but I have heard that she is now married to an Australian Naval Officer and that she has the rank of Lieutenant Colonel in the Australian Army! If that is correct, it should be easy for you to make contact with her and her husband! So, Anh, please find these two people for me and help Vietnam to rectify the wrongs that we inflicted upon them!" Anh replied, *"Yes, father, it shall be done as you wish! I shall find these two people and their current families, no matter where they are living now. It may be easiest to find Cung, if the reports about him having a successful fertiliser and farm machinery business at Howard Spring are correct."*

The following morning, Anh went to work at his police station and began to research the marital status of both Cung and Hoa as well as their addresses. By the end of the day, he had the address of both families, and he sought advice from his father about the best way to approach Hoa and Cung about compensating them for what had happened.

Meeting his father that evening, Anh said, *"Father, I think that I could have the addresses of both Hoa and Cung by mid-morning of the next day. I now need to get your advice on how best to approach both parties without scaring them off! After all, they have not had pleasant experiences with the national government of the Democratic Republic of Vietnam! Therefore, I need you to guide me in how best to approach them both, can you please help me to do this?"*

His father, Nguyen Van Tan thought about the matter, and he said, *"My son, I feel that it may be for the best if we leave the actual getting in touch with both Hoa and Cung to me, because both of them are more likely to trust someone whom they either know or know of. In the case of Hoa, she will know me because I was her commanding officer back during the fight against the American bully! In the case of Cung, he will have heard of me, and that could help to break the ice, so to speak! I still need you to investigate both these people, but it should just be a formality!*

For the service records of Cung, just obtain the personnel records of the 2nd Battalion, 31st Infantry Division of the Peoples' Liberation Army of the Democratic Republic of Vietnam. For the service background of Hoa, you will find it easiest if you get hold of her personnel file from my old battalion, D440, also known as Long Kahn's, own Battalion. You shall find that I recommended her for two 'Conscious-conduct-while-under-enemy-fire' awards! When you investigate her history, you should find that she was raped repeatedly by an AVRN sergeant called Ho Anh Sang. He was brought to justice, and he died before a firing squad commanded by Hoa! Her other rapists are still at large.

I have investigated those who took part in the rape and infection of Hoa with a venereal disease. I found out their identities by going through old personnel records of the American supply units located at Long Binh during 1966 to 1971. They are Americans and their names are Master Sergeant Ronald Buick, Corporal John Kelly, Privates Neville Williamson, and Brian Jones! Hoa does not know the names of the men who committed the war-crime of raping her! She only knows of Sergeant Ho Anh Sang!

She was black-listed as a traitor by the family of the ARVN sergeant called Ho Anh Sang and she fled to Australia in order to remain free! Yet she is an outstanding heroine of the struggle against the American Capitalists! I want her case to be reviewed and for her to be welcomed back to Vietnam as a heroine. That is because the Americans who took part in her rape and infection with a venereal disease, are still at large and they appear to think that they have gotten way with their war crimes! I want you to begin proceedings to extradite them as American-War-Criminals who are guilty are guilty of unspeakable acts against humanity. If we can get them here, we shall put them all on public trials as the war-criminals that they are! I also want you to fully investigate Sauget et Sang! In fact, after you have investigated him, I want to be the man who prosecutes him!"

Anh Duong Van Tan replied, *"Yes father, it shall be so, however, I do not hold out much hope of the Americans actually sending their criminal soldiers to us for justice. Usually, the Americans only cover up things and put the blame upon us because we have a communist administration! Still, I shall do whatever is possible.*

If it turns out that the Americans will not comply with the request to send us their war criminals, we must look at alternative ways of bringing them to justice, even if that means kidnapping them if they happen to travel somewhere in the southeast of Asia! If that becomes necessary, we shall have to wait until such time as the war criminals are travelling in Indonesia, Laos, Vietnam , Cambodia, India, Pakistan, and other places outside of Australia, Japan, and Singapore where police activity is too intense for us to successfully kidnap them!"

Nguyen replied, *"Thank you, my son, please do what you can in this regard, even though it will result in a diplomatic incident! It must be done, and Vietnam must rectify the wrongs committed against our heroes! Please do whatever becomes possible and we will again fully discuss this at out next meeting in one month from today!*

Once you have given me the latest news about where things stand , and what the postal address of Hoa Lan Xuan who has married and is now called Hoa Lan Roberts, I shall contact her! Therefore, it may be possible to send her a registered letter by writing to her using the name and address of Lt. Colonel Hoa Lan Roberts, c/o MILPO, Townsville, QLD, 4810, Australia."

The thought of contacting Hoa once again, excited Nguyen and he began to draft out a letter to her. It took him a long time as he was unsure of how best to get the information to her in such a way as to not upset her too greatly, because he was aware of her suffering at the hands of the American war criminals! Also, he took into consideration that the letter to her would in all likelihood, be opened and read by the Australian security services.

So, he wrote, *"Dear Hoa, I am Colonel Nguyen Van Tan and I distinctly remember recommending you for decorations on two occasions. The reason that I am making contact with you is to inform you that I have been successful in obtaining a review of the cases of the state against both yourself and also, a hero of the Kampuchean War called Cung Whyat.*

I have investigated your rape and infection with gonorrhea, and we have found that the names and ranks of the Americans who did that to you by checking the personnel records of the 3rd US Ordnance Battalion which was based at Long Binh at the time when your rape occurred! The men were, master sergeant Ronald Buick of Miami, Florida, USA, Corporal John Kelly of San Antonne in Texas USA, Privates Neville Williamson, and Brian Jones, both from New York, New York, USA. Our national government has gone through diplomatic channels to bring these war criminals to justice in a Vietnamese court! However, it is more probable that this will result in yet another diplomatic incident involving the God-damned Yankee!

We expect that our extradition requests for these men to be sent to Vietnam to answer for their war crimes, will result in the Americans either denying that their soldiers are guilty of such things and refuse to hand them over or else they will gloss over everything and just say that such accusations are what Americans expect a communist country to say! They will also attempt to strongly deny that such things ever happened!

I have also researched Cung whom I am told went to Australia with you on board the Giang Kein. His problem is more simple in that it does not involve the USA! In his case, his denouncer was Sauget et Sang who has been arrested for embezzling National funds and treason. It also came to our attention that he bore false witness against Cung Whyat for the purpose of having him removed in order for Sang to take-over Cung's business. I want both you and Cung to return to Vietnam to give evidence against Sauget et Sang in early January of 2012. Please me know if that suits you and if not, and when you can come here to give evidence. It should not take very long.

Whatever you decide, please let me know by return mail to the personal details below: Colonel Nguyen Van Tan, PO Box 11045, Hanoi, Vietnam. I hope to see your answer soon. My personal email is Col.VanTan@gmail.com and I have included that in case you find it more convenient to use email.

Kind regards – Colonel N Van Tan.

His letter to Lieutenant Colonel Hoa Lan Xuan was given to her when she collected her mail from the military post office in Townsville. Hoa was excited by finally receiving a letter from her former commanding officer. She hurried back to her married quarters in Hubert Street of Townsville. It was located outside of the base area of Townsville.

Having finally arrived at home, she opened the letter and became thrilled to read it. The events of her time as a freedom fighter in the Viet Cong D440 Battalion was still fresh in her mind as she read the letter from her former commanding officer. In her answer to Colonel Nguyen Van Tan, she gave the correct mailing address of Cung and Daiyu Whyat at Howard Springs northern Territory, Australia. She also let her former commander know that she was going to be in Vietnam between December 2011 and January of 2012 and that Cung and his family would be with her and her husband.

Fourteen (14) days later, an answering letter from Colonel Nguyen Van Tan arrived. Hoa opened it and she found that Nguyen was asking her and Cung to give evidence during the trial of Sauget et Sang for corruption and treason which was scheduled to begin at 09:00 hours (Vietnamese Time) on Thursday, the 8th of January 2012. This letter also stated that a similar letter had been sent to Cung and Daiyu Whyat at Howard Springs, asking for Cung's help in bringing Sauget et Sang to justice.

Meanwhile, Daiyu and Cung discussed the implications of giving evidence against Sauget et Sang. Daiyu said, *"Cung, we are now Australian citizens and perhaps it is time for us to forget all about what happened to us in Vietnam. The trial date is far too close to when we have to return to running our successful business at Howard Springs and I would rather be here doing that than staying in Vietnam to give evidence!"*

Cung, on the other hand, was more inclined to fight back against those who wronged him, in particular now that he finally had the means of so doing. So, he said, *"Daiyu, I have no fear of the unknown! I do have strong feelings of injustices carried out against me by various people in Vietnam and I want to get even! I have already sent Colonel*

Nguyen Van Tan a letter which tells him that I am honoured to return and give evidence against Sauget et Sang and others who caused such misery for us after my actions against the Khmer Rouge of Pol Pot!

I have already issued instructions for our staff of our business at Howard Springs to close the business until February 2012. I have also notified Colonel Nguyen Van Tan that it will not be possible for us to remain in Vietnam after the 2nd of February 2012 and that we must leave prior to then."

Daiyu, having expressed her concerns about these dates and times, then was silent. A week later, a letter arrived from Colonel Nguyen Van Tan in which he and Vietnamese authorities agreed that Cung and Daiyu would not be required to remain in Vietnam beyond the 30th of January 1982. The letter also clearly stated that the Government of the Democratic Republic of Vietnam would pay for the accommodation of the family of Cung and Daiyu at the Au Lac Charner Hotel in Ho Tung Mau street of Ho Chi Minh City.

Upon the receipt of the letter and reading it, Cung spoke to Daiyu. He said, *"My love, we shall remain in Ho Chi Minh City until February if need be! The Vietnamese Government shall pay for the cost of our hotel which is the Au Lac Charner Hotel in Ho Tung Mau Street for as long as we are required to give evidence against those who caused us such misery in the first place! I feel good that we are finally about to receive justice for the wrongs carried out against us!*

I also think that we should take this opportunity to travel to our former country of Vietnam with both of our children. Can you please get in touch with our son

Nguyen and our daughter Nguyet, and ask them if they would like to accompany us on the visit? Now that they are both qualified and experienced in the fields of medical and veterinary surgery, they may find that opportunities will await them if they decide to practice in Vietnam!"

Daiyu answered, *"Cung, I shall do that soon. By the way, Hoa Lan Xuan, Ho Hiep, Ahn Hong Kanh, Cung Le Sam, Hanh Liem Tru, and eight other people have been in touch, and they have all confirmed their attendance at the re-union followed by travel to Vietnam and back to Australia. We are all set to leave from Darwin Airport at 14:00 hours, Central Australian Standard Time on the 2nd of January!*

The flight shall land at Ho Chi Minh City in the morning of the 2nd of January 2011. From there we travel to our hotel and then we visit my parents at Cho Lon . After that, we return to our hotel and our children shall also stay the hotel where we are staying . We will introduce our children to their grandparents when we all visit them . At 09:00 hours of the following day, we will be at the Supreme People's Court of the Democratic Republic of Vietnam in Ho Chi Mihn city. We will go there from our hotel by taxis, which have already been booked to arrive at the hotel by 08:00 hours to ensure that we get delivered to the court on time!"

The re-union of the refugees on board the Giang Kein was held on the second level of the Victoria Hotel in Smith Street in Darwin as arranged. A good time was had by everyone present and it resulted in an additional two people to visit Vietnam as a group during late December of 2011 and stay there until early in 2012.

Cung & Daiyu Introduce their Children

After arriving in Ho Chi Minh City, the entire Whyat family travelled to Cho Lon and arrived at the home of the parents of Daiyu located along Hem 154 Phong Phu Street. Arriving by taxi from the city's airport, Cung, his wife and two children walked to the main door and pressed the door-bell. After a short time, the door was opened by Cung's Father-in-law called Aiguo.

As he opened the door, Aiguo exclaimed with pleasure, *"Daiyu my daughter and Cung, my son-in-law, how good it is to see you! Are your daughter and your son with you?"* Cung said, *"Yes Aiguo, they are!"* He had barely said that when Daiyu came forward and said, *"My loving father, how wonderful to see you! This is Nguyet, our daughter, she is a highly respected Veterinary surgeon and successful at what she does!*

Daiyu then introduced her son saying, *"My father, this is our son in whom we are both highly pleased as we are with his sister. He is a respected medical doctor and surgeon in Australia. Australia has been good for us, and we operate a fertiliser and farm machinery sales business in the north of Australia at a place called Howard Springs! Both of our children are married.* Aiguo came out of the house and into the sunlight in order to better see his grand children and their partners. As he came further out, he was spoken to by Millicent, who was the wife of Nguyen. She said, *"Than you so much for receiving us, Aiguo, I have heard much about you from Daiyu and Cung, who are my in-laws. It is a pleasure to meet you at last!"*

That was followed by Daiyu introducing a man to Aiguo. She said, *"Father, this is John Mc Douglas, and he is the husband of my daughter Nguyet! Now that you have met all members of my family, I want to see my mother and my sisters if they still live here!"*

Aiguo replied, *"That would be fine sweet daughter, however, your dear mother shall be with you soon, and it is indeed fortunate that you are here now. With regards to your sisters, they have both moved out to their own living areas. I shall contact them, for I am sure that they will want to see you! Please tell me where you are living, and I will let them both know so that they can visit you at your hotel."*

Daiyu answered, *"Father, we are staying at Au Lac Charmer Hotel in Ho Tung Mau Street of Ho Chi Minh City. Please visit us there with my sisters, but please make it after six in the afternoon because Cung and I have business with the Supreme People's Court of the Democratic Republic of Vietnam during business of the next few days. Cung is giving evidence against his denouncer known as Sauget et Sam! As of 09:00 hours of tomorrow."* Aiguo said, *"Very well, my daughter it shall be as you desire!"*

Trial of the Denouncer of Cung

At 08:50 hours of the 8th of January 2012, Cung and Daiyu were guided to their seats within the court house where they had to give evidence. The clerk of the 'Supreme People's Court of the Democratic

Republic of Vietnam' read out the charges against Sauget Sang by Democratic Republic of Vietnam, he said, *"The Supreme People's Court is hereby in session! Judge Nguyen Cuong is presiding! All Stand!"* That was followed by the judge walking into the court room. When he arrived at his throne, he said, *"Thank you, please be seated!"*

That was followed by the Clerk of the Court saying, *"This entire hearing shall be completed within the jurisdiction of the Court at Ho Chi Minh City with inputs from other areas, including Hanoi! Sauget et Sang, you are charged with corruption, with destroying the livelihood of peasants between 1952 and 1975. You are also charged with Crimes Against Humanity for your activities of supervising the mistreatment of prisoners at the French prison on Con Son Island in that you actively supervised and took part in splashing caustic substances upon the skin on those people whom you put into the 'Tiger Cages' on Con Son Island behind the walls of the old French prison. As well, you are charged with treason!*

The fact that you helped to incarcerate people in the 'Tiger Cages' measuring nine feet in length and four feet in height by three feet wide shows that you were totally without pity for those who had the bad luck to be under your supervision! By making people live in such tiny measurements, they would never be able to stand up. They also would have had extreme difficulty in just turning around! That led to them developing pressure sores all over their bodies! These people whom you tortured were the heroes and heroines of the First and the early part of the second Indochina Wars! How do you plead in answer to the charges against you?"

Sauget et Sang replied, *"Not guilty! Anyway, I do not recognise your right to hold me to account in any way, shape or from! I was only following orders from the French and American masters of the Republic of Vietnam (South Vietnam)! Therefore, it is the French and Americans who are to blame! I only followed orders, therefore I innocent of all of your charges against me!"*

The Clerk of the Court then shouted at Sauget et Sang! He yelled, *"Sauget et Sang, all charges against you shall proceed! A Defence attorney has been provided for you, and in my opinion, that is more than you deserve, but it is what you are entitled to under Vietnamese law! You shall be provided with meals, showering and other bathroom facilities at your current place of incarceration at the main watch house of Ho Chi Minh City!*

While the hearing is underway, and that means as of now, you shall remain silent! If you do not remain silent, you shall be taken back to your jail cell and your trial will continue without you. If that happens you will have the right to watch the legal proceedings on a closed-circuit TV which shall be placed into the reception area near your jail cell. Prosecuting shall be Colonel Nguyen Van Tan!"

Colonel Nguyen Van Tan Prosecutes

The court hearing was ended for the day and Sauget et Sang was returned to his cell under guard. He was in despair as he contemplated the events of the day and how he had inflicted pain and misery upon the people of southern Vietnam when a guard came to his cell and spoke. The guard said, *"Sauget et Sang, you have a visitor! He is your court appointed lawyer! You are to have unrestricted access to him, and you have the right to consult with him at most times, as long as he is available. You shall now accompany me to the interview room, where your meetings with your legal advisors shall take place! Come with me now!"*

Sauget et Sang accompanied his guard to the interview room and he was dismayed by the sight of a young man. He thought, *"Oh lovely, the defence lawyer that the State has given me is a young fool! I do not think that I can get justice in any Vietnamese court now!"*

As he was thinking that the young man stepped forward and said, *"Sauget et Sang? I am Duong Sam Lee! I am your court appointed lawyer! I have briefly looked over your file and I note that there are serious charges against you! Are there things which the authorities do not know about your case which may have the effect of mitigating the charges against you? Please tell me everything because unless I know your background, I cannot help you!"* Sauget answered, *"Duong, where do you want me to begin and what do you want to know?"*

Duong replied, *"Let us begin with what you were doing during 1951 onwards at the French prison on Con Son Island! Firstly, tell me what your job was and what your duties consisted of!"* Sauget replied, *"When I first begin working at the old French prison on Con Son Island in 1951, my role was that of a prison guard. Those who were imprisoned there did not receive any training or other means of being re-habilitated or improved in any way! Everyone who served time on Con Son Island was there as punishment for what the French called treason against France!*

In those days, I wore a French uniform given to the prison guards and we were always instructed to make life as difficult as possible for all prisoners! We were ordered to make prisoners get up and out of their cells at 05:00 hours while it was still dark! That was followed by the prisoners having breakfast and some tea. After that we put them to work. At times that meant we would take the prisoners to locations in areas where no-one wanted to go. There we would force them to construct roads and bridges. The prisoners were fed, but it was only a small amount of food and they worked very hard for it!

Things were already bad enough for the prisoners but then Ngo Diem became the Prime Minister of Emperor Boa Dai! Diem enthusiastically applied terror in an attempt to control the people of Southern Vietnam. Remember that during the peace talks held at Geneva about Indochina in 1953, after France had lost the Battle of Dien Bien Phu, the convention decided that there would be an interim government for the southern part of Vietnam and that free, internationally supervised elections would be held and that would result in the re-unification of Vietnam. Instead of that happening the Americans used their influence over Diem to have him set up the new country, called Republic of Vietnam (South Vietnam).

With direct American help from their CIA, Diem organised and succeeded in launching a revolution against Boa Dai. Diem then had himself installed as the first president of South Vietnam.

Meanwhile, from 1952 onwards, he did the bidding of the USA! One of the worst things he did was to have constant raids taking place upon the families of the south. These at all times involved torture and kidnaping.

After receiving instructions to do so, he had three hundred men and two hundred women enclosed in small 'Tiger Cages'. They were only three feet wide, nine feet long and their height was four feet. That resulted in the prisoners not even being able to stand up. Another direct result of it was that the people who were imprisoned in the 'Tiger Cages' developed pressure scores.

As of 1952, I paid the necessary bribes to be promoted from private to corporal within the prison system. After that, I paid the bribes and was eventually promoted to higher ranks, and I was finally appointed as a Police captain at the Bien Hoa area. After Diem was made Prime minister, I was already experiencing discomfort in the way I was asked to treat prisoners, and then came the order from Diem for the prison guards on Con Son Island to splash caustic substances on to the skin of the prisoners. I objected to that, and I was told to do it, or I would be placed into a 'Tiger Cage' and have that done to me! I am not a hero, so I did what I was told, and I splashed the caustic substances onto the skin of prisoners as ordered by Diem!

Duong said, "I see! What you have told me means that the file I have about you is in fact correct! I am your Defence Attorney, and I shall do whatever I can on your behalf! However, be warned that I find your personality abhorrent, and I do not like you at all! Make sure that you give me all necessary information, no matter how much discomfort that may bring you! The man who is prosecuting you is Colonel Nguyen Van Tan, and he does not at all like you or what you appear to stand for! He is calling for you to face the death penalty!"

Sauget replied, *"So, I am to be prosecuted by the famous Colonel Nguyen Van Tan of the D440 Battalion! Duong, please object to him prosecuting me, because if I get prosecuted by him, it will result in me not having a fair trial because he is a hero, while I am a known coward! Whatever I may be guilty of, I was only following orders! Other people are responsible for issuing those orders, and so, I am innocent of these charges against me!"*

Duong replied, *"Sauget, the State says, and I agree, that everyone is responsible for their own actions. However, we shall proceed with the argument that you were simply doing what you were ordered to do! However, it is a weak defence and I do not hold out much hope that it will completely save you, but it may lessen an otherwise extreme sentence for you. We shall see. If you are unhappy with me, please say so, and I will happily wash my hands of your case! So, do you want me to continue as your defence lawyer?"* Sauget was feeling panicked by that, and he said, *"Yes Duong, please continue as my Defence Lawyer!"* Duong said, *"In that case, when you again appear at court at 09:00 hours of the next day, you shall plead, 'Guilty-to-all-charges-with-mitigating-circumstances!' Do you understand?"*

At 09:00 hours of the following day, Sauget and his lawyer were seated in the court when Colonel

Nguyen Van Tan walked in. Duong asked for and received a court recess while he spoke to the colonel and the trial judge about plea bargaining. He said, *"Your Honour, I have spoken at length to my client! He has agreed to plead guilty to all charges against him on the proviso that the clause of mitigating circumstances is applied! I have made it clear to him that is the only way that he will avoid the death penalty for continuous treason and crimes against the people! That being the case, I am authorised to plea bargain on his behalf! So, let's get the ball rolling! What can you offer?"*

Nguyen thought over the matter at hand and then he spoke. He said, *"What has to happen now is that Vietnam comes out of all of this in a much better position than what it was in. I know that Cung Whyat is a decorated hero of Ba Chuc and that he had a successful business in Cho Lon after the war with Kampuchea and that was taken from him by the false accusations of Sauget et Sang. I also know that his daughter is a successful Veterinary surgeon and that his son is a successful medical surgeon.*

So, if Cung was to publicly forgive Sauter et Sang and Sang was to repay Cung for the money he has lost, I am sure that all could be well. I shall recommend that to the administration of Vietnam that we go down this path, and I shall also ask that Vietnam offers to hire Nguyet, the daughter of Cung as the Veterinary surgeon for the Mekong Delta Region. I also want his son, called Nguyen to be offered a post as a medical surgeon in either Ho Chi Minh City or else in Hanoi for two years." Duong answered, *"I am relieved to hear you say that Nguyen! I thought that you would press to have Sauget et Sang executed!"*

The old Colonel said, *Duong, long ago, that would have been the case, however, the whole country has moved along, and we now enjoy good relations with countries which were once fighting us. Our relationship with Australia, for example is very good. And I put it to you that we have in the children of Cung Whyat, an opportunity to have highly skilled medical and veterinary surgeons to help out this county. Even if we can only have them both here for a period of two years, it will greatly help our country and people to become even more qualified and able to do what has to be done! As well, we may be able to get the grandchildren of the Whyat family to come to Vietnam as possible immigrants and so, make our country even better!*

So, as for Sauget et Sang, I propose that for the crime of treason, he is sentenced to twenty years prison. However, due to his age and the probability of him dying in prison I suggest the that his sentence be commuted leaving only six months to serve. In order to spare the public expense of his incarceration, I propose that he be placed under house arrest. Reference to the charges of his Crimes-Against-Humanity, those charges must be dealt with by the Vietnam's administration, but if you plead that he has following orders against his own sense of decency and that he is most sorry for what he did, then this country may go easier upon him!"

That was readily agreed to by Duong on behalf of Sauget et Sang. Then at 10:45 hours of the same day, both the prosecuting and defence team met in the chambers of Judge Nguyen Cuong.

He listened to what had been agreed between the prosecutor and the Defence Lawyer and he agreed to it. He said, *"Well, gentlemen, do not hold back! Just go into the court room and ask Cung if he can forgive Sauget et Sang if he pays Cung compensation the amount of which shall be determined by this court! Further, I want to ask Cung if he could ask his two children to consider working in Vietnam for two years to help us to develop our medical and veterinary services.*

I understand that both his daughter and son are presently in the Ho Chi Minh City. Perhaps, they may even come to this court in order to observe proceedings. If so, I want them both to be offered the two-year contracts that we have discussed!

Duong said, *"Your Honour, I have seen that Cung, and his family are seated in the court room. Why don't we ask them all to come in here and immediately consult with us about this matter? While we are doing that, we could also have Sauget et Sang bought in and we can ask him to pay the compensation that you speak of!"* That was agreed to and Sauget et Sang was brought into the Judge's Chambers.

Colonel Nguyen Van Tan spoke directly to Sauget et Sang. He said, *"Sauget et Sang, be advised that I do not like you and what you stand for! If I had my way, you would be charged with High Treason and then after you are found to be guilty, you would be taken to a place of execution and shot! People such as you disgust me!*

However, I do not administer the law and you now have the chance to partly make up for what you

300

have done! Do not waste this opportunity, for if I ever can do so, I shall bring you down and you shalt face the death penalty!" Sauget et Sang replied, *"And just what is it that you think I can do to make amends which shall be seen as my salvation?"*

At this point, Judge Nguyen Cuong spoke up! He said, *"Sauget et Sang, remember that you are currently charged with treason, with Crimes against Humanity, Embezzlement of State-Owned funds, and Income Tax evasion! These crimes singularly are already bad enough, but when added together, they say that you are the worst kind of criminal and that you deserve the death penalty.*

The only way that you can stop your execution from happening is to make amends with those whom you have wronged! In the case of the people whom you helped to torture at Con Son Island and put in to the 'Tiger Cages' it is too late to do anything for many of the people you wronged and your options of making amends to the people whom you wronged is limited to those people who are still alive. However, there are also the cases where you have falsely denounced people as traitors, even though they were in fact decorated heroes of Vietnam!

In this regard, I am referring to the case where you bore false witness against the decorated hero of Cung Whyat because you coveted his successful business! You were successful in obtaining his business at Cho Lon and you have made much money from what is the property of the Whyat family! The Supreme People's Court of the Democratic Republic of Vietnam has ruled that you must do the following if you are to avoid the full penalty for your crimes! If you do not do as we ask you, then all of your bank accounts, including your secret numbered Swiss Bank accounts shall be used to redress the wrongs practised by you against many people.

If that happens, then you shall be sentenced to death with your execution to be scheduled within the next fourteen days! So, here is what you shall do and what will happen after this has been actioned! (1) You shall immediately pay Cung Whyat and his family the sum of two million American dollars. Don't say that you do not have that amount of money for we know that you actually have close to eight million US dollars!

(2) You shall on the 12th of January 2012, apologise to the people of Vietnam for being a low-life piece of scum that you are! You shall withdraw at least US three million dollars from your Swiss bank account And pay that into the fund for the resettlement and reimbursement of the people who had their lives made a living hell by you and other guards on the Con Son Island prison! Again, you shall beg the forgiveness of the people whom you have wronged!

(3) You shall set up an education fund for the children of the families whom you have wronged with whatever is left of your money. That shall leave you without any funds from anywhere and you shall have to live as best you can in the same way as other citizens of Vietnam!"

That resulted in the prosecutor Colonel Nguyen Van Tan saying, *"So Sauget et Sang, you place more value upon money and riches than your own life? Do you really want death more than life without your riches which you have stolen from the people? Is there no end to your greed and corruption? Very well then, as far as I am concerned, you can have your riches which we shall simply take off you and then distribute to all of these having claims against you! Then we shall take you to your place of execution and shoot you to death! Remember if that is what you want, we can easily do it!"* Sauget et Sang then reluctantly agreed to what the court wanted to happen.

Colonel Nguyen Van Tan said, *Sauget et Sang, you shall start making amends by confessing your crimes in public here in the court room when the reporters from around the world arrive! They should be here soon! You shall only say what is printed on the papers in front of you and there shall be no deviation from the script! Right now, you will apologise in person to Cung Whyat for falsely accusing him of treason and robbing his business from him and the family of his wife! You shall right now pay him US$2,000,000.00! If you do not do so, all charges against you shall proceed and you will die!"* So, it was that Sauget et Sang organised the withdrawal of US$2,000,000.00 and had that paid to Cung's bank account at Westpac in Darwin.

The colonel now spoke directly to the judge. He said, *"Sir, as you may recall, Vietnam urgently requires the services of medical cardiac and veterinary surgeons! Cung Whyat and his family have produced two such people and both of them are here in this court now! I have pleasure in introducing Nguyen Whyat, the cardiac surgeon and his sister, Nguyet the veterinary surgeon.*

He paused and then said, *"Nguyet and Nguyen please come forward and introduce yourselves to the Judge!"* They both did so, and then he said, *"Nguyet and Nguyen, here in Vietnam are great opportunities for people with the skills that both of them have. Vietnam can really use the likes of both of them. I want both these people to please consider working in this country on a two-year contract."* He then spoke to Cung's children. He said, *"Housing and transport can be part of the contract if you choose to accept this employment. As for the payment of your services, you shall be paid the upper salaries available to Vietnamese surgeons! I am sorry, but this country cannot afford to pay more because we were systematically robbed by the French, the Vichy French and Japanese followed by the Americans and their allies!*

I want both of you to see me later on today at say, 16:00 hours when I shall give you the names and addresses of the organisations and for which you would be working Vietnam! Does what I am presenting to you meet with your approval, and also, do either of you have children who may accompany you for the period of your employment here?"

Nguyen replied, *"I shall see you at 16:00 hours in order to obtain details of whom we must contact and where to do so. In answer to your previous question, I have one child aged ten years while my sister and her husband have two children, whom they may bring to Vietnam when Nguyet starts working for you as a veterinary surgeon. Now then Your Honour, I am very hungry, and I need to eat, so if that is all for now, I wish to go to a restaurant where we can have a meal! We shall return by 16:00 hours for the names of people and organisations we must get into contact with in order to work in Vietnam!* Both of Cung's children then departed in order to have meals.

Hoa's Rape Case is Terminated

After they had left, Colonel Van Tan got into contact with his son, Duong. Speaking to him by the use of a mobile phone, he said, *"Duong, this is your father speaking, I need to know about the status of the extradition request to the USA of the Americans who took part in the rape of Hoa Lan Xuan. What can you tell me of how things are progressing or otherwise?"*

Duong replied, *"Father, I have recently been in touch with American authorities, and I do not like what I have been told. I am sure that you shall also not like what the American attitude about this matter is. The arrogant Americans have apparently passed a law which now states that American soldiers cannot be prosecuted for war crimes that they may have inadvertently carried out during war service overseas from the USA! We can be sure that they will hide behind that and inflict ever more crimes against all people with whom they may be at war with!"*

His father said, *"That is what I have expected! We shall have to drop this case! Hoa's tormentors have been Successful in getting away with it!"*

Ende.

Bibliography

Beryl, Williams; Smith R. B., (2012) *Communist Indochina Volume 53 of Routledge Studies in the Modern History of Asia.* Routledge ISBN 97804 15542630

Dommen, Arthur J (2002). *The Indochinese Experience of the French and Americans: Nationalism and communism in Cambodia, Laos, and Vietnam.* Indiana University Press USA

Jennings, Eric T. (2001) *Vichy in the Tropics: Petain's National Revolution in Madagascar, Guadeloupe, and Indochina, 1940 -1944.* Stanford University Press.

Giap V. N. (1971) *The Military Art of Peoples' War.* Monthly Review Press, New York, USA.

Vien N. K. *Vietnam A Long History,* The GIOI Publishers, Hanoi Vietnam.

www.ingramcontent.com/pod-product-compliance
Lightning Source LLC
Chambersburg PA
CBHW011655010726
47499CB00011B/3273